or
Nice

BOOK YOUR PLACE ON OUR WEBSITE AND MAKE THE READING CONNECTION!

We've created a customized website just for our very special readers, where you can get the inside scoop on everything that's going on with Zebra, Pinnacle and Kensington books.

When you come online, you'll have the exciting opportunity to:

- View covers of upcoming books
- Read sample chapters
- Learn about our future publishing schedule (listed by publication month *and author*)
- Find out when your favorite authors will be visiting a city near you
- Search for and order backlist books from our online catalog
- Check out author bios and background information
- Send e-mail to your favorite authors
- Meet the Kensington staff online
- Join us in weekly chats with authors, readers and other guests
- Get writing guidelines
- AND MUCH MORE!

**Visit our website at
http://www.kensingtonbooks.com**

Naughty
or
Nice

SHERRI ERWIN

ZEBRA BOOKS
Kensington Publishing Corp.
www.kensingtonbooks.com

ZEBRA BOOKS are published by

Kensington Publishing Corp.
850 Third Avenue
New York, NY 10022

All Kensington titles, imprints, and distributed lines are
available at special quantity discounts for bulk purchases for
sales promotion, premiums, fund-raising, educational, or
institutional use.

Special book excerpts or customized printings can also be
created to fit specific needs. For details, write or phone the
office of the Kensington Special Sales Manager: Attn. Special
Sales Department. Kensington Publishing Corp., 850 Third
Avenue, New York, NY 10022. Phone: 1-800-221-2647.

Zebra and the Z logo Reg. U.S. Pat. & TM Off.

ISBN-13: 978-1-4201-0106-5
ISBN-10: 1-4201-0106-4

First Printing: October 2008
10 9 8 7 6 5 4 3 2 1

Printed in the United States of America

Acknowledgments

Thank you, Nick and Elissa, for filling my days with joy and laughter, despite the occasional challenges. Special thanks to Lea-Ann Gordon-Cooke for refreshing my memory on the unique abilities of babies in their fourth month. And a big thank you to readers everywhere, and especially to the Whiners, friends of the Whine Sisters, who keep coming back for more.

Prologue

"But, soft! What light through yonder window breaks? It is the east, and fair Kate is the sun." *Hermes ended his soliloquy with a mocking Shakespearean flourish and a deep, low laugh. He never tired of teasing his poor lovelorn uncle.*

Hades sighed, cast a wicked glare in the direction of Hermes, and diverted his attention back to his gazing ball.

The previous year, Hades had embarked on an affair with a human only to be forced to leave her and never set foot on earthly soil again. He'd struck a bargain with Zeus. In exchange for consigning himself solely to hell's environs, Hades had been able to offer his ladylove what she'd wanted most: a child. Now, unable to be with them himself, Hades watched over Kate and their daughter with near-obsessive interest.

And with a growing sense of pity for his powerful uncle, Hermes watched Hades give in to fits of humanlike emotion.

Hermes couldn't imagine a love great enough to sacrifice any of his godly gifts. Traveling among the clueless humans was chief of his amusements. Despite his penchant for stirring up mischief, he had been spending a lot of time there as messenger to Hades. His uncle frequently sent him down to monitor his various business ventures, and more recently to check on Kate.

So far, he had managed to keep his distance and merely observe mother and child from afar. As a rule, Hermes preferred to avoid children, the tiny things with their grasping hands and never-ending babble. They taxed his nerves and annoyed him with their vulnerability.

"Hermes." At last, his uncle turned from the gazing ball and spoke. "I've a mission for you."

"Yes, I'll make the journey." Hermes anticipated the request, so he only half listened as he filled his cup with some more of his uncle's excellent wine. To go with the wine, he ripped a hunk from a nearby loaf of bread and looked over the well-set sideboard for the delectable gouda he had devoured, save for a small wedge, earlier.

One thing about the lord of the underworld, he kept a magnificent house. Only the best for Hades. Mount Olympus had nothing on hell, which was why Hermes had no quibble with his lot, ending up in his uncle's employ instead of being stuck in his father's house. Like his uncle, Hermes had an appreciation for the finer things.

"I'm not after the usual reports."

Hades's tone of voice commanded Hermes to attention. He cocked a brow. "Not the usual?"

"I want you to spend some time with them, get to know them. See how they fare day to day."

"They, meaning Kate and"—*his voice broke, revealing his distaste*—*"the* baby*?"*

"My child grows at an alarming rate. She's already holding her head up and starting to observe the world around her, but I can't manage any insight to her mind yet."

"She's four months old in the mortal sense of time. That

barely puts her on par with a satyr as far as displaying her mind-set goes."

Hades tightened his mouth to a grim line and Hermes felt the momentary prickle of fear that he was about to be felled by a lightning bolt. None came.

"My concern is that Eliana may not be entirely human. What if she's harboring godlike powers? She could be at risk were she to display her skills. You remember the Salem Witch Trials?"

Hermes bit into his bread and washed it down with cabernet before answering. "Humans have grown more tolerant of uniqueness in their midst. Besides, she's but a babe."

"Exactly." Hades leaned forward and pressed his fingertips together. "She has no control of her gifts, no idea they even exist. Anything could happen."

Hermes, recognizing true parental concern in his uncle's tone, stifled a grin. "I'm sure she's entirely human. Zeus barely agreed to lend you the power to create human life. He certainly wouldn't have entertained the idea of gifting her with extraordinary powers on top of everything."

"You're probably right." Tension lifting from his features, Hades rose to pace the room. "Nonetheless, I want you to walk amongst them. Use the premise of taking over at Glendower Enterprises. It will put you in proximity to Kate and you can find an in to get closer to her from there."

"It's nearly their Christmastime," Hermes noted with revulsion, stealing a glance at the gazing ball. "They'll be in fine spirits. Singing, celebrating." Doting on the children. He choked back a wave of nausea. "Perhaps it could wait until spring?"

"It can't wait. Make haste. Prepare to leave at once. I want a full report as soon as you're settled."

Hermes prepared to argue his case, then stopped in his

mental tracks as he caught sight of something extraordinary through the gazing ball. Who's that? He didn't say it out loud. Not yet. Why tip his hand to his uncle?

A vision. *She leaned over Eliana's cradle, the curve of her lush bottom on display from the fall of her low-rise jeans. Genius human invention, low-rise jeans. And when she stood up, she gave him a chance to check out the rest of her. Not Hades's Kate, thank the gods, but she had something of Kate's appearance. With slightly smaller breasts. She had to be the sister.*

She looked enough like Kate, and yet different. Long legs, those breasts, slender waist, angelic smile, a prime example of everything Hermes liked best about the human race: sensual, lovely women.

And she would be willing. At least, they were usually willing where he was concerned. He seldom met with refusals. Ah, he had found his "in," just the way to insert himself into Kate and young Ellie's life.

"So be it, Uncle." *He barely allowed himself a wolfish grin.* "I'll leave straightaway."

Chapter One

"Charge it!" Wilma Flintstone and Betty Rubble, the original wives gone wild, had instilled the thrill in me at a very early age. Their solution: *Charge it!* With the exception of "I love you," was there a nicer combination of words in the entire English language?

My credit card poised at the ready, I debated between the black patent platform Louboutin pumps, *cheaper but so last season,* and the red Dolce & Gabbana ankle boots, *too hot for words with a price to match.* WWWD? What would Wilma do?

When I was a kid, I used to get up early, before everyone in the house, and enjoy the company of my cartoon friends in the family den. My favorite, Wilma Flintstone, offered valuable insights to the way things should work for a modern Stone Age family. My family had been Stone Age all right. We didn't even have cable.

Didn't Wilma deserve her few indulgences, after all? She put up with a lot being married to a caution-to-the-wind type like Fred. And I'd put up with a lot, too. A widow for almost a year, I knew what it was to suffer, and I deserved a few indulgences of my own. Only six weeks to Christmas, but as long as I made sure Santa brought my kids everything on their lists, I was free to spend.

I looked at the boots, red-hot tops sticking out of lavender tissue wrap, and sighed. My role model, Wilma, was too practical to put her budget off balance so close to the holidays.

Practical? I would only get as far as the first snowfall with the pumps before I had to stick them in the back of the closet for another six months or so. And honestly, who knew if they would still be stylish by the time designers introduced their spring lines? By contrast, I could get a good five months out of the Dolce & Gabbana boots, and maybe a few months of the following autumn. Even though they were pricier up front, they would be a much better bargain in the end.

Pleased with my decision, I left the pumps in the box under the Christmas tree adorning the table at the side of the shoe department chairs and headed for the register with the boots. My heart lifted to the strains of "Silver Bells" playing in the background. Wilma would be so proud.

But Wilma wouldn't be the one helping me go over my expenses at the end of the month to make sure all my bills were paid. That honor would go to my sister, Kate, and Kate was no Wilma Flintstone. Not even close.

"Charge it!" was not a part of Kate's everyday vocabulary. The last time she indulged and bought herself a new pair of jeans, stone-washed had just been reintroduced to the market. Kate was uptight with a capital UP. Especially after baby Eliana came

along and gave her a real taste of the challenges facing single mothers.

It was so much easier for Kate when she could tell me how to handle my kids without having to worry about caring for one of her own.

When I emerged from Macy's into the Natick Mall parking lot, I couldn't find where I'd parked the car. I looked around the lot, certain I'd spot it any minute.

Then I saw a guy loading an SUV onto a tow bed. My heart stopped. I almost dropped my shopping bag in the mad dash across the lot. "What are you doing? That's my Lexus!"

"We're repossessing." He flashed me paperwork, some kind of order. "You're behind on payment."

"That's not possible." I thought back over the last few months. Didn't I pay the bill? I *had* to have paid it. Sure, I'd skipped a few payments on nonessential things to free up some cash to pay down the credit cards, but I wouldn't skip the car payment. I needed wheels!

"Three months," he added in a lifeless voice.

I flashed him *the glare*, the same look that had Spence and Sarah admitting to minor household misdemeanors and running for their rooms within seconds. He only shrugged, apparently immune to tactics that worked wonders on the preteen set.

"Hmm," I said, giving him the up-and-down appraisal. He was slim, well put together, about an inch taller than me, or taller than I would be *in my new boots*. "You don't look like the *normal* repo guys."

He raised a slim, curved brow. Obviously a waxer.

In my experience, any guy who believed in regular spa treatments was not in the business of repossession. More like renovation, a designer like my sister, Kate. Or a cat burglar? Maybe a professional thief!

"I've seen *Cops* on TV." I poked him in the chest. He had to know he wasn't dealing with some clueless housewife. "And repo shows, like the one with the Big Pussy guy from *The Sopranos. You* look too neat. Normal. Tame as a TV weatherman."

He tossed, or tried to toss, his immovably sprayed J.C. Penney catalog model hair. "So you're familiar with my kind?"

"Weathermen?"

"Ugh." He shook his head. "With *repo men.* Not that I'm surprised, considering your payment history." He laughed at his own snarky dig in the sort of self-conscious male model way that made me pause and look around.

"Are we on TV?" I asked, wondering if maybe it was all a gag, like the TV news was doing a *Candid Camera* type of segment for the holidays. "So then, you're not really taking my car?" *Big sigh of relief.*

I was glad I'd recently reapplied my lipstick, and it had been a pretty good hair day. I looked around to make contact with the camera. No unsuspecting fool, I. Mentally, I went down the old pageant poise checklist and considered my bio in case they asked for information to add a personal touch to the broadcast.

Repo-Ken caught his breath on the tail end of a throaty guffaw. "Uh, no. I need to get the car. You can sort it all out with the GMAC folks. If you hand over the keys, it'll be easier for me to avoid damaging anything when we get her back to the lot."

Damage? Now *my* breath caught in my lungs. "*GMAC?*"

It sounded familiar. Then it hit me—I'd thought GMAC was the billing code for MAC cosmetics, which I'd switched to over the summer in an effort to replace my more expensive Lancôme. I was *so* all about saving money. So when the bills came in, I figured I could skip a few payments to GMAC. What were they going to do? Repossess my midnight navy mascara?

Besides, I always caught up on my debts when a new check came in, one every few months. I guessed it was time for a new check. Patrick had provided for us, and my sister had set up the investments. I tried to make sense of it all, but I had no idea I'd let things slip so badly.

"Sorry, hon. The car folks say you owe. I don't get involved. I'm just a paid go-between."

"Yes, but—I'm Bennie St. James. Little Miss Massachusetts 1986. Mother of two. Recent widow." My press-ready bio came shooting out my mouth, along with a few real tears. *"It's Christmastime!"*

"Lady, I wish I could care."

"But—we're at the mall. How did you find me? Don't you usually do this in the middle of the night, from people's homes? Like the Grinch?"

"We've done our homework. You're always at the mall."

I glared. This time, it had some effect. He sobered instantly. "We prefer to follow you around and grab at the best opportunity. It cuts down on the chances we'll get shot at or attacked if we avoid the primary residence."

I could imagine.

"Can't you just pretend you didn't find me?" I gave him my best come-hither stare and a pout. Flirting would be a lot easier if he looked more Abercrombie and less J.C. Penney. I tried to use my imagination. "I'll pay tomorrow morning, first thing."

"Have a nice holiday." Lexus loaded, he turned to join his pimply faced friend in the front seat of the truck. Too late to salvage any pride, I ran and tugged at his sleeve. "Please. How much? I can pay you now."

I let my shopping bag slump to the ground and started rummaging around for my checkbook in my purse. A car behind me honked, obviously desperate to get the newly vacated parking space where my champagne gold Lexus RX330 used to sit. Checkbook in hand, I leaned into the window of the truck brandishing a check.

"I can't take payment." He shrugged, handed me a card with the name of someone at GMAC, and nudged my hand out before pulling away. "Merry Christmas."

"I'm a widow!" I shouted after the truck. As if on cue, the honker pulled into my space, just missing my shopping bag of new boots. "My husband always paid for everything."

I felt the sting of tears streaming down. The honker, an old fat man obviously missing Santa's joviality, got out of his car, avoided eye contact, and huffed off toward the mall entrance.

I was left with no choice. I had no excuse, no way to get home.

No job, no prospects. No money.

I needed bailing out again. I reached for the cell and dialed Kate.

* * *

"I don't understand," Kate said over a loudly crying Ellie as I opened the front door about to climb into her Lincoln Aviator. "How could you have forgotten the car payment? It's due on the sixteenth of every month. You have to mail it by the ninth to get it there in time. We've been over this."

I opened the back door to stow my bags, but then I realized that Ellie's cries drowned out most of Kate's lecture. I closed the front door and decided to sit in the backseat with the baby. Over the sound of Ellie's cries, Kate sounded like the teacher on *A Charlie Brown Christmas*. *Wah wah-wah, wah-waaah.*

"Where are the kids?" No sign of my two.

"I left them home," Kate shouted over the din. "It's a five-minute ride. They'll be fine."

"I guess." I'd never left them home alone. I knew it was a five-minute ride, but who knew what could happen in five short minutes? Some maniac could break in, shoot them both, and be gone in two minutes or less. Or kidnap them. Or, okay, even just scare them. Finding a strange guy in your house trying to steal your presents, how terrifying is that? In real life, the little Whos down in Whoville would have been absolutely traumatized, not merely amused.

It had only taken Patrick a moment to lose control of the car, veer off the road, and end life as we knew it. I'd been left behind, with a new sense of the power of time, even the barest intervals.

I turned my attention to comforting Ellie in an effort to ignore my own urge to let the tears flow. I gave her the crook of my thumb to suck while I checked in the folds of her snowsuit for her woobie, which Kate insisted I call a pacifier. Too many parenting manuals and long, lonely nights had turned Kate on to all the "proper" parenting techniques, like using adult words, no baby talk. I'd baby-talked to my kids and they were just fine, thank you. Spencer had always been at the top of his class, and Sarah was honor roll every report card. Wasn't it more important you talked to them at all?

I couldn't find Ellie's woobie, but I couldn't resist sticking my finger in her belly button region just to see if she was poppin' fresh. All in white, she looked like the Pillsbury Doughboy. She laughed like him, too, all of a sudden. No more crying. Ellie and I had always had a special bond. And why not? We shared a common enemy, her mother.

Not that Kate was my enemy, most of the time. Only when she thought she knew it all, which was at least half of the time. I caught Kate's glare in the rearview mirror. I couldn't figure out if the malice in her gaze was because I made Ellie stop crying without much effort, or because she was still stuck on the car thing, or both.

"I lost track of time," I said, sounding helpless and young, and feeling stupid. "I didn't realize I hadn't paid."

The tears hovered, but didn't fall. I kept a meticulous kitchen. I'd had the holiday cookie baking schedule charted out weeks ago. Why was it so hard for me to stay organized when it came to money?

"I know, honey. I know," Kate said, all traces of anger vanishing. "We'll take care of it."

I noticed her "we" instead of "I" and it made me feel better that she meant to include me in the process. So often, she steamrolled right over me in her attempt to fix things and make it better. That she was such a capable fixer made the know-it-all part of her more tolerable.

Patrick used to do the same thing. He would fix things so that I didn't have to trouble or worry myself. He thought he was protecting me. To be honest, he made me feel incapable. I wasn't sure if it was worth having things fixed only to have lost that part of me that believed I could straighten things out for myself.

"I'll fix it. I appreciate your help, but I have to start working things out on my own." I had no idea where the voice came from. Was it even mine? But I guessed it had to be mine, didn't it? Ellie wasn't old enough to talk.

Kate, apparently as surprised by the declaration as I was, found the road again in time to brake instead of running the light. At the sudden stop, Ellie's baby face crumpled as if she was about to bellow again. I tweaked her stomach and she laughed in response.

"You have the money to work it out? How far behind are you?"

"Three months," I admitted too easily. "I have it. It's no big deal."

I didn't have it. It was a huge deal. I had no idea what I was going to do, exactly.

"Do you? The way we've set up your investments, you don't have a lot of cash for frivolous spending and I notice you've been doing a lot of shopping lately."

"True. It's Christmas. I have a lot of gifts to buy." I shrugged. Kate had no response. For all she knew, I could be telling the truth. I could imagine her in the Dolce & Gabbana boots. *Merry Christmas, Kate!*

"You should have another check coming in for the first of the year. In the meantime, why don't you let me go over your accounts, see what we can do? I can move some things around, set up the car payment as an automatic withdrawal, and maybe even free up a little extra for holiday spending."

My mind latched on to the part about the check coming on the first of the year. As in, *after* Christmas. What good would it do me then? I had to make it through six weeks when I knew Kate's idea of "a little extra for holiday spending" wouldn't begin to cover all the things I planned to buy for the kids. I miscalculated when the check was due to come in, my own stupid mistake. Again.

My lip started to quiver and I took a shaky breath. As if sensing my desperation, Ellie raised a chubby fist, held out her missing woobie, and smiled as if she were offering me the moon in consolation.

I couldn't help but smile back. I might have been lacking in finances, but I had a little angel niece who loved me and two growing angels of my own at home. I could be the biggest failure in the world, with no money to buy presents, and the children in my life would always love me. Maybe my situation wasn't so dire after all.

I thought the worst of my day was behind me.

And then Kate dropped me off and I entered my bedroom in time to catch my adolescent son trying on my lipstick.

"It's not what it looks like," he said, quickly putting the cap back on my favorite tube of Lancôme's Ginger Flower.

"What does it look like?" I asked, thinking it looked like I might have to hide the new boots, and any of the designer dresses he might decide to try on with them. At twelve, he was barely old enough to go to the movies alone with a girl, let alone consider his dating preferences.

"I'm not gay," he said matter-of-factly as he reached for the eyeliner. "I'm going Goth."

"Goth? Like, walking dead, black is the new black, vampire wannabe stuff?"

"Like, *Shelley Miles is experimenting with becoming a witch and she needs a warlock* stuff. I like her, Mom. I think if I do the Goth thing, she may get interested."

I stifled a sigh of relief and took a seat on the edge of my bed. "So you're wearing makeup *for a girl*?"

"You got it." He pointed at me with two fingers and a cocked thumb, game show host style. "A really, really hot girl. You've seen her, Mom. She's got—" His hands moved to his chest, then dropped as if he'd suddenly thought better of offering a vivid explanation. "Style. She's got style."

"Big bundles of it, I'll bet." I rolled my eyes. My little boy was growing up. As much as I hated the idea of him leaving the house in makeup, my protests would most likely drive him to do it behind my back. "Stay away from my good cosmetics. I'll go to CVS and get you some makeup of your own, if you like." Tomorrow. Once I got my car back.

"Good idea." He turned back to the mirror. "I don't think Ginger Flower's my color. Maybe they have black. I could deal with black lipstick."

If Patrick were here, he would be freaking out, but was it so different from the eighties, after all?

I'd been a Duran Duran fan. Those boys knew their way around a makeup palette.

"Black might be a little harsh with your fair coloring." I'd pictured having this conversation with my daughter in a few years, but never with my preteen son. Fortunately, Spencer tired easily of trends. He would be done with the Goth makeup and on to the next big thing in a matter of weeks, maybe days depending on the reactions of other kids at school. "We'll run out tomorrow and try a few on. For now, I really need a nice long bath. Scoot. And make sure the dogs get out for a walk."

Once Spencer shut the door behind him, I stripped. I needed a long bath to think about how I was going to pay for lipstick among other necessities like food, gas, and Miss Clairol Strawberry Sunset number 116. My roots were beginning to show.

It was time to face the cold, hard facts. I needed to get a job.

The phone rang as I was about to sink chin-deep into bubbles.

A glance at the caller ID told me it was Kate. I dried my hands and picked up. The sound of Ellie crying in the background told me why she was calling before she even said a word.

"I think she may be teething," I offered. "Her gums felt hard in the car tonight."

"Plus, she's drooling all over the place. And the crying." Kate's voice broke off in a groan. "But isn't she a little young for teething?"

"A little, yeah, but they all go at their own pace. Spencer and Sarah were both late bloomers, but

Ellie has her own style." If she was anything like her mother. "Where is she now?

"I put her in her crib for a few minutes. I need to know what to do, Ben. You're the expert."

I smiled. *You're the expert.* This was a big admission from the perfect sister. I inhaled deeply of my favorite almond coconut bath bomb from Basic as I took a minute to appreciate the comment. Kate had always been the overachiever, the smart one. I was the "pretty" one. Finally, there was an area in which she could recognize my superiority in something more substantial than hair and makeup.

"Frozen bagels," I said, after a minute. "The topical ointments never seemed to do much for the kids, but giving them something substantial to gnaw really helped."

"Frozen bagels? What if she bites off a piece and chokes?"

"With swollen gums? Yeah, *that's* going to happen. Look, I got it from T. Berry Brazelton. He knows his stuff. It worked for Spence and Sarah. If that makes you nervous, you could try a frozen washcloth."

"Okay." Kate sounded a little nervous. "I'll go try that."

"Call later if you need more help. You two can always come and sleep over here."

Just after Ellie was born, Kate spent the night quite frequently. Kate's house was only a few miles away and nothing rendered her near helpless quite as effectively as her own screaming child. With me, *the expert*, close at hand, she never really had to go it alone for long. Fortunately, Kate kept her own hours at the office and she was often able to return the favor and pick my kids up from school in the event that my Pilates class should go long or, more often, I decided to stop and pick up a new outfit on the way home.

I clicked the phone off and dropped it on the towel at the edge of the tub. As good as it was to have a sister to share in the parenting, she was not a substitute for a real partner. I slid down into the bath, felt the silken water smooth across my thighs, and ached for my missing husband, my dear departed Patrick.

I remembered the way he used to come home late from work sometimes to catch me just slipping into the bath. He would stand just there, across the room in the doorway, with a smile of appreciation crossing his lips, making the freckles dance across his crinkled nose. God, I missed those freckles.

More than just missing my husband, my best friend, I missed being loved. I missed being kissed in a way that made a tingle go right down my spine. I missed feeling like a woman. I was almost thirty-three years old, for goodness' sake, and the mother of two. I loved my kids, but would they be my entire life now? Was I ever going to have something for me, just for me, ever again?

The mere idea of dating made my palms sweat. I wouldn't mind a little romantic attention, but how to meet suitable men? I wasn't about to go looking for love in singles bars or matchmaking Web sites. Colin Firth as Fitzwilliam Darcy wasn't about to trot his white horse down my path. Maybe a job would be good for me, more than just a way to fund my shopping habit. Maybe I would actually find something I liked, something to fill the void. But what on earth would I possibly be good at?

Before I got out of the bath, I heard my sister's car pull into the drive, followed by the sounds of Ellie's cries getting louder all the way up the walk. Good thing I'd anticipated their arrival before Kate had even called. My freezer was fully stocked with washcloths.

Chapter Two

The next morning, Kate came down to breakfast wearing a relaxed smile. I'd stayed up with Ellie so that she could get some sleep. It wasn't much of a hardship. I was wide awake worried about my Lexus, my son in lipstick, and my employment possibilities.

According to Kate, her daughter always rose with the first rays of the sun, a fact she attributed to her being named Eliana, Greek for "daughter of the sun." Considering that Ellie was also up for hours after sunset, I wasn't convinced that the name had relevance, but it hardly mattered. I was a morning person, too.

I had coffee brewing, my pugs, Bert and Ernie, out in the fenced yard for their morning business, and Ellie fed by the time Kate found her way downstairs. She was in a good mood, or so it looked, and all the better for me. I needed her help, not her scorn.

"I paid your car bill last night while you were rocking Ellie. Three months behind. I set your account to pay it automatically. After I made a deposit, of course. You were overdrawn." She said it with a smile, as if this bit of news had no impact on her good mood.

"Hmm. I wonder how that happened." I shook a toy in front of Ellie in her baby Exersaucer. Ellie's brown eyes shone like little suns. Maybe there was something to her name, after all.

"Probably the three-hundred-dollar blouse from Neiman Marcus," she said, a trace of sarcasm sucking the cheery out of her tone.

"Was it that much? I guess I didn't look at the price tag." I stifled a sigh of relief that last night's boot purchase hadn't shown up yet. "I'll have to be more careful."

"You think?"

"Christmas shopping." I sighed and worked up a good pout. "I bought it for you, but I guess the surprise is ruined."

I peeked from beneath my lashes to see if she believed me, but I wasn't so sure. *I* wouldn't believe me. I had no idea my shopping habit had gotten so out of hand. It was time to stop using the excuse of retail therapy as a form of grief counseling.

"No problem." She poured coffee. Casual. Avoiding eye contact. She didn't believe me. "Take it back. You know I don't need fancy presents."

I nodded, but I'd already brought it to the dry cleaner to remove a small stain on the cuff. Kate set down her coffee and leaned over to say hello to her daughter, lifting her from the seat to cuddle.

"She's had her bottle," I said, glad for the change of subject.

I refused to use the opportunity to criticize Kate for switching to formula so early in Ellie's life. Everyone knew breast milk was best, but pumping took time, something busy Kate could hardly spare. The same woman who would agonize for hours over fabric swatches to find the right shade between eggshell and ecru couldn't take an extra twenty minutes to pump. To her credit, it probably wasn't easy running a business and being a mom. I'd never had to juggle motherhood and a career, but maybe I would learn.

"Who's a happy girl? Wook at da big smile." Kate lapsed into baby talk.

My smile was bigger than Ellie's at catching Kate's slip. Aha! *Perfect? I think not.* "She's had a good morning."

"I have to hand it to you, Bennie, you always know just what she needs. You're a whiz with her." She looked wistful, almost sad, as she settled Ellie into the crook of her arm.

"I've got years of experience. You'll catch on. After you've done it awhile, it's a piece of cake."

"I guess. You make it look so easy."

I could practically feel the swagger in my step as I crossed the floor to refill my coffee. Then I turned around in time for my ego to make a crashing fall back to earth. Spencer stood in the kitchen door, head to toe in black. His beautiful blond hair was dyed jet-black, which matched his kohl-rimmed eyes. His skin looked extraordinarily pale in contrast to the black and his slash-red mouth. Lipstick. I guessed he must have raided my makeup drawer again, and settled on my L'Oreal Cherry Red, something I picked up on sale and had worn only once because it looked cheaper than the sale price.

"Yeah," I repeated, gesturing to the doorway. "Piece of cake."

Kate nearly jumped out of her chair. "Are you auditioning for The Cure?"

"The who?" Spence asked.

"No, The Cure," I said, desperate to keep my cool. "The Who still tours with the original lineup. Except for the bassist. He died. The Cure's the band with the wild singer in trademark red lipstick. I thought we agreed black was more your color."

"Seemed a bit much with the outfit." Spence, charming as ever, winked on his way to the fridge. "I needed to break up the black with a hint of color."

"Smudged liner really brings out the blue in your eyes," I said, looking for the bright side.

"You think?" Spence asked before reaching for the juice.

"Definitely. She'll notice."

"She?" Kate looked stunned, looking from Spencer, to me, and back again.

"He's going Goth for a girl," I said, trying to match Spencer's casual mood. Freaking out would be the surest way to drive him more solidly into the look. Humor was the only response I could rely on. If I couldn't make me laugh, I was going to cry. Spencer's beautiful blond hair! *Hair grows*, I reminded myself. "Bold move, don't you think?"

"More like insane. You're not letting him go to school like that, are you?"

"If he's willing, I'm willing. As long as he conforms to the school decency standards, why not? Don't you remember your Madonna phase?"

Kate wasn't far enough along in the parenting game to understand. "That was different. It was the *eighties*."

"So was The Cure." I shrugged. "Everything old

is new again. Spencer's going Goth to win a little witch's heart."

"Mom's not insulting her," Spencer explained, taking a seat. "Shelley Miles wants to be a witch. She found an old spell book and everything."

"Where, exactly, does one find a spell book?" Kate asked, raising a brow. Or tried to, anyway. She never quite got the gesture down, but she had been trying for years.

"EBay," Spencer said, sparing his aunt the extra "duh" that he usually added to punctuate.

"Be careful," Kate warned. "You never know what you may be getting into with that occult stuff."

Kate liked to joke that Ellie's father was the devil, now absent because of his return to rule in hell. Personally, I agreed that Owen Glendower, whom she fell head over heels for, might have been the devil. In fact, I'd even warned her. But it seemed far more likely that business took precedence over his personal life. He was probably too busy building new empires in Europe to live up to his paternal responsibilities. *Jerk.*

"Spencer's got a good head on his shoulders. I'm sure he'll do the right thing."

Spencer smiled and I could almost see my son's freckled splendor under the ghostly pallor.

An hour later, we dropped the kids off at school and were on our way to the impound lot, armed with the computer printout receipt of my now-paid bill. Ellie, snug in her car seat, slept soundly. Kate was strangely quiet, probably dying to offer more criticism or advice but too afraid to wake her baby.

We pulled in to the single available space outside the lot, a fenced-in dump so jam-packed with cars that it was a wonder any remained out in the general population. 'Tis the season. Christmas must have been their prime time.

"You can stay in the car." A knot formed in my stomach as I looked at the trailer labeled OFFICES. I could do this. I could do it all on my own. "I'll just take a few minutes. No need to risk waking Eliana."

"No freaking way." Kate shut the car off. Apparently, not even the fear of waking the screamer would deter Fix-it Kate. She got out and grabbed Ellie's seat.

Together, we stepped onto the crumbling pavement and headed for the trailer. Inside, it was as dingy and pathetic as I'd imagined, complete with stale tobacco smell and vinyl chairs, most likely salvaged from the Goodwill down the street. Determined to bail me out, she handed me Ellie and charged right ahead with my receipts balled in her fist.

A dead ringer for Danny DeVito's Louie in *Taxi* stepped up to the Plexiglas window, only to tell Kate there was an extra fee, the per diem lot charge for parking. What a racket! After Kate paid the fee, he told her that all agents were out for the day and we would have to come back Monday—Monday!—to pick up my Lexus.

"But—I need it now," I said, tired of hanging back to let Kate straighten it out.

He looked around Kate right at me. "I'm sure you do, princess, but we got rules. Can't release the car without an agent to check her out of the lot. It's a busy day. I'm short a few agents."

"Why can't you do it?" Kate demanded, stepping in front of me again. "So you can suck another thirty dollars a day in parking fees out to cover the weekend?"

I sidestepped her in time to see his shrug in response. "I have to man the desk."

"When do you expect an agent back in?" she asked, steel in her tone. "We'll wait."

Kate's modus operandi was to push back. Mine was to size Louie up, and my guess was that he was not the type to cave to pressure or demands. So what would work?

As if on cue, my charming baby niece startled awake and launched into a full-blown wail. There was my girl.

"You're out of luck for the weekend," Louie, unmoved, shouted over the din.

"It's right near the exit. I can pull it out on my own." Kate's words bordered on a threat, as if she fully intended to just do it, wheel-popping spikes in the road be damned.

"No one drives cars on the lot but my agents. Liability issues." He had no problem making himself heard over Ellie's din, and he seemed entirely unmoved. I wasn't deterred. Every man had his Achilles' heel. What could get to a tough little lump of Boston attitude like Louie?

I handed the baby to Kate. "Take her outside. I'll handle it."

She looked at me as if I'd lost my mind.

"Seriously. Let me talk to the man."

Clearly skeptical, Kate took Ellie and headed for the door. "I'm going to quiet her down and be right back."

I made my way to the window and took a moment to breathe. "I'm sorry. For my sister. She's—she's used to getting her way."

His eyes relaxed and he laughed. "I know the type."

Laughter was a good sign, but my work was far from done. I sized him up.

Baby cries left him unmoved. He probably had a big family, lots of children, maybe a few grandkids, enough to have learned to tune out kid sounds. I pegged him as a younger child from a big family. I could picture plenty of bossy older sisters in his background, and maybe one or two younger ones if I was lucky. And perhaps a crabby wife. He hated it when she nagged, but more than anything, he could not stand to see her cry. Aha. Immune to baby cries perhaps, but a woman? Now, that was something.

I felt the tears start to burn at the back of my eyes. Not until I could feel the drops clinging to them would I lift my lashes, at just the right second. *Ready for my close-up, Mr. DeMille.* "She's—she's only trying to help. My husband recently passed away. I haven't been able to keep up with my bills."

With every word, the tears came harder. My voice started to shake. I turned away from the window and fanned my face, as if I was trying so hard to stop.

"I'm sorry, lady." His voice held an edge of impatience along with the barest trace of sympathy.

"My first Christmas without him. The kids still ask—" My voice broke. Perfect. I paused and sucked in a breath. "They still ask when Daddy's coming home."

The emotion wasn't all that hard to fake. My nerves were frayed. My feelings had been close to the surface for months. Tears were never more than a minute away. Patrick would have understood. "I don't know what I'm going to do."

Besides sob uncontrollably for dramatic effect before I pulled it together in the nick of time to ask for a tissue, apologize for taking up his time, and turn to leave.

"Just a sec," he called with a sigh before I got to the door. "I'll meet you outside."

"How on earth did you get him to budge?" Kate asked once the Lexus was running in park outside the impound gates and Louie was headed back inside.

"I gave him a blow job," I said, with a completely straight face.

"You did not!"

"Of course I did. Didn't you see that smile on his face?"

"You played the widow card." She nodded knowingly.

"Yes, I informed him of my sad personal situation. I guess it struck a chord."

"Incredible." But, for once, Kate chose not to criticize. Instead, she grinned and patted me on the back. "Good job! Now what? I've got to meet with clients, but it's informal. I can take Ellie with me, unless you're headed home?"

"No." She wasn't the only one on her way to work. "I've a busy day ahead."

"Getting your nails done?" There wasn't a trace of sarcasm in her voice, as if she had merely come to understand this as the way I lived my life.

Well, not anymore. I turned on my heel, started

for the driver's seat, then looked back and waved my perfectly French-tipped fingers. Manicure was last week, ha. "I have some appointments to keep."

It was all I intended to say. And it wasn't a lie. I'd been due to return to the Habitat for Humanity office for months to finish up on some volunteer fund-raising activities. If anyone could help me get a job, it was Leslie, the Habitat office manager, a twenty-something firecracker who knew everyone and everything in and around Boston.

When I arrived at the office, I was informed that Leslie was out working on a build site in Newton, close to home. I'd come all the way into the city for nothing. For a second, I considered giving up on the job search and putting my trip into Boston to good use: shopping. Instead, I asked for directions to the house under construction and headed right over. *Progress!*

The house was on Mill Street, near Boston College's Newton campus, close enough to take advantage of the college's library but far enough to be a comfortable family neighborhood. Like most of the Habitat sites I'd worked on, the house was a bright new breath of air on a stale, old street. It screamed *hope* and *possibility*, all the things I liked best about working with Habitat for Humanity. The whole "up with people" vibe always got me. Of course, I hadn't done much more than help write a few fliers and tap some resources for funding. The one time I tried to help at a build site was an unmitigated disaster. At least, according to Josh Brandon, the site manager.

So I wasn't the best builder. Yes, my nails never

went in straight, and power tools weren't exactly my thing. But the man needed to relax. What did he expect from untrained volunteers, anyway? If he'd let me paint, as I'd suggested, everything would have been just fine. I could accomplish amazing things with a brush or roller.

As I got out of the car, I caught sight of Josh across the site. Even though he had covered his shock of prematurely silver-gray hair with a hard hat, I could tell it was Josh by the way the flannel hugged his broad, construction worker shoulders. He was five feet ten inches of dense muscle, built as solid as any house he worked on. Though he annoyed me personally, he was an undisputed master of his profession. Even from a distance, he looked a lot calmer today than he had the last time I'd seen him.

Until he looked up and spotted me. Though his facial expression was hidden behind protective eyewear, his body flinched as if I'd sucker punched him in the abs.

"Hide the power tools," he called across the site.

His Boston accent was as thick as his soccer player thighs, so it sounded more like powah tools. He was a good ol' Boston boy, the type that worked hahd and enjoyed a few beeahs aftah work. Just a few. His work ethic matched his build, rock solid.

Heads looked up, then down again when they saw nothing but a harmless little lady in a power suit. Donna Karan, navy pin-striped, fluted skirt, worn with some serious heels. Pilates had given me great calves. If it helped sway any executive decisions in my favor, so be it.

"Good morning to you, too, Mr. Brandon," I said to show his little teasing had not unnerved me as I closed the distance, effortlessly stepping over wood beams and cords in my stilettos. *I am woman, see me walk.* Skill with power tools had nothing on the skill required to walk in heels.

From the corner of my eye, I spied Leslie waving at me from the top of a scaffold on the side of the house. I flashed a smirk at Josh and headed in Leslie's direction.

"Hey, looking to sign up for our phone bank this weekend?" she said, obviously assuming I had come for volunteer purposes. "You didn't have to come all the way out here."

"Actually, it's a social call. But I am looking for some advice."

"Great. What can I do you for?" She climbed down and brushed dust from her hands.

"I need a job." I forced confidence into my tone, as if I got great jobs all the time. Jedi mind trick, as Spencer would say. "Something light, easy, not very important, but it has to pay well."

"If I knew where to find that job, I guarantee you it would be filled. By me! Hello."

I resisted rolling my eyes. Leslie's conversational quirks were one of the reasons I never sought Leslie on a social basis, even though I enjoyed her company at volunteer sites.

"Not that it isn't a perfect description of what I do now at H for H."

"Your job's important," I said, by way of defense. "What would all the families who need houses do without you?"

"Actually, you have great timing. I need to scale down my hours."

"No way."

"Way." Leslie nodded. "My Web design company is taking off and I need to give it more attention. Besides, it pays more than H for H. I charge up to a hundred bucks an hour, and I end up getting it. Go figure."

"Go figure."

"Don't get me wrong, I love working here. But it's too much. If I could cut my hours and give some of my duties over to an assistant— Interested?"

"In being your assistant?"

"More like codirector. It wouldn't pay much. Probably my salary split in half. But it's a start, right?"

"I don't think I'm qualified. I don't even have a résumé. Yet. But—"

"You're plenty qualified. You practically raked in the funding for all of last year on your own just by tapping your trusty acquaintance list. All the board needs is my recommendation and you're in. Plus, you'll have me to show you the ropes. Eventually, who knows? Maybe you can take over and I can bow out."

"Just like that?" It was true that I'd used my community contacts, numerous thanks to Patrick's job in real estate, to drum up a lot of interest and money for the cause. I was a pretty good communicator, and a real people person. I was *perfect* for the job.

"Just like that. Consider yourself hired. I mean, as soon as I run it by the board and all."

It couldn't hurt that I was on a first-name basis with most of the board. The job was mine!

"Leslie, you're incredible!" A weight lifted right off my chest. Really, it was amazing news. I didn't have to look for a job. I didn't need a résumé. No longer would I have to cry about being widowed and beg for mercy just to get an entry-level position doing who knew what? I was spared! "Thank you. Thanks so much."

"Yeah, just come in on Monday dressed for work and we'll get you started."

"Monday? So soon?"

"I'll get the board together and put it to a vote, but yeah. Pretty much. It may not be official right away, but close enough. The sooner you take over half my duties, the sooner I can scale back."

"Okay. I'll see you Monday."

I turned, lost in thought, lost in excitement, lost in the process of deciding what to wear . . . and lost my footing. I felt my ankle twist at an awkward angle. I felt my body going down. I felt an unbelievable wrench of white-hot pain shooting through my leg. And then I didn't feel a thing.

I must have blacked out a minute. When I opened my eyes, I was staring into the most incredible leaf-green gaze I'd ever seen. I was—off the ground, being held by a pair of incredibly strong arms.

"Let's get you to my car, shall we?"

Foreign accent? British? French? I couldn't make it out. The throbbing of my ankle distracted me. But nothing could take my mind off the fact that I was in the arms of a handsome stranger, being carted off to his car. Which, hello (to steal one of Leslie's trademark phrases), was an enormous black Town Car, complete with a driver who came around to open the passenger-side rear door.

No doubt about it. I was still out cold, probably sprawled on the ground in an ungainly heap while caught up in this beautiful dream.

Chapter Three

I blinked and opened my eyes. A blond, broad-shouldered god held me in his arms, seemingly unconcerned with wrinkling his perfectly tailored suit.

Who was he? How did he catch me just in time? But if this wasn't a dream, why couldn't I think straight? Concussion? Did I hit my head when I went down?

The god settled me into the rich leather of his car seats. I took a second to assess him from shoes up. Nice shoes, expensive-looking, probably Italian. Black trousers. Armani? Overall, a *very* nice package.

He laughed.

Tell me I hadn't said it out loud.

"I think I dropped it," I said quickly to cover. "My package."

"She's delirious. She didn't have any packages," Leslie said, suddenly appearing at my side. Or had she always been there, and I just didn't notice? Who would, with Daniel Craig standing next to her? Or was he more David Beckham? "Just her Coach bag."

She handed it to the god, who placed it on the seat beside me.

I glanced again. Oh yes, definitely a longer-haired David Beckham. Probably between thirty and thirty-five. Tall, blond, and built, with green eyes that sent an instant charge right through me.

"I think she'll be all right," the Beckham-god said. "As far as her head goes, I didn't see her strike it on anything. Now, the ankle, that's another story."

He leaned down to inspect the ankle up close.

"Ow!" I couldn't help shrieking when his fingers caressed my delicate skin, and unfortunately, it wasn't out of excitement. It hurt.

"It may be broken." He made his skilled assessment after trying to gently move it from side to side. I bit my lip to keep from crying out.

"Broken?" I feared pain. I feared disability. But more than anything, I feared my ankle becoming an ugly swollen mound right under Beckham's touch.

He unbuckled the ankle strap of my shoe and slid it off.

"Precautionary," he said, with a wink that made me melt into the seat.

"Thank you." I tried not to wince as my newly freed foot went limp along with my backbone as I melted at the romance of it all. He'd carried me. All the way to his car.

"Nick Angelos," he said by way of introduction.

Leslie, belatedly realizing she'd been lax in introductions, jumped in. "Mr. Angelos, one of our corporate donors, has graciously offered land and supplies for new buildings. Including this one, in fact."

Nick nodded. Angelos. My own personal angel. "I happened by to check on progress, to see if Leslie needed anything else. I'd just stepped out of the car when I saw you going down."

My head swooned. The thought of "Nick Angelos" in the same sentence as "going down" sent an instant erotic shock right through me.

"I can't imagine how bad it would be if you hadn't caught her," Leslie said, her cheeks coloring. "You moved so fast. As if you had wings on your feet."

"Unfortunately, it looks bad enough as it is," he said.

I followed Nick's concerned gaze back to my own ankle. It had indeed swollen, and some highly unattractive purple bruises colored the inflamed skin. Yuck. How embarrassing. I made a move to cover it, but recoiled in pain. I couldn't contain the yelp that shot to my lips from the effort.

"These damn shoes." The voice came in the form of a snarl from behind Nick. Josh Brandon stepped forward, bent to fetch my shoe, and held it up. "Wearing these around a construction site is suicide."

"As usual, Mr. Brandon, thanks for your concern." I was reminded of the thorough dressing-down I received from attempting to use the electric sander without protective eyewear on a past volunteer endeavor.

"Well, I'm foreman here and from now on, I establish a rule. No walking around a site without proper footwear."

"My footwear is very proper," I said, defensive. "The perfect match for my suit, and quite in style for the season."

"I mean, appropriate." His full lip rose in a sneer, lending his stark blue eyes an air of menace. "Appropriate footwear. Work boots, with steel-reinforced toes. No heels, no soft Italian leather."

He lowered his eyes to Nick Angelos's feet and lifted them to meet my gaze again. "Next time you show up without steel-toed Timberlands, you'll be banned from walking around the site."

Nick snorted. Clearly, he wasn't going to let Josh Brandon tell him what to do. Unfortunately, I couldn't afford to flout the rules if I planned to accept employment.

"May I have a look?" Josh asked, stepping around Nick to gesture toward my ankle. I nodded.

Josh knelt and ran his hand over the ankle with a whisper-light touch. I barely felt it. I didn't even wince. It appeared he'd had experience with this, and no doubt he had from working construction sites. "Do you think it's broken?"

He shook his head, not taking his gaze from the bruising. "No. Just a sprain, maybe just a really bad twist. You would be in a lot more pain if it were broken."

"I'm in *a lot* of pain," I said. How could he dare steal some drama from the situation by declaring it not broken! "I hide it well. It's a parent thing. Mothers are good at hiding pain."

Josh smiled, a wide grin so unexpectedly tender it disarmed me. "You may want to drop by a hospital and have it checked out, just to be sure."

Nick moved in again, nudging Josh aside. "I'll see to it she gets what she needs."

My gut clenched with anticipation. What exactly did he think I needed? For the first time in a long while, I felt the spark of romantic interest and the thrill that came with instantaneous attraction, and I liked it. A lot.

"I'll be fine." I slid forward to get out of the car. "I'll just drive home and call my sister."

"You're not driving anywhere with that ankle," Josh said.

"He's right," Nick said. "I'll take you."

I looked up and got lost in the lush green gaze. I didn't want to protest. "All right."

"Good." He eased me back and took a seat beside me.

I leaned forward. "Leslie, I'll see you Monday. I'll come back for my car later. Don't worry."

"Monday." Leslie waved. Josh Brandon stood beside her, hands on hips and wearing the usual cross expression. The driver shut the door and walked around to get behind the wheel.

"I've got healing in my blood," Nick said, turning to me. "One of my brothers perfected some medical techniques and I've spent plenty of time watching him work."

Gulp.

"I hate to be a bother." I tried to adjust myself more comfortably in the seat as the car pulled away from the curb, but my ankle throbbed with the slightest movement. I bit my lip to keep from crying out.

"You're no bother. Let's get you home. Where do you live?"

I gave him the address, only a short drive away. He repeated it to his driver. "There now. Sit back. Relax. Swing your feet up into my lap."

My heart raced. I couldn't help glancing at his lap, trousers hugging lean-muscled thighs.

"I'm not going to bite." He laughed. "Don't look so scared."

"I'm sorry." I tried to steady my breathing. "It's the pain. I think it's making me light-headed."

"That's why I need to get my hands on that ankle. I can stop the pain. Now, come on." He patted his leg. "Up."

I shifted back, careful to keep my knees together as I swung my feet into his lap.

"Very good." He smoothed his hand over my good leg, from foot to knee and down again, before reaching over to tend the bad one. "Pilates?"

"How did you know?" I sat up a little, pleased that he had noticed.

"Long muscles. Your legs are beautifully toned."

"Thank you." I couldn't wait to tell Kate how wrong she was about me "wasting all those hours in the gym." Looking good was never a waste. Especially when a handsome man appreciated the results.

So easily, I could have given up on my body and wallowed in self-pity over countless pints of ice cream. Not that I didn't indulge in the occasional Cherry Garcia pity party. I wasn't *that* perfect. But I knew I had to work at looking good and I wasn't ready to throw in the towel and go the *Body by Ben and Jerry* route.

He rubbed my ankle, working magic to take away the pain. My legs looked so white against the tan of his hands. The bruising seemed less pronounced.

"Oh. That's good."

"I'm going to need to wrap it," he said, stripping off his jacket, tossing it aside, and starting to work at the buttons of his shirt.

"What are you doing?"

"I'll use my shirt. Not to worry. I have plenty of them."

"But—no. I'll have something at home to wrap it. Don't trouble yourself."

He shrugged out of the sleeves and ripped. "Too late."

Speaking of ripped. I drank in the sight of his bare chest. He might have been a god by the looks of him. The man took excellent care of himself. His skin glowed bronze against the creamy leather seats. Every inch of him was taut, his muscles well defined right down to the washboard abs. His biceps worked as he tore the white fabric into strips. My mouth went bone dry.

I watched him, unable to speak as he began to wind the strips around my ankle. Finally, I found my voice. "I can replace your shirt. I'm sure it could have waited, but you're right. It feels much better."

"Nonsense." Shirtless, he shrugged back into his jacket. "I don't want you to feel uncomfortable."

"Amazing," I said, wiggling my exposed toes, and so glad I'd kept the pedicure appointment earlier in the week. My pearl-pink toes looked adorable peeking out from the makeshift bandaging. "You really are a miracle worker."

"My pleasure." He reached for my hand, lifted it to his lips, and kissed the tops of my fingers curled over his.

"Actually, I think it's mine." I giggled like an idiot schoolgirl. What was I thinking? Who *could* think sitting next to an Adonis?

"I never cared much for Adonis," he said. "Honestly, he's rather full of himself. No doubt, fueled on by Aphrodite and Persephone fighting over him so often—sickening."

Had I said that bit about Adonis out loud? I must have. Oh. God.

"I'm fine," I said, desperate to change the subject. "So, how about that Josh Brandon, huh? Talk about full of himself."

"Mr. Brandon?" Nick's lips curled up in a sly half smile. "So you're not all that fond of him, eh?"

"Not exactly." I blushed, feeling suddenly guilty for throwing Josh under the bus to save myself. "I mean, he's okay. He's a master of his profession. But he gets a little bossy on the job site. On occasion. Nothing I can't handle."

"With the shoes, perhaps? I thought I saw you bristle at his comments there. As if a woman doesn't know for herself what constitutes proper footwear?"

"Exactly. Could you imagine me in Timberlands? With this suit? Ha!"

"I can imagine you in just about anything." His lip curled as if in some sort of secret sexy invitation. "You could pull off Timberlands. Or anything you choose. But that's the point, isn't it? Your feet, your choice."

"Yeah," I responded, feeling empowered. I liked it. "My feet, my choice." Never mind that Josh was probably right and I should invest in a good pair of work boots. But still.

"And such adorable feet they are. Feeling better?"

"Actually, yes. Much better. Your wrap did the trick."

"Good. I believe we're on your street."

"Oh." So soon? I glanced out the window. My street. "Wow. Your driver's good."

"I hope Morrison didn't hear you. His head's big enough as it is."

I glanced toward the front. Was that a smile

reflected in the rearview? "Thank you, Morrison," I said, then turned back to Nick. "Must be nice to have a driver. I hate driving in the city."

"I love it, but it's too risky on company time. I get a lot of tickets." His eyes lit with a golden sparkle. "I like to go fast."

My pulse accelerated. I bet he did. "Thank you again. I don't know what I would have done without you."

Besides have Leslie drive me to the ER and probably go back later to get my car. As it was, my poor newly freed Lexus was left abandoned on another street. But at least this time, when I needed Kate's help to pick up my car, I could say it was because I had a job. Yes! That's right. Bennie St. James, employable after all.

"You don't think I'm going to let you walk away, do you?"

"I—um, I think I can manage."

"It's too soon to put weight on that ankle. Sit still." He opened the door, got out, and leaned back in to scoop me up in his arms.

"Oh no. Really. I—" Felt so good in his arms. So light and tiny. His arms were incredible. "I mean, I probably just need a little support."

"Nonsense. Morrison, bring her bag," he called behind to his driver after he'd lifted me and started for the door.

I turned to shout to Morrison, "My house keys are in the front pocket of the Coach bag," and that was when I saw Kate's SUV in my driveway. Kate? Here?

"What on earth?" She opened the front door in

time for Nick to slide right by her, with me in his arms. "What happened to you?"

Her bewildered expression said *and who the hell is he?* But she didn't ask out loud.

"I had a little accident," I answered. "You can put me down on the couch there."

"An accident? What?"

Nick set me down as instructed, our eyes meeting as he settled me, a nearly palpable shock of attraction sizzling through me. He found a throw pillow to prop under my foot and tucked me in under the hand-knit afghan, a gift from Gran I kept draped over the back of the couch.

"Thank you," I said.

"No need for thanks. I'm just glad you're okay." There was a marked tenderness in his tone. "She took quite a spill," he said to Kate. "I'm Nick."

Morrison deposited my Coach bag on the chair inside the door and headed straight back out again.

"Nick Angelos," I interrupted, still enchanted with the idea of having my own personal angel. And why not? Kate'd had her devil, Ellie's father, who she claimed had run off to reign over hell. "He has been doing some charitable work with Habitat for Humanity and I ran into him on a build site. Rather, I ran into some wood and lost my balance, and Mr. Angelos just happened to catch me."

"A build site for Habitat for Humanity? What were you doing there?"

I smiled. "Getting a job. Meet the new community outreach codirector."

Kate's eyes widened. "Seriously?"

"Yes, seriously. Is it so hard to believe?"

She didn't take the bait. "And you, Mr. Angelos? Did you donate your shirt to the cause?"

"He used it to wrap my ankle." My hero!

Nick shrugged. "What can I say? It was all I happened to have handy at the time. I'm a sucker for a damsel in distress."

Kate shot me a look. I answered with a waggle of my brows.

"I'm not always so clumsy. Would you like a cold drink? Kate can get us some lemonade or something? Kate?" The weather reports might have called for a November chill, but my internal furnace had been on the rise since meeting Nick.

"Oh, absolutely. Maybe some coffee?"

"Nothing for me, thanks. I should be getting back to the office. But I'm glad to see the color return to your cheeks, Mrs. St. James. May I come back to check in on you later? Would you mind?"

I feared Kate was about to butt in and say we minded. Fortunately, she stayed quiet.

"I wouldn't mind at all. You're welcome anytime. Oh, and call me Bennie."

"Excellent. Then, I'll bid you both a good afternoon. Lovely to meet you, Bennie. And you, Kate. Will you see me out?"

"Until we meet again," I called out after him.

"Very soon, I promise you," he answered without hesitation. "Make sure she stays off that ankle for a day or so," I overheard him say to Kate on his way out.

"Oh, Kate! Isn't it romantic?" I said, sitting up more as soon as I heard the door close. "He caught me in his arms and carried me to his car. Just like in the movies."

"Ankle injury, yeah. That's romance for you. He's kind of an odd one, don't you think?"

"Oddly appealing, perhaps. Did you get a load of that bod?"

"I couldn't exactly avoid it, the way he was putting it out there for display."

"Well, he did try to cover up. He put his jacket back on, anyway. What else could he do?"

"Oh, I don't know. Stop at a pharmacy to pick up an Ace bandage? Maybe drive you to an ER?"

"I don't need a hospital. I'm fine." Not too fine. The ankle felt great, but I liked the idea of staying off my feet and letting everyone take care of me for the afternoon. Why not? I got a job! I deserved a few perks before I had to join the working class. "I mean, it's still sore, but—he said I would be fine and he seemed to know his stuff."

"Right, with the degree from WebMD and all."

"You're such a cynic, you know, Kate? Can't you just be happy for me, for once?"

"Because you met a man? You like him that much?"

Maybe. "No. Because I got a job. How cool is that?"

She sighed. "You're right. I'm sorry. It's extremely cool, if a little unexpected."

"I told you I wanted to take care of myself."

"You did. You're right. And after you got your car out this morning, I would say you're on a roll. Oh! What about the Lexus?"

"I had to leave it at the construction site. We'll have to go back for it later. Once I feel better. Maybe you could pick the kids up from school for me? What are you and Ellie doing here, anyway? Shouldn't you be at work?"

She shook her head. "I finished my morning

appointment. It was a success, and now there's
another new open house on the schedule before
the holidays. While I was on the way back to the
office to work out floor plans with Val, Sarah called
and said she forgot her gym clothes."

"Oh. She called you? Why not me?"

"She tried you but she didn't reach your cell."

"I set it to vibrate so the ring wouldn't interrupt
me at my interview." So it wasn't exactly an interview.
I couldn't let Kate think Leslie had simply handed
me a job. Bad enough that I felt guilty my daughter
had to call Aunt Kate because her mom was otherwise engaged. "She must have left a message."

"Not a problem. I zipped here, brought her
clothes, and then came back here because Ellie left
a nice little bundle of her own for me and your
house was closer. After I changed her, she conked
out, so I figured I would hang here awhile and let
her sleep. Val and I exchanged ideas over the phone.
I hope you don't mind."

"You know I don't mind. My house is your house."

"And the reverse. Unless you're going to make a
habit of bringing home shirtless hunks of man
cake like that one. Then we'll have to work out an
arrangement." Kate smiled.

"Ha. Yes. Because shirtless hunks of man cake fall
in my lap on a daily basis."

"It was my understanding that you fell into his lap."

"Yeah." I blushed. "Whatever. So, as long as you're
picking the kids up from school, why don't you and
Ellie stay for dinner? I've got a lasagna in the freezer."

"Sounds good. I'll bring the wine. Your getting a
job calls for celebration."

Chapter Four

While Kate was out picking the kids up from school, a knock sounded at the front door. My heart leapt. Nick Angelos? He'd come back to see me so soon?

"Just a minute," I called out from the couch as I debated if I should shout for him to let himself in or make a good show of limping over to answer. With Kate's help, I'd changed out of my suit to my shlumpy sweats and a tee. Better to stay on the couch. I fluffed my hair, licked my lips, and called out a seductive "come in."

The door opened slowly, as if he hesitated, unsure. Suddenly I didn't want to look the overeager one. I leaned back into the couch, my best Sleeping Beauty pose, eyes closed but not quite asleep. I imagined him approaching and kissing me fully awake. A little role play never hurt in a relationship.

The floorboards creaked with the approaching footfalls. Closer, closer. I breathed slowly, making sure my lips were plumped out, tempting. He stopped right over me. Should I open my eyes, say hello? Or wait for him to get the hint?

"Ugh!" Something hit me solidly in the chest, something small enough not to hurt much but big enough to make me jump. I opened my eyes. "What the—"

"Your keys." Josh Brandon stood over me, a small crooked smile on his lips. "Who did you expect? Prince Charming?" With his Boston accent, it came out "chahming."

He laughed. Laughed! At me.

I picked keys out of my cleavage and sat up. "I was resting my ankle. Remember? I kind of got hurt at your work site. Maybe I should sue?"

"Yeah. That's going to happen. You're gonna sue your new employer? I don't think so, Princess." Without waiting for an invitation, he plunked down in the opposite armchair. "Congratulations, by the way. Leslie told me the good news. So, how's your ankle?"

Maybe it was the way the hulking brute took up the entire chair, legs spread, no concern for the Andrew Martin fabric or delicacy of the English wingback-style frame. Or perhaps it was the way he'd made air quotes with his thick workman's fingers when he'd said "good" news. Or the simple fact that he laughed at me upon entry. Whatever it was, Josh Brandon made my blood boil. "My ankle's fine. Just fine, thank you."

"You went for X-rays? The doctor said it was fine?"

"I didn't need X-rays." I shrugged. "Nick Angelos took care of me."

He huffed loudly, as if annoyed, and ran his hands through his shock of prematurely gray hair.

"He's a doctor now, too, is he? Along with his other lofty credentials? Philanthropist, entrepreneur, architectural engineer."

I sat up straighter. "You really don't like him, do you?" Apparently Nick and I were two of a kind, both having earned the Josh Brandon stamp of disapproval.

"Nah, it's not that." Josh stared across the room at the framed prints of my family lining the staircase, or into space. He didn't seem particularly focused. "Never mind. So, your car's out front now, if you need it. I didn't think it would be safe on the street near the site all night."

Instantly, I was flooded with a mix of gratitude and remorse. "My keys! That's right. Thank you. Thanks so much. That was really nice of you. But—what about *your* car?"

"Leslie's borrowing it for the night. She's got to drive up to check on her mom in Vermont."

Leslie, a city dweller, relied on public transportation, but she needed wheels to get to her mother's place. I remembered that Leslie's mother had been going through treatment for breast cancer, bringing on a second wave of remorse. I'd been so focused on myself I hadn't even thought to ask Leslie how her mom was doing. "How is her mother? Is everything okay?"

Josh finally stopped staring into the distance and met my gaze. The brightness of his silver-blue eyes made me blink a little in surprise. I'd forgotten how those eyes could penetrate, as if he could see right into me. He really did have amazing eyes, especially in contrast with the silver of his hair.

"She's recovering," he said, after a minute's hesitation, as if he was trying to decide if I really cared about Leslie's mother, or anyone other than myself. "They did the double mastectomy but nothing seems to have spread. Leslie's spending the weekend up there with her."

"So how are you getting home? If Leslie has your car and you brought my Lexus, then you need a ride?"

He shook his head and stood up, as if taking it as a cue to leave. "It's a nice day for a walk."

"Don't be silly. You live miles from here."

"Four miles. It's no big deal."

"And then for the weekend? You'll be stuck."

He looked surprised that I was even capable of giving any thought to someone else's predicament. "I've got my bike."

Yes, that fit. I could picture him as the leather-clad biker type. He probably spent his weekends at Harley bars surrounded by big-haired buxom types. I debated if I should repeat the offer of a ride or thank him again, and then became distracted by the image of Josh Brandon as tough guy biker tooling down the highway. To my imagination's surprise, he looked pretty good in black leather.

I startled at the sound of the door opening. Kate came in, followed by an exuberant Sarah and a dark-haired smiling Spence, who looked miles apart from the sulky image he was so desperate to project. You couldn't keep a good St. James down.

"Hey, gang." Josh was first to greet them. He'd met the kids when we volunteered as a family earlier in the year. He knew Kate from a previous acquaintance. *Ellie's father.* "Whoa, what happened to you?"

"I'm a Goth." Spencer beamed and tossed his dark spikes of hair. "Cool, huh?"

"He's doing it to impress a girl," I added quickly. I wasn't sure what Josh might think of Spence's new look, but I didn't need to give him more reason to criticize.

"Ah." Josh nodded. "Did it work?"

"I think so. Shelley's coming over to do home-work tomorrow."

"Well, all right, my man." Josh did some kind of guy salute move, a fist in the air. "Good for you. And, Sarah? What's new with you?"

Josh might have called me a princess, but he didn't mess with Sarah. No "little lady" or "angel" or any of the girlie nicknames that drove her crazy, even though her delicate face and long red hair put most people in a girlie frame of mind. At last, I'd found something to appreciate in Josh. He had a seemingly innate sense of how to deal with my kids even though he'd only met them briefly on a previous occasion.

"I made the hockey team," she said in a matter-of-fact way that did nothing to disguise the fact that it made her so proud. "We've got our first game in a few weeks."

"Whoa, hockey. I love hockey. Would you mind if I came to watch a game now and then?"

"No problemo." Sarah returned the fist salute that Josh had shared with Spence earlier. "So, Mom, Aunt Kate says you took a donkey. You okay?"

"I didn't think Aunt Kate spoke in such colorful terms. But yeah, I'll be fine. Just a little ankle twist. Where'd Kate go? She was just here."

"She's getting groceries out of the car," Spencer

said. "We're dropping off our book bags and going back out to help her. Then we'll be in our rooms, and out of your way."

"More like out of the way of boring adult conversation."

"That, too." Spence smiled. "Good to see you again, Mr. Brandon."

"Call me Josh. No need for formalities."

"Later, Josh." Sarah slapped him a high five and followed her brother out through the kitchen door.

A minute later, Kate came in accompanied by Bert and Ernie, two fawn pugs with nearly identical features. Sensing new blood, the ferocious duo wiggled their way over to Josh, where they proceeded to roll over for tummy rubs.

"My fierce protectors. They seem to have forgotten that immediately rolling over for intruders does not exactly establish their dominance."

"They know an alpha dog when they see one," Kate quipped.

"Hey, Kate." Josh lifted his square masculine jaw by way of greeting.

Josh and Kate's warm familiarity set my mind to work instantly. Did I sense some chemistry? My matchmaking skills, long dormant, sprang back into action. Josh and Kate? It had possibilities. Sure, she was seeing Marc Ramirez off and on, but it never hurt to play the field, so to speak. I took some pride in the fact that Marc, a linebacker for the Patriots, was actually one of my past fix-up attempts for Kate, from before she'd even hooked up with Owen Glendower and had Ellie. Not that I'd had anything to do with them hooking up again once Owen vanished from the scene, but I *had* introduced them. It counted for something.

"Hey." She smiled big, as if Josh was her favorite new friend. "Thanks for bringing over the Lexus. I owe you one."

I nearly fell off the couch. "*You* owe him one?"

She rolled her eyes. "Of course. How do you think he got the keys?"

"So, on the way to pick up the kids—"

"I stopped by the Habitat site and asked Josh if he could drive your car over. Fortunately, he was willing."

Josh smiled. The two of them shared a glance. "Kate, you know I'm always willing."

Wait a minute. *Kate* asked Josh to drive my car over? Maybe she was beating me to the fix-up game. Turnabout was fair play. Was I rubbing off on her? Did she somehow see a future for me with, *gulp*, Josh Brandon? I looked from Josh to Kate and back again, trying to figure it out. No. I was being ridiculous. Kate hated matchmaking far too much to get wrapped up in it. And Josh? No way he was attracted *to me*. But then, he drew in close and knelt at my side, those blue eyes a gas flame burning into me.

"We've established that Nick Angelos says you're fine, for what that's worth." Josh laughed. "But I'd like to have another look. Do you mind?"

"Look? At my ankle? You?" I tried to contain my gasp of surprise. Josh didn't even *like* me. Kate, poor thing, was so bad at this sort of thing. Bless her for trying, but—why was he looking at me like that? Why did he even agree to bring my car over? What alternate universe had I ended up stumbling into? I remembered the gentleness of Josh's touch after I'd first fallen and I knew I could at least trust him to make an assessment, yet why did I feel so cornered? "And what makes you any more qualified than Nick?"

His gaze steadily held mine. Unsettled, I looked away and sought his lips, which curled with amusement. He had nice lips, actually. Full, soft. Not as rough-looking as one might expect considering the time he spent in the sun. "Years of experience. I've seen all kinds of injuries through the years."

"Hmm." I contemplated his words, or rather, his lips as he formed them. "And you think you can heal me?"

"I'd like to try," he said, and his words seemed to hold so much more meaning than a desire to fix my ankle. For a second, I looked at Josh and saw a man. Just a man, not the dictatorial construction foreman. But it passed just as quickly. It must have been my admiration for his well-formed mouth.

Silly of me, really. There was no way I could actually imagine even going on one date with Josh Brandon. No doubt his idea of romance would be to plunk me on the back of his bike, take me for a spin around the block, and stop off at his favorite bar for a few *bee-ahs*. Or maybe he was more into the whole *Lady and the Tramp* Italian dinner scenario, one plate of spaghetti, two meatballs. My gaze caught on that mouth and I had a sudden vivid image of being caught on opposite ends of the same strand of spaghetti.

"Whatever," I said, to hide my blush, lifted my ankle outside the blanket, and tugged up the leg of my sweatpants to the knee. "Do your worst."

"Only my best for you, Ben." He winked before

he turned his attention to the strips that bound my injury. "What's this?"

"Nick's shirt," I said, flushing at the memory of his bare torso, those perfectly sculpted abs. "He ripped it to make bandages for me."

Josh snickered. "Get real."

"My thought exactly." Kate joined the conversation, bringing cold drinks out from the kitchen, a sparkling water for me, a beer for Josh. "You should have seen him carrying Bennie across the room like a delicate heroine from a romance novel. Blech."

"It *was* romantic." I had to protest their disapprobation. "He was really sweet."

"And shirtless." Kate nodded. "Under a suit jacket. He looked like something straight out of *Saturday Night Live.* You know, those brothers that Chris Kattan and Will Ferrell used to do."

Josh removed his fingers from my ankle as he boomed laughter. "The Butabi brothers. *Night at the Roxy.*"

"Yes!" Kate joined in. "Those morons. Ha!"

"More like Daniel Craig," I said. "From *Casino Royale.* Or David Beckham."

"Or Fabio." Another wisecrack from Josh. More laughter from Kate.

"You just don't like him." I pulled my sweatpant leg back down.

"Who does? He swans around like he owns all of Boston, for God's sake. Now, come on, I wasn't done looking. Give me your leg."

"What, so you can make fun of Nick's gallant efforts again?"

"I'll be nice. I promise. Let me look. I want to make sure you don't have to go to a hospital."

"All right," I allowed, on a sigh, as I pulled my sweatpants back up to reveal my leg.

"Ellie still asleep?" Kate gestured to the baby monitor at my side.

"I hobbled up to check on her a little while ago and she was sleeping soundly. She lets out the occasional snore as if to reassure me that she's not waking any time soon."

"I'll go check on her." Kate excused herself, leaving me in Josh's hands. Literally.

Again, Josh's touch was light. When he looked up from his examination, he seemed genuinely amazed. "It looks great. How does it feel?"

"Better," I said, eager to defend Nick's efforts. "But it still hurts," I added, enjoying the thought of an evening on the couch being waited on. It didn't hurt at all, actually. It was as if nothing had happened. Kate returned with a still-sleepy Ellie in her arms.

"Unreal. I would have expected the bruising to last for weeks, but it's nearly gone," he said, over my head to Kate. "No more swelling. Maybe Nick did know what he was doing after all."

He followed the assessment with a long swig of beer, as if the concession had left a bad taste in his mouth.

"Good," I said, covering back up with the blanket. "I hate hospitals."

Who didn't? But the room grew quiet around me as if everyone silently acknowledged why hospitals might be worse for me than for the average bear. Kate had given birth to Ellie in a newfangled birthing center, keeping me a safe distance from the horrible place where my husband had died in my arms.

Oh. God. The thought took me by surprise. Not

that I wasn't used to random flashbacks of being with Patrick, of suddenly missing him, of bursting into tears unexpectedly. But lately, it had happened less often, and I'd started to think I had it all under control. And then, in a heartbeat, it all came back to me, flooding over me, threatening to drag me down into that desperate, dark, and swirling pool of grief all over again. I choked, gasping for breath, feeling as if I were about to drown.

Before I knew what was happening, Josh was on the couch beside me, cradling me in his big strong construction worker arms. "It's okay, Bennie. I'm sorry. I didn't mean to—just let it out. It's okay to cry."

"No, it's not okay," I said, breathing at last. In, out. In, out. "No. I thought—jeez, it's been a year almost."

"A year's not really that much time," Josh said. "You loved him."

"Very much, yes." Breathing became easier. As easy as it was to dissolve into grief, it had become that much easier to snap out of it. I wiped my face. "But I'm fine. Really. I'm sorry to scare you."

"It takes a lot more than a woman's tears to scare me," Josh said, removing his arm from my shoulder. "But I'd better get going."

Suddenly I felt very grateful to Josh Brandon. Most guys would have fled for the door the second I became hysterical. Not Josh. He'd jumped right in to comfort me. It was a nice quality. "Stay for dinner. We're having lasagna."

"Yes." Kate hovered near the end of the couch. "We've got plenty. Marc's coming over, too, so it will be fun. Just the four of us and the kids."

"Marc's coming?" Just when I thought it was safe

to relax, I sensed a double date scenario brewing. No problem. I would just have to make sure the kids took center seats, creating some space between Josh and me. They would make up any lulls in conversation and remove any of those awkward moments that might pop up if I had any renewed reason to believe he was attracted to me.

"He called earlier and I couldn't resist asking him. The Patriots play Monday night this week, and it's a home game. Not that he'll be on the field with his knee acting up, but he still has to make it an early night, the perfect night for staying in with family."

He was practically family by now. What was I thinking to even consider fixing Kate up with Josh? I wondered when Kate was finally going to give in and get as serious about Marc as he obviously felt about her. She hadn't gotten over Owen. Yet. But I could see it was only a matter of time. To Marc's benefit, he was like a father to Ellie. He'd even beat my parents to the birthing center for her delivery.

And in this corner, Josh Brandon.

I sipped my water and wondered if Josh had ulterior motives or if he truly was just a guy having dinner with friends.

Marc arrived for dinner with a big bunch of wild-flowers in tow. Score one for Marc.

"They're beautiful! Thank you." Kate kissed him on the cheek. I glanced at Josh. No reaction. He stared straight ahead in the direction of the fireplace.

A second later, Josh was on his feet to do the guy greeting thing, a handshake and slap on the arm. "How you doing, man?"

"Not too bad," Marc said. "Hanging in there. You?"

"Eh. Hanging in there," Josh said. Men were so creative with words.

"Busted ankle, huh? Tough break." Marc leaned over and rumpled my hair.

I'd almost forgotten about it. "It's feeling a little better now. I should be able to hobble over to the dinner table without much trouble."

"That's my girl. Taking one for the team. And where's my favorite little lady?" Marc looked around for Ellie, found her playing with her toes in the baby seat, and scooped her up in his arms. "Oo-wee, touchdown. Kate, I'm taking her up to give her a change."

"How long has it been since you've had a fire in the hearth?" Josh asked after a minute, as if the question had been on his mind for some time.

"Oh, a long time," I answered cautiously. Josh wasn't exactly acting the part of the romantic suitor, but it was too early to tell what he, or Kate, had in mind. "Patrick was allergic to burning wood, so I've put decorative candles in there. It's something."

"Something, but not the real thing. There's nothing like a blazing fire on a cold winter's night."

"True. I do miss it, actually. We'd thought about converting it to gas."

"Gas?" Josh wrinkled his nose in disgust. It was a fine nose, not too angular, slightly wide. An Irish nose, I decided. Like Patrick's. "But then you don't get the outdoorsy aroma. And the flames aren't the same. No. You've got to stick with wood."

"I don't know how to light a fire."

"Would you mind if I had a look? Not tonight, I

mean, but I can come over next week, get a look at the chimney in daylight. Clean her out, get a fire lit."

"You want to clean my chimney?" It sounded like a lot of work.

"I want to light your fire," he said, and the gleam in his eye matched the spark of any blaze. My stomach flipped. Was that a line? Please tell me he wasn't resorting to cheesy lines. But he clarified. "I don't have a fireplace of my own. It would be nice to have a fire. If you don't mind."

Sigh of relief. Maybe he was just hot for my fireplace. "No, not at all. You can come over and play around with it. I'm not sure about where to get wood and supplies."

"You free Tuesday? We can go out together. I know a good place for wood. A guy out in Natick, he cuts it himself. He can deliver it, for a price, but it's cheaper if I bring my truck out and fill it up there. It's a bit of a drive, but it's pretty this time of year."

"Yeah, sure," I agreed. "Tuesday." Tuesday. Nothing dangerous about heading out for firewood on a Tuesday, right? It wasn't like it was a date. It wasn't a date. Was it?

I made a mental note to make sure Kate was around on Tuesday. Safety in numbers. Just in case.

"Great, I'm going to go see if I can help your sister in the kitchen. How about I refresh your water while I'm up?" He reached for my glass.

I looked up and got lost in the blue of his eyes. It took me a minute to recover and speak. "Sure, but how about something stronger? There are some bottles of red in the kitchen, maybe a California cabernet?"

"California cab with lasagna? Are you kidding me?"

I rolled my eyes. Not another wine guy. Patrick would have said the same thing. "So, what do you suggest?"

"A nice throaty barolo."

"I may have one of those. Feel free to look through the selection under the bar." I gestured to the heavy, old-fashioned wood bar in the corner, a gift from Kate several Christmases ago that had delighted Patrick to no end. Maybe that was my problem with thinking of Josh as a romantic interest, that he reminded me a bit of Patrick. Or maybe it was the Italian wine. He was probably a fan of the North End, while I was more of a Southey kind of girl.

"Mmm. It all looks wonderful," I said, looking over the bounty laid out on the table once I hobbled my way into the kitchen, embellishing a bit to maintain my status as the injured party. It wasn't the usual spread I would have laid out for company, with my finer china and extra decorative touches, but Kate had used one of my nicer tablecloths to complement my everyday dishes, the heavy rustic earthenware. "Salad, too?"

"Courtesy of Josh."

"Caesar is a specialty of mine," he said proudly as he stopped filling glasses to dash over and help me to my seat at the head of the table. "I have a secret formula to make sure you get a crouton with every bite."

I looked up, astounded. He had no idea that I had a similar secret formula, about which Kate teased me mercilessly. Kate and I exchanged a glance. Maybe I'd met my salad-making match.

Josh took the seat next to me, across from Kate, Ellie in her high chair, and Marc, who had put himself on baby duty for the evening to give Kate a break. The kids joined us and filled in the rest of the seats.

We passed around dishes, filled plates, and made comfortable conversation. The kids told us about their days. Josh complimented my lasagna, my mother's recipe. I returned the compliments on his salad.

"If I'd known I was coming for dinner, I would have brought a loaf of my famous home-baked bread."

I cocked a brow. "Right, like the kind you pick up at the store, stick in the oven for a few minutes, and voila, home-baked bread?"

His fork paused in the air, midway to his mouth. "Uh, maybe that's what *you* do, Betty Crocker. I actually take the time to measure, mix, and knead." He met my surprised stare with a shrug. "It's therapeutic after a hard day on a construction site. Kneading is incredible stress relief."

"I can't believe you actually get home from a long day of building and bake bread," I said, out loud, then wanted to kick myself for directing my stare to his strong, workingman hands. Thick fingers.

"Something about punching down dough just takes the edge right off." He put down his fork and pounded a fist into his other open hand. "You should try it sometime."

"Oh, I have. I can see that it might be therapeutic. But you just don't seem the type." I sipped my wine to chase away the image of Josh working dough with his hands, sleeves rolled up over muscular forearms.

"What type do I seem?"

"The biker bar type." I laughed, thinking of my earlier image of leather-clad Josh knocking back a beer with a buxom blonde at his side. The wine had relaxed me and loosened my tongue.

"Ha!" He laughed. "Just call me Easy Rider."

His eyes twinkled in the way that made me think of my birthstone, aquamarine. They held me rapt, the way the light refracted from his glistening pupils. Those eyes were dangerous! They should be declared a lethal weapon. It took a minute to break my stare and realize that we were carrying on a conversation as if we were the only two at the table. "So, um, Marc, who do you play Monday night?"

"Indianapolis. The Colts are also undefeated, so it's going to be a good one. I wish I could get on the field."

"The knee's still giving you trouble?" Josh asked.

"Yeah. Every now and then. The coach is good about trusting my instincts. I tell him when it's good to go and when I need to take it easy."

"You're lucky to be with an understanding coach. A lot of teams might keep putting you out there, testing your limits."

"I know it. I do like it here. For so many reasons." Marc looked at Ellie and then up at Kate, warmth lighting his brown eyes to a golden amber glow.

Kate smiled, but didn't seem to pick up on Marc's meaning. How clueless could she be?

I tried to throw Kate a look, but Sarah piped in. "Mom, my teacher's going to call you next week."

Aha, that was never a good sign. I noticed she

waited for the right time to strike, with friends and family around and Mom building a nice wine buzz. Smart.

"About what?" I said, keeping it casual. She knew I wouldn't lose my temper now.

"Math. I'm having trouble. I kind of failed my last quiz."

"Kind of failed?" Josh and I asked in unison.

She blushed. "Did fail. But the teacher said I can make it up. It's not that I don't understand balancing equations. It's that I go too fast and make stupid little mistakes, so that the answer ends up wrong in the end."

"I used to have that problem," Josh said. "My teacher solved it by teaching me to play cribbage, believe it or not. Playing sharpened my adding skills, but it also helped me to focus, to slow down and see the big picture."

"Cribbage?" Sarah asked.

"It's a card game. You play with a board."

"We have one," I said. "Patrick and I used to play. He always won. It's in the game cabinet."

"Cool. So, Josh, will you teach me after dinner?"

"I don't see why not."

As if tired of being neglected in favor of food and conversation, Ellie let out a wail.

"I'll get her." Marc jumped up. "You stay, Kate. Eat."

"Oh no. That's fine. She probably needs mommy time." Kate stood, but Marc scooped Ellie up in his arms. As if to prove her mother wrong, Ellie stopped crying and let out a delighted coo once in Marc's arms.

"You see?" Marc said. "I can handle it. You enjoy

your dinner and I'll have my turn once she's settled."

"Wow, thanks." Kate seemed pleased. I glanced over at Josh, who was watching the sweet domestic scene play out between Marc, Kate, and Ellie.

"So, kids," Josh interrupted the silence that settled over the table as everyone finished eating, "before we have that game of cribbage, we're going to get your mom settled again in the other room and then the three of us will do the dishes and clean up."

"Josh, that's really nice of you. But I think I'm fine now. It won't be much for me to get back and forth in the kitchen. You've done enough."

"Not nearly. You still need to take it easy. I'm good in the kitchen. Trust me."

I felt a wave of guilt at playing up my injury. "It's not that I don't trust you." A man who could bake bread and make one of the best Caesar salads I'd ever tasted certainly didn't need to prove himself in the kitchen. "But I can do it. Really. I would feel better if I could help out."

"Sorry, Mom," Spence said, "Josh is right. We're going to handle kitchen duty tonight. You get to rest on the couch."

"Wow, I think some of that hair dye may have invaded your brain cells. Are you feeling well?" The kids never wanted to help in the kitchen. I could only guess they were on their best behavior because we had company.

"Or maybe it's that an alien has taken over his body." Sarah never passed up an opportunity to razz her brother.

"Ha-ha," Spence said. "Seriously, Mom, you deserve a break now and then."

Sarah looked at her brother as if he'd grown a third head, never mind the alien takeover. But I agreed to go back to my couch and let them have at the dirty dishes. Who was I to argue?

Chapter Five

An hour later, as I lay sprawled on the couch digesting the enormous meal, the doorbell rang. Spence was on the phone with Shelley. Sarah and Josh played their game of cribbage. Kate and Marc, fascinated with Ellie's latest trick of rolling over from back to belly, were in the family room trying to see if she could master grasping the carpet fibers to pull herself to a crawl.

Still feeling guilty for avoiding dish duty, I made sure to limp a little as I headed over to answer the door. Nick Angelos stood on the front porch, devastatingly handsome in a black suit and white shirt open at the collar, as if to remind me of the exquisitely muscular expanse of chest beneath it. As if I needed reminding. He twirled a single red rose between his long, capable fingers.

His forest-green eyes widened, as if in appreciation, upon seeing me. Instinctively, my hands flew to my hair. I realized that lounging on the couch in sweats all day might not have left me looking all that inspiring.

"*Ciao, bella,*" he said, obviously in an Italian frame of mind. The language of love? Or was that French? Did it matter? Anything this guy spoke seemed to be the language of "melt Bennie to a puddle on the spot."

"Nick." I smiled and hoped I looked better than I suspected. "Come in."

"I thought I left you with explicit instructions to stay off that ankle."

"Sorry, old habits die hard. I happen to be used to answering my own door."

With a feral grace, he prowled past me, batting me on the nose with the flower. If that was some sort of wildcat mating sign, I was in.

"Don't make me send the minions over to keep you in line."

"Minions?" I asked, my mouth going dry. The man had minions? I could use minions. As long as they were of the doing-all-the-housework variety, and not the actual evil steal-your-soul kind of minion. "How would that work exactly?"

"The minions? Oh, you know, they would do all the boring, mundane things that you can't stand to do. They're quite handy, actually. For instance, they might take this rose I brought for you and put it in water while I"—he paused long enough to lift me in his arms, causing me to give an involuntary squeal—"carry you back to the couch."

"What's wrong?" Josh, apparently concerned, came running at the sound of my shriek. "Oh. Good evening, Mr. Angelos."

"Ah, there. You see? Minions," Nick said, settling me back on the couch. "Handy buggers. Josh, my man, do me a favor and put this in water, hmm? Not cold water, though. Make it warm, but not too warm."

Josh's mouth turned up at the corner. I couldn't tell if he wanted to laugh or haul Nick out back to start a brawl. But he did take the rose that dangled from Nick's fingers. "I'll make it a temperate eighty-six degrees. Will there be anything else?"

Nick took a seat at the end of the couch, propping my feet in his lap. "No." He waved Josh off with annoyance. "That will be all. I'll spare you the lecture on letting our little miss hobble to the door without any assistance."

Little miss? I liked it, but Josh's face turned the color of my homemade marinara. Okay, *now* he wanted to hit him. But he didn't. He turned on his heel and stomped off to the kitchen with the rose. I trusted Sarah would help him find the appropriate vase.

"Wow, that was impressive," I said with a giggle once Josh was out of earshot. Wait, had I actually giggled? Out loud? "I've never seen Josh Brandon take orders. From anyone."

Nick adjusted his cuffs. "You just have to know how to command."

I lost my breath. Nick definitely knew how to command. He had my heart standing at attention, ready to take orders. And the rest of my body, too.

"You are a commanding presence," I finally said.

He ignored the compliment and began to massage my feet. "Looking much better. I couldn't wait to come over and check on you."

"Really?" I didn't mean to sound as surprised as I felt.

"I was at an excruciatingly boring business dinner and I finally just said *enough. I can't take it. I must go check on my lovely new friend,* and I made my excuses and ended the evening early."

"I hope it wasn't an important dinner."

He shrugged, leaned his head back on the couch, and studied me. "What's important next to new friends? We are going to be friends, Bennie. Aren't we?"

He seemed to inch closer as he said it. I didn't mind except for worrying about the kids happening into the room. What would they think? Hey, kids, meet Mom's new *friend.* Hubba. "Yes, Nick. We're going to be friends."

He seemed to get the message to keep a little physical distance, but his eyes oozed pure sex as he met my gaze and rubbed my foot more suggestively. "I'm looking forward to getting to know you better."

My stomach tightened. I felt a tingle where I hadn't tingled in a very long, long time. Before I could roll my head back and give in to the sensation, the kids bounded out of the kitchen with Josh Brandon holding the rose in a vase.

My stomach did a flip of another kind as it suddenly occurred to me that Nick Angelos might be turned off by the single mother thing. I came with what some men might consider "baggage." Serious baggage.

I shot a look at my kids. Sweet, red-haired, tough-as-nails-for-her-nine-years Sarah. Formerly blond and angelic about-to-hit puberty Spence. If they were baggage, I didn't mind lugging them around.

"Who do we have here?" Nick said, rising to greet the children. So far, so good. He hadn't run screaming.

"My children," I said, immediately claiming responsibility and putting all doubt to rest. "Spencer and Sarah, this is Mr. Angelos. He helped me out earlier today when I twisted my ankle."

"I thought *Josh* helped you?" Sarah crossed her arms over her chest. "Weren't you at *his* construction site?"

"I was," I said, forcing a smile in Sarah's direction to camouflage *the glare*, an unspoken signal to be polite. "But Mr. Angelos was there, too. He's donating supplies and land to Habitat for Humanity. Lucky for me, they were both on hand when I needed a little help."

Spencer narrowed his gaze, sizing up the new visitor. "Nice to meet you." Done with his assessment, but still looking unsure of Nick, he reached out to shake his hand. I smiled at my son's easy manners and natural charm. "Thanks for helping my mom."

"It was my pleasure," Nick said, but he glanced at Josh before slipping his gaze back to Spence. "Good to meet you, too. And the lovely lady." He bent at the waist, a slight bow. I feared he would reach for Sarah's hand to kiss it, but he seemed to sense the misstep in advance and he straightened up in time. "Sarah, I'm charmed."

Sarah snorted. Out loud. I shot her the glare. She shrugged. "Yeah, hey. Josh, can we finish our game now?"

All right. One out of two wasn't bad. We'd have a little talk about appropriate greetings later.

"Yes." Josh smirked at Nick, as if Nick had failed some kind of test in his mind. I wondered what. "We'll go and finish the game." He looked at me. "If you don't mind."

Why would I mind? "Of course not. Go ahead."

"I'm going back to my room to work on some homework," Spence said.

"But it's Friday." Nick frowned with disapproval. I guessed he wasn't an all work and no play type, which suited me fine.

"No doubt Spence is preparing the groundwork for tomorrow. He's having a girlfriend over to study." I didn't want Nick to think that my son had no sense of fun.

"She's not a girlfriend." Spence rolled his eyes. "But yes, I want to finish my science so I have all day tomorrow for English."

"Ah, is that what they're calling it these days?" Nick's lips curled up in a wolfish grin that made my heart flutter.

"Um, yeah. See you later, then." Spence headed for his room.

"Your daughter looks like you." Nick sat back at my feet, took my hand, and smiled warmly as soon as we were alone again. "What a beauty. Prepare to put a solid lock on the doors."

"We already have solid locks. All secure."

"Smart move." He moved in closer, pulling my feet back onto his lap. "I want to think of you as protected at all times."

Flustered, I shifted back into the cushions a little but let him hold on to my hand. "Normally, I do a better job of staying out of harm's way."

"Oh?" He cocked a golden brow. "Right now you're in danger of making me want to kiss you and that's probably not a good idea with your family all around."

My palms started sweating. I hoped he couldn't tell. "Probably not," I conceded, but considered daring him to take a chance when Kate bounded into the room, followed by Marc cradling Ellie against his sturdy shoulder as if she were a football.

"Oh. We have company. Mr. Angelos, nice of you to drop by again." Kate didn't seem to think it was as nice as she let on.

"I was eager to check on your sister. And please, call me Nick."

"Nick, this is my friend Marc."

"Marc Ramirez, of the Patriots?" Nick got to his feet. "Or should I say, of the undefeated Patriots? You're having an excellent year."

"The team is," Marc allowed. "Personally, I would be happy to spend more time on the field."

"Knee trouble." Nick nodded knowingly. "How awful to be held back by physical limitations."

Marc gave a look that said he wasn't certain if he liked Nick Angelos. I hated for him to make a bad impression.

"And this is my niece, Eliana," I said, hoping Nick could win Marc and Kate over by complimenting the baby.

"Ah, the precious angel." Nick tilted his head to get a better look at her sweet face mashed against Marc's shoulder. As if sensing interest in her, she lifted her head and looked up. "But she has a bit of the devil in her eyes, doesn't she?"

Under ordinary circumstances, it was a perfectly harmless comment. But Kate's fixation with Ellie's father had been anything but ordinary, and there was that devil thing. But that Nick seemed to sense it, to zero in on it, right away?

Kate's eyes narrowed. She gnawed her lower lip as if concerned. "Yes, well." She reached over to Marc and took Ellie into her arms. "She seems to be getting sleepy, so I think Marc and I will take her up and get her ready for bed."

"Sure, Kate," I said, eager to get her away from Nick before he said anything else to upset her. "Good idea. She looks exhausted, poor thing."

She looked wide awake, and I was certain her three-hour afternoon nap had everything to do with it. Kate might be upstairs with Marc and the baby for a good long time. For now, Josh was busy with my daughter. I had Nick Angelos all to myself.

"I always wondered what she'd look like," Nick said, still looking off to the stairs. "Beautiful child."

"Ellie? Oh yes. She is." I was only half listening, wondering how I could get him to sit back down again. I'd practically been in his lap when Kate and Marc interrupted.

"It runs in the family."

I blushed again. "She actually looks quite a bit like her dad, too."

"I know. That's what I meant."

"Oh, Marc's not Ellie's Dad. Though, of course, he has been there since the night she was born. He might as well be."

Nick took my hand. "I know Ellie's Dad, Bennie. I work for the man. He's my uncle." My heart stopped. He *knew* Owen Glendower?

"Your—" Oh. God. Not good. My knees shook. I lowered myself to the couch before I fell. One high-profile stumble a day was my limit. "Your uncle?"

"Mmm-hmm." He sat beside me again, but by now I'd all but lost that lovin' feeling. "Owen Glendower, of Glendower Enterprises, where I'm serving as temporary CEO in my uncle's unfortunate absence. I've worked for him for years. My father actually sent me to live with him ages ago."

Oh dear. "Really? So you're close? You lived with him."

"Not that I didn't prefer it. My father's an uncompromising sort."

"Compared to Owen Glendower?" I remembered Patrick's long nights and lost weekends working for Owen Glendower. Uncompromising didn't begin to describe his demanding nature.

"My uncle's a lamb next to my father."

"Wow." I made a mental note to put off any meet-the-family scenarios with Nick for as long as possible. Maybe forever. How could I even think of seeing him when it would bring such agony to Kate to face a constant reminder? Unless . . . I could somehow keep it from her? Meet Nick on the sly, a tawdry affair, nothing serious. Hot sex, no strings. My lips curled up in a naughty smile. But I was getting ahead of myself. *Way* ahead. "So, Angelos must be your father's name? Owen is your mother's brother?"

"No, my father's. My uncle took a new name to go into business. We all did. Angelos is Greek for 'messenger'. I liked the sound of it."

"And Glendower?"

"There was a Welsh nobleman accused of being the devil. It's a favorite of my uncle's." He smiled as if enjoying a private joke. Maybe that's where Kate got the idea of Owen being the devil.

"So, what's your real name?"

"Let's not trouble ourselves with details of the past." He leaned in and brushed the hair out of my face. Suddenly everything became a lot less complicated. It was as if all questions were swept straight from my mind, unimportant for now. All I wanted was to give in to the feeling of his touch.

"That's it," he said, his voice low and seductive as he continued to stroke my temple. "Relax. We have a lot of time to get to know each other better."

"Ahem, Mom?" I startled to look up and see Sarah standing at the end of the couch. I hadn't even heard her approach. "Do you want a chance to play Josh at cribbage? He says he could beat you with his eyes closed, though I don't see how since he won't be able to see the cards."

"Play Josh?" I straightened up and cleared my throat. My head was fuzzy, as if I were waking from a dream. "At cards?"

Sarah plunked down in the opposite chair. "Duh. I don't mean at thumb wrestling."

"Sarah." I sat up straighter still, the warning tone in my voice.

She rolled her eyes. "Yes, Mom."

Josh, hands jammed in the pockets of his tight-fitting jeans, emerged from the dining room. "It's okay, Sarah. Your mom's probably a little rusty on the rules of cribbage. Maybe you can show her later."

"Rusty? I am *so* not rusty," I said, suddenly defensive. "When you come over for the fireplace, I will show you how to play cribbage, Mr. Brandon. And you're going to need both eyes open."

"Why, so you don't cheat?" His penetrating eyes crinkled at the corners as he laughed. Sarah slapped him a high five.

"I never cheat," I added calmly. "I don't have to cheat to win."

Nick's hand spread out flat and slipped down to

my lower back. Instant heat shot through me. I struggled to sit up straight and remain coherent, but for the life of me, I couldn't recall what I'd just been saying.

"I'm going to hit the road, then," Josh said, the blue of his eyes working like beacons to lead me back out of my dazed fog. "It's late, and I'm due on-site early tomorrow."

"Tomorrow's Saturday," Sarah said.

"Winter's coming. We have a few things to finish up before the first snowfall."

"Bummer." Sarah stood up. "Good night, then. I'm going up to look for Spence. Great game, Josh. I'll beat you next time."

"Keep practicing. I'm sure you will."

"Unlike her mom, huh?" I wanted to stand up to say a proper good-bye, but I didn't want to risk Nick worrying over my ankle again. "Wait, you can't leave. You need a ride."

"It's a short walk. No problem."

"In the dark? And it's cold out now. I didn't see you wearing a jacket when you came in. I won't have you walking." Nick still had his hand on my back, but somehow Josh's gaze held my attention and kept me from slipping back into blissful oblivion. "Have another beer. Take a seat. Marc will bring you home. He'll be ready to go soon, too."

Josh seemed to consider it.

"No need," Nick said. "I have to be going. I can drop you on my way."

"Oh." Josh bristled visibly. "No, really, another beer sounds great. I'm sure Marc will be right down."

"I insist." Nick stood, and the warmth slipped out of my belly at the loss of physical contact with him.

"It's probably on my way. No problem at all. It seems we both have early mornings at the office. I've got a report due. You've got your building."

A report. In his office. At Glendower Enterprises. I stifled a groan. I finally met a man that made my heart beat faster, that made me think I could be ready to consider dating at the very least, and he was related to my sister's devil. Just my luck. I probably shouldn't even see him again.

Josh chuckled from low in his throat. "You really should come to volunteer in construction sometime, Nick. Every man could benefit from learning how to work with his hands."

"My hands are more experienced than you'd ever guess." He winked in my direction before turning his attention back to Josh. "I dabbled in lots of fields before I ended up working with my uncle. Cattle herding, music."

"A regular Renaissance man," I said, trying to contain my drool as I continued to picture him at home on the range, his wild blond mane blowing in a dusty western wind.

"Actually, I wasn't stoked on the Renaissance. All those flowy fabrics and billowy breeches? Damned uncomfortable."

Josh and I exchanged a glance. What? Apparently, I didn't understand Nick's sense of humor. Yet. "You worked on a ranch?"

"More of a pasture."

"What kind of music?"

"Stringed instruments. It was experimental." He didn't seem willing to elaborate. Conversation stalled. I could imagine him with a guitar.

Younger, leaner, longer hair. Yum, talk about a rock 'n' roll god.

"Well," Josh said, breaking the awkward silence. "I'm glad your ankle's on the mend, Bennie. I had a fun evening. Thank you."

"I did, too." I wanted to memorize every inch of Nick's muscular frame, but I caught and held Josh's intense gaze. What was it about his eyes that I found so riveting? So they were an unearthly shade of blue, so what? "Thanks for staying. And for returning my car."

"See you Monday. I'll, um, just wait outside." Josh must have sensed the sensual tension brewing between Nick and me.

"I'll tell Kate you said good-bye," I called after him, more to remind myself of Kate and why I couldn't agree to see more of Nick.

Nick drew in closer. My breath came in sharp, shallow stabs. Alone at last. Would he kiss me? I ached for him to kiss me. I imagined his lips meeting mine with a sort of fevered, all-devouring urgency. One kiss, what was the harm?

He leaned down and dropped a chaste peck on my forehead. "Until we meet again. Soon, I hope. I want to take you to dinner. Just the two of us."

"Mmm." A tingly warmth radiated out from where his lips had touched, heading straight for the pleasure centers of my brain. "Let me know when and I'll be ready."

Erasing my brain, apparently. *I'll be ready*? What was I saying?

He smiled, not the wolfish half grin but with a genuine beatific shine. "I like that you don't play games, Bennie. No pretending to have to check your schedule or acting as if you may or may not be interested. There's no holding back with you, is there?"

"Life's too short." I shrugged. "I know what I like." And apparently, I liked living on the edge. Kate would kill me if she knew I was flirting with Owen's nephew.

"I know what I *want*." His eyebrow arched suggestively. "You take care of your ankle. I like you in heels. I'll be in touch."

With that, he swept out the front door. I stayed on the couch for an extra few minutes staring off at the picture window across the room, wishing the drapes were open so I could watch them drive away, and enjoying the heat that still danced through my veins.

Now I wished I'd bought the Louboutin peep-toe platform pumps. They would have gone perfectly with the slinky plum cocktail sheath I'd bought on sale at the end of last season. I wondered when I would get my first paycheck and if it wouldn't be too late to get the pumps in time for dinner with Nick Angelos. Which I absolutely couldn't do, because of Kate. I would just have to say no when he called. I only hoped I could be that strong in the face of temptation.

Once I had a chance to catch my breath and calm down, I headed upstairs to make sure the kids were settling in for the night. I decided not to tell Kate about Nick's relation to Owen Glendower just yet. There was no need to upset her. It wasn't as if we were dating. If we were, and the time came to confess, I could just imagine her reaction. *Oh, by the way, Kate, Nick Angelos is Ellie's cousin. Small world, huh?* No, I didn't think the news would thrill her.

Hearing voices, I paused at the top of the stairs. Arguing. The exchanges came fast and sharp, low pitched, as if the speakers didn't want to be over-heard, or perhaps didn't want to disturb a baby. My stomach clenched. I hated for Marc and Kate to be at odds.

I crept down the carpeted hallway and listened at the door.

"Don't keep apologizing," Kate said. "I'm the one who started it. I just don't know where I'm headed."

"You're still not ready." Marc's voice sounded re-signed, but not bitter.

"I know it's not fair. You said you were fine with being friends. I hate to keep you hanging on, wait-ing for me to come around."

"Kate, I *am* your friend. I'm not simply coming over hoping to change your mind one day. I'll always be here for you and Elle." I smiled. I liked how he called her Elle while the rest of us stuck with Ellie. It was something special between the two of them alone. Marc deserved something special.

"You're such an incredible man. I hate to keep turning you down. You should be with someone who appreciates you for all you have to offer, not just a part of it." Apparently, Kate agreed that Marc de-served something special. And she wasn't giving it to him. She was still too stuck on Owen Glendower.

Not that I blamed her. She'd once confided to me that they'd had the kind of love that endured, the kind I'd shared with Patrick. We'd talked about her feelings for Owen all through her pregnancy. She'd fallen hard for the man. All the more reason not to tell her about Nick's connection. Also, all the more reason I wanted her to have the chance to love again. It wasn't fair for either of us to have lost the men we loved so early in our own lives.

"To be honest, Kate, I can't think of anywhere I'd rather be than where you are. I've been with other women. I know the score. I'm not looking for anything but what you're willing to give," Marc said, a note of consolation in his voice.

"You say that now. How long can we go on like this?"

"As long as it takes."

"Aha, you see. You're still hoping it comes to more."

"As long as I live and breathe I'll be hoping it comes to more. So shoot me. I'm in love with you."

"Don't say that. Don't say you love me," Kate hissed.

"But I do love you. And I don't care if you don't love me back."

"I love you. But not like that. I wish I did." We *all* wished she did.

"I know, babe. I know."

It was quiet for a few moments then. I stayed frozen to my spot. Maybe she was crying and he was holding her in his arms. Why couldn't she wake up out of her Owen haze and see that Marc was the one? In my opinion, Owen Glendower was not all Kate had cracked him up to be. Even if he was, he wasn't here. *Love the one you're with.* Kate and I deserved to love again. The difference was that I knew it was time to move on. She seemed stuck in a dream that Owen would someday return.

Ellie began to fuss. "I think it's too early for her to go to bed," Kate said, opening the door. "Let's bring her back downstairs for a while. Oh, by the way, Josh is going to need a ride home. Do you think you could drop him off?"

"Sure, no problem."

I backed away from the door as if just coming up the stairs. "No need. Josh just left. Nick took him home."

"Josh and Nick in a confined space, together?" Kate said. "I hope it doesn't come to blows."

"Nick has a big car," I said. "I'm sure there's plenty of room for them to avoid each other."

"The last thing we need is to have grown men fighting over you, Bennie."

I laughed. How else to respond to such a ridiculous statement? "Just call me Helen of Troy."

Chapter Six

The weekend passed uneventfully, with the usual laundry, housework, kids, and homework issues. Love, or the hopeful pursuit of it, was in the air for some.

Spencer's crush, Shelley Miles, spent most of Saturday with us. I suspected she kept her parents ignorant to her witch pursuits, as her spell book had been buried at the bottom of her book bag and her own Goth makeup didn't get applied until after she'd arrived, and mysteriously disappeared right before she went home. I would have to keep an eye on that. I didn't want her parents after me for being an enabler and I had a feeling she would be spending more time with Spencer in the future.

Marc came to dinner again on Sunday with the intention of clearing the yard of fallen leaves, but most of them had blown to the neighbor's lot before we got outside. Instead, Marc tossed a football around with the kids before heading back to Kate's house for the evening with Kate and Ellie. I still waited to hear how that turned out.

The good news was that I managed to get the kids ready for school and myself ready for work with plenty of time to spare. I drove to work full of excitement at the prospect of being a respected member of a hardworking team. Habitat for Humanity provided good homes for people who'd struggled in life. It was a great cause. I would be making a difference, and one day, who knew? Maybe it would lead to new opportunities, my own office with my name in big letters on the door. A girl could dream.

And—hello, gorgeous—the stuff of dreams was riding down the street up ahead, a cyclist out for his morning exercise wearing bike pants that hugged all the right places. I drove slowly with the hope that people would think I was just being cautious when I was actually checking out those muscle-bound thighs.

The guy must do a lot of cycling because his whole body was lean, muscular, and just about perfect in the unforgiving spandex outfit. It was a shame he wore the proper headgear, helmet and tinted glasses, because it denied me a chance to check if the face went with the too-perfect rest of him. I shot a glance in the rearview. One last look. *Whoa, baby.*

Maybe it was true that a woman reached her sexual peak at thirty-five. The closer I got, the more I seemed to think about sex. If it was this bad now, what would it be like in a few years? Lost in thought, I slammed on my brakes in time to avoid colliding with the car stopped at the light in front of me.

As I watched the cyclist's tight ass cruise past me a second time, I realized that traffic lights served a higher purpose. This time, he waved. Heat filled my cheeks. He must have known I was appreciating the view. And now, green light, I got to pass him one more time. But this time, I tried to keep my eyes on the road to avoid the embarrassment of being caught staring or starting a major accident. I managed a small peek, anyway.

A few minutes later, I parallel-parked down the street from the Habitat construction. Over the weekend, Leslie had called to tell me to meet her at the Newton site instead of at the office. All hands were needed to wrap up building projects before the weekend's predicted snowstorm. Just my luck, my first official order of business wouldn't be my specialty, charming donors over the phone, but what I dreaded most: building. With Josh Brandon telling me what to do.

At least, I knew he wouldn't be able to quibble with my attire. I wore a heavy flannel shirt loose over a long-sleeved tee tucked into my favorite Rock & Republic jeans with—the pièce de résistance—pink steel-toed Timberlands. Let him try to complain about my footwear. Personally, I didn't have any complaints. My ankle felt well enough. The crunch of gravel under heavy soles as I stepped out of the car reminded me that the Timberlands were a lot easier to walk in, and I was more comfortable than I'd expected to be for my first day of work.

Work. The word still held me in awe. I hadn't held an actual job since my first summer out of college, right before my wedding to Patrick, followed all too closely by my pregnancy with Spencer. Since I'd had so much trouble with morning sickness and Patrick was thriving in the real estate market, we decided I could forget the job search and quit my interim position as a bank teller to prepare for becoming a stay-at-home mom.

I took a breath of crisp November morning air, looked up the street at the sturdy Tyvek-wrapped frame that would soon become someone's lovely new house, and prepared to report for duty. I thought of the house's structure as a symbol for my new life. The bones were good, solid, waiting to see what they might yet become.

As I walked down the street to the house, I had to slide into the row of parked cars just in time to avoid being mowed down by the cyclist, whose route had again taken him into my path. Maybe it was a sign? I smiled lecherously once I could be sure he was far enough ahead to not look back and catch me ogling.

He turned into the house's winding dirt driveway. Interesting. Perhaps he was one of the crew. I wouldn't mind getting a chance to see if the face matched the incredible body after all.

I could see him up ahead, swinging a leg over the bike and bringing it to a safe spot to lock it up. His helmet and protective glasses were still on as he pulled a duffel bag off the back, probably his work clothes. No self-respecting construction worker would be caught on the job in cycling gear, especially those formfitting padded shorts that had me hoping it wasn't *all* padding.

I rounded the edge of the drive just in time to see him take off his helmet to reveal—a thatch of thick gray hair. My stomach did a flip. Josh Brandon. So when he'd said that he had his bike, he'd meant Schwinn, not Harley. Well, it wasn't actually a Schwinn. I squinted at the lettering on the light metal frame.

No doubt it was some fancy bike manufacturer I'd never heard of.

Fortunately, I had a chance to get my bearings before speaking to him.

"Josh," I said, a hint of scorn in my voice. "That's hardly the proper footwear for a build site." I dropped my gaze tellingly to his biking shoes, but my eyes lingered for a moment to the incredible bulge in his shorts.

I looked up to find his eyes hung up on my gaze. Oh God. He'd caught me staring. I blushed from head to toe.

"Not to worry, Mrs. St. James." He held up the duffel. "I was just about to go change."

"Oh. Right. Good idea." Very good idea. I hated thinking of Josh Brandon as, well, as a potentially desirable man. The sooner he hid his well-defined muscles under a bulky work shirt, the better. "Safety first."

"Why don't you come to the trailer with me?"

"While you change?" I hoped my voice didn't crack.

"I will be changing in the back, well out of sight of the front office. Where you can catch up with Leslie."

"Oh." I caught on so embarrassingly slowly. "Leslie's there."

"Yes. That's generally where she starts her day. And there's coffee. If we're lucky, she was in a good mood this morning and also picked up a dozen donuts."

"Donuts?" I raised a brow. I was a sucker for donuts. "Plain glazed?"

"There's a good chance. Those don't go quite as

fast as the Boston cremes. Maybe you'll get lucky."
He winked and I was reminded of the power of
those incredible eyes.

A tingly warmth erupted in my core. "Maybe."

Maybe? I was referring to the donuts, of course. I
hoped he didn't think I was attracted to him. So he
had an unexpectedly firm physique, and those
eyes, but that didn't mean I was interested in Josh
Brandon.

We walked across the driveway to the beat-up old
trailer parked near the house in the dirt.

"Here we are," Josh said, opening the door for
me. When I brushed by him, I jolted with electric
shock on contact. He laughed. "Spandex. It's a good
conductor."

"Right. Spandex." And my eyes involuntarily
dropped down to examine his spandex again. What
was wrong with me?

If Josh noticed my gawking, he didn't let on. "Ah,
you're in luck. She brought donuts." He stepped
into the office that barely had room for a desk, side
table, extra chair, and Leslie, let alone two extra
bodies. "Good morning, Leslie."

"Hey, guys. Yeah, Bennie, grab some donuts and
coffee. Take a seat. We have to fill out some new
hire paperwork."

"Paperwork? So it's official?"

"It's official. Congratulations. The board approved.
You got the job."

I'd taken it as a given that the job was mine, but
now it was much more real. So incredible! As if, despite having been a wife and mother for years, I was
taking my first big independent step into adulthood.

"I got the job."

* * *

Why did I want a job, again?

Hours into the day, the most important thing I'd done was sort screws into piles. For easy access, Josh had explained. It was important the guys could just grab what they needed without having to take time to sort. I had a sneaking feeling I'd been given busywork just to keep me out of the way.

Leslie got to help with cutting wood, but I apparently couldn't be trusted with a power saw. I stood off to the side, watching, trying to assess where I could jump in and be useful before Josh saw me unoccupied and had a chance to assign the next mundane task.

The framing had been completed on Friday and the roof went on over the weekend. A subcontractor was coming in tomorrow to direct volunteers on installing the doors and windows. Today, Josh's crew worked on the porch. They were getting ready to lay the floor on the frame, and I knew I would be useless there. I decided that my best bet was to check on Leslie and see if anything needed sanding. I was sure I could master the power sander if I had another go at it. When I turned out to be a success with sanding, maybe Josh would give me more credit and let me move on to bigger things. But I only got about three steps forward before Josh rounded a corner and nearly bumped right into me.

"Aha, there you are. Screws sorted?"

I rolled my eyes. "It was a tough job but I managed."

"That's my girl." He patted my shoulder. "Now I have a new job for you. Slightly more challenging."

I perked up. "Really?"

"Mmm. One of the most important jobs on-site. Lunch."

"What?" I narrowed my eyes.

"The crew needs food to stay motivated. I took the liberty of writing down all the requests." He held out a slip of paper. "You just have to call it in and go pick it up."

"Seriously?"

His eyes, nearly colorless in the bright glare of the sun, twinkled like glass under lights. "Leslie usually does it but she's cutting out early today."

"Leslie fetches lunch for the crew?" She hadn't mentioned it as one of the job duties, but she did say things worked a little unconventionally when she helped at sites. I had a feeling I would prefer the regular nine-to-five office part of the job, Leslie's usual duties.

"And snacks. Plus, she keeps up with brewing fresh coffee. I don't know if you've gone for a refill lately but"—his nose crinkled in disapproval—"we're down to the dregs. You're going to be using the office phone to call in the lunch order. You might as well put on a new pot of coffee while you're in there."

"Oh, I might as well," I said with forced cheer.

"Good. When you get back with the order, just come on over to the porch to pass it out."

"Great. See you then." At least I got to go for a drive. Better than sorting screws.

By the time I returned with lunch for eight, the porch was finished and the volunteer crew ended up taking their food to go. Even Leslie had bailed. With me on the scene, she was able to cut out early to check on her fledgling Web business. She left Josh his car and caught a ride home with one of the guys.

Josh seemed in no hurry to leave. He leaned against the side of the trailer with his lunch bag, pastrami and swiss on rye.

"Not the healthiest choice," I said, eyeing his bag.

"I could say the same about yours. One measly container of yogurt? You could stand to gain a few pounds."

"Ha. Right. Haven't you heard, thin is in? And forty is the new thirty."

"But you're not close to forty."

"And I'm not too thin." I flashed him a patronizing grin.

"I know. You're healthy. I was just busting you in retaliation. I biked eight miles to work this morning, so I think I earned a little extra indulgence."

"Of course." I blushed with the memory of Josh in shorts. But come to think of it, his jeans didn't leave a lot to the imagination, either. The Levi's, well worn and faded, hugged his thighs in all the right places. Which would be the wrong places for me, since I was *so* not interested. "I was just busting you, too. Habit, I guess."

"It's probably well earned. I don't think you quite appreciated the importance of screw duty this morning."

"Not exactly. You know, I *can* be trusted with more complicated tasks. I'm actually pretty good with my hands."

"I know, or, I mean, I guess you are." Was it his turn to blush? Or just indigestion? "That's why I'm hoping you'll stick around after lunch to help me with a few things."

"Me?"

"You're the only one here. I sent everyone else home. The subcontractors are coming in tomorrow, so no need to come back then. You can report in to the office instead."

"The Boston office?"

He nodded. "Leslie's got some fund-raiser calls lined up for you, I think. But for today, I just need opinions on a few things."

"And you're asking me?" I couldn't believe it. He wouldn't trust me with power tools, but he wanted my opinion?

"I'm trying to picture the finished product, to imagine what the house might be like for the family who gets it. You have kids. You know what a busy family needs."

"I'm not sure I'll be much help, but I'm willing to try."

"We'll go through the house after lunch. I'm going to head inside to eat. Join me?"

"Sure." I followed him to the office, took the seat across from him at the desk, and watched him pull his pastrami sandwich out of the bag and unwrap it. Suddenly my yogurt seemed a lot less satisfying. I tried to distract myself with thinking of how many miles I would have to walk on the treadmill to burn off pastrami. Too many.

"Want some chips?" he asked, ripping into the bag of Ruffles. The decadent fried potato aroma filled the small space.

"No. Thanks. I'm fine." Fine, as long as I stopped at the store on the way home and bought some chips, and maybe some pastrami.

"Suit yourself." He shrugged and bit into his

sandwich. We ate in companionable silence. At last, I couldn't take the silence and had to talk just to keep my mind off stealing his chips.

"So, Josh, you have kids, too, right? At least, I seem to recall you mentioning a daughter at some point. How old is she?"

He startled as if surprised I remembered, or surprised I brought it up. I couldn't tell which. "Yes, I do. She's nine."

"Oh. Almost Sarah's age."

"But she's nothing like Sarah."

"You mean she's not a tomboy?" I laughed.

"Let's just say she's not going to try out for hockey any day soon. No, she's very girly."

"Like her mother?"

"Like her mother." He nodded. "I have her every other weekend."

"So." I hesitated. I didn't want to be too nosy, but it was interesting to imagine Josh as a single father. It explained why he was so perceptive with my kids. "Is it a divorce situation?"

"Molly and I weren't married long. We were more good friends and something happened that didn't last. We still get along pretty well."

"That's good."

"Yeah. It's healthier for Kyrie that way, too."

"Kyrie? That's an unusual name. Pretty."

"Kyrie Elieson is Greek for 'Lord, have mercy.' If you grew up Catholic, you may have heard it in church."

"Not Catholic."

"Neither is her mother." He laughed. "She was a Mr. Mister fan."

"The eighties band?" I smiled. It brought back some memories. "Kyrie. I remember the song."

"Hmm. So Molly named her Kyrie. I didn't mind. It fits her, actually." He dug in his back pocket and pulled out a wallet. "Here's her picture."

"Wow." She was a stunner, slender with white-blond hair and bright eyes. "She looks like a story-book fairy."

"She does, doesn't she? She's a great kid. I'm a lucky man."

"It's nice that you think so."

He beamed with pride. It added a new facet to appreciate in Josh that he was so obviously pleased to be a dad.

"She's a lucky girl."

"She lives in Providence."

"Not too far away. And you get her every other weekend, so that works. You should bring her over to meet Spence and Sarah sometime. Just because they're different doesn't mean they can't be friends."

"True. She could always use new friends." He picked up his trash, threw it away, and dusted off his hands. "So, shall we go check out the house? You ready?"

"Ready." I tossed my yogurt container and followed him outside. We crossed the dirt to the house. "It will be much prettier in the springtime with a fresh green lawn, maybe some shrubs and flowers planted around the porch."

"Do you garden?" he asked.

"Not really." I laughed at the thought. "I used to have a landscaper come in, but Kate recommended it would be more economical to tend the yard myself. I'm afraid I have a brown thumb. Marc has been helpful, though."

"Marc's over that often? With Kate?"

"Always with Kate. To me, he's like a brother by now."

He nodded, but his gaze lit with something like relief. Or was I imagining? "And to Kate?"

"Something more, I hope." I shrugged. "I think Kate actually misses him when he's on the road with the team, but she tries to hide it."

He reached for my hand as we neared the steps. "Be careful."

"Why?" I pulled my hand back to prove I could manage just fine. "Are you afraid I'll take another tumble?"

"Not in those shoes. Those are some serious work boots. I'm glad you took my warning to heart."

"I was tempted to show up in my new red Dolce and Gabbana boots with the stiletto heels, but I wasn't sure you could handle it. Plus, they didn't go with my outfit."

He shook his head and opened the door at the top of the steps. Inside, I took a look around. Though it was lacking finish, it was easy to see the layout, an open floor plan with the family room leading right to a dining room and the kitchen in the back corner. It looked like there would be a half bath in the space under the stairs on the right. "Small, but it will make a lovely home."

"I like to think so," Josh agreed. "What I really need is your advice on the bedrooms, upstairs."

We walked carefully up the rough wood stairs. I was afraid of getting splinters from the makeshift temporary railing, so I avoided it. The top of the stairs led to a small central hallway, the master bedroom straight ahead from there.

"Nice." I took a look around the walls, still just beams without drywall.

"But pretty basic, right? I was wondering if you thought a window seat might be nice. It's a big window."

"I love window seats." I looked around and tried to imagine bedroom furniture in the space, a queen bed along the back wall, maybe some end tables.

"Some built-in bookcases would be nice, too, but we just don't have the budget."

"Maybe a combination window seat and shelf unit to frame the window, something that wouldn't cut into the space too much but might provide a little storage?"

"Right," he said, catching on to my vision. "A seat with a cabinet underneath. Great idea. I could do it without much trouble. But now in one of the other bedrooms." We walked the short stretch of hall to the next room. "There's practically no closet space. I really would like to add some shelving. Nothing fancy, but something to provide a little extra storage space."

I checked out the one small closet. "Yes. Kids have so much stuff now, toys, games. I think some shelving would be nice. I can look over the budget."

"I wouldn't really need extra supplies. Just a few things. I could probably get most of it from spare wood and scraps left around the site."

"But what about time? Would it eat into your schedule?"

He shook his head. "I can take a few extra hours. The main concern is to have the major outdoor stuff done before the snow comes."

"I can't believe it's already time for snow." I used to like snow, but now it brought to mind treacherous driving conditions and that brought to mind Patrick. Not that it had been snowing on the night he ran off the road. He'd been driving drunk. It was still a hard fact to face that the accident that took him from me had been his own careless fault.

"Five shopping weeks until Christmas. Are you done with yours?"

"With my shopping?" I asked incredulously. Hadn't he heard? "Um, no. That's probably not a safe topic with me."

"Shopping. Ah. Well, you and most women."

"Sure, stick to stereotypes."

"No, I actually like to shop, too."

"You do not."

"I do. I swear."

"But for, like, tools and television sets and stuff, right?"

"No. Believe it or not, I enjoy shopping for clothes. I even enjoy watching women shop. Well, when it's Kyrie, anyway. Her face lights up when she finds an outfit she really likes. She could try on stuff for hours."

"And you don't mind?"

"Like I said, I enjoy it. I must have got the shopping gene from my mother. But don't tell anyone. I'll be a laughingstock among the guys."

"I won't tell. I promise. But I may make you prove it sometime."

"Say the word and I'm there. Actually, I could use some help shopping for Kyrie. I'm not quite sure what's in fashion for the nine-year-old girls this season. Plus, if I go to a clothes store and ask, I get the most unbelievable looks."

"Why? I think it's sweet that you want to shop for your daughter."

"Yeah, but a lot of people aren't so trusting these days. They seem to think a forty-year-old guy walking into a shop that specializes in clothes for preteen girls must be a pedophile."

"Oh. Ouch. I guess I can imagine. I do know what's in for most preteen girls, but not Sarah. She has a style all her own. Or total lack of it, but I've learned to pick my battles."

"You're a good mom." He looked thoughtful, hands in his pockets, as if he wasn't quite sure what to say all of a sudden.

"Thanks. I try. It's not easy. You know how it is."

"Molly's great with her." He shrugged. "I do my best."

"That's all any of us can do."

He smiled awkwardly. "I guess we're done here for the day. Thanks for the help."

I checked my watch. It seemed almost too early to go home. "Kate probably already picked the kids up from school, so I'll get home in time to make sure they do some homework before dinner."

"It's nice working with you, Bennie. Congratulations again on the new job."

"Thanks. It's nice to have a job. I think I'm really going to like being part of the workforce. Oh, hey, do you need a ride?"

He shook his head. "Leslie left my car. I'm going to hang around here a bit, finish a few things up. You go on ahead."

"All right. Bye, then." I let myself out of the house, but somehow I wasn't ready to leave. I felt a weird ache from low in my belly. I told myself it had to be the desire to have made a good first impression at work, but I wasn't so sure. Maybe it was hunger. Josh was right. Yogurt wasn't much of a lunch. I needed to get home, grab a snack, and think about what to make for dinner.

Chapter Seven

I parked in the garage, walked in through the kitchen door, and was met with the startling sight of my sister leaning over a huge pot.

"Oh, you're early," she said, disappointment in her tone.

"Sorry. I could go back to work."

"No." She rested her spoon on a plate, ran over, and gave me a big hug. "Congratulations on your first day!"

"Thanks."

"Stay in here with me a minute. The kids have been working on a surprise in the living room."

"A surprise?"

"For your party. A surprise *congratulations on your job* party. They're so excited."

"I can go back out and come in the front door when they're ready. So, what are you up to?"

"I made chili."

"Oh." I barely contained my sigh of relief. It was one of the only dishes Kate could manage without ruining it. "Chili. Smells good."

"And explains why your dogs are out in the yard instead of greeting you in the kitchen as usual. Chili apparently doesn't agree with their little puggy stomachs."

"Really? Who knew?" I tried to sound surprised. Who in their right mind feeds dogs chili? Kate. That's who. They would be having stomach problems for the next week. "Where's Ellie?"

"In her bouncy seat, out with the kids. They're keeping a good eye on her."

"I'm sure they are." I'm sure Spencer was. Sarah was going through a phase where she wanted nothing to do with babies. Not even with Ellie. Too drooly. "So, you're staying for *Monday Night Football*? Are you and Ellie here for the night?"

"My house is so big and lonely. We missed you all last night."

"Aw. It was quiet here, too."

A minute later, Spencer came tearing into the kitchen with Shelley Miles on his heels. "Mom, you're home!"

"Looks that way."

"Guess what we did today?"

"Prepared an extraordinary surprise for your newly employed mom?"

"Yeah, that." He shrugged. "But something even cooler."

"Cooler than I am?"

I smiled. Shelley blushed. I could see her cheeks getting pink even under her pale Goth makeup. "So cool. We made water freeze without a freezer."

I looked at Kate. She shrugged. "I was focused on the chili."

"How did you manage that? Some kind of science experiment?"

"No." Spence sneered, as if science experiments were silly kid stuff. "With magic."

"Magic?" I raised a brow.

"From Shelley's spell book. There's this spell on turning water solid."

"Uh-huh." It probably involved the old switcheroo, a glass of ice hidden under the table.

"You have to see it. It's super cool."

"So let me see."

"Fine." He tilted his chin, determined, and headed for the sink to fill a cup with water.

Shelley looked up the spell in the book.

"To make sure we get the words right," she said, then joined hands with Spencer, forming a circle around the cup. Eyes closed, they began to chant. *"Liquido a solido, l'acqua di ghaccio."*

"Like something out of *Harry Potter*," I said, before being shushed by a very serious Spence.

"*Harry Potter*'s kid stuff, Mom. Don't break our focus."

After a few repeats of the chant, they opened their eyes and looked at each other.

"Take a look," Spence said, gesturing toward the cup.

"I have to admit that I never even saw your hands move. Maybe it really is magic." I picked up the cup. "Um, or maybe not. It's still water."

"No way." Spence stood and grabbed for the cup.

"Where did we go wrong?" Shelley asked.

"Maybe my mom's interruption did break our focus." He shot me a glare.

Ellie, in the other room with Sarah, started to fuss as if she knew she missed out on all the fun.

"I'll get her." I knew Sarah wouldn't want to pick her up. I came back out to the kitchen balancing her on my hip, ready to see a repeat performance.

Sarah followed me in and stood back to watch the show.

"Here we go," Spence said, before reaching for Shelley's hand and beginning the chant over again. *"Liquido a solido, l'acqua di ghiaccio."*

Sarah stifled a laugh and made the cuckoo gesture with one finger spinning at the side of her head.

"Try now," Spencer commanded.

I hated to disappoint them, but I could see that it was water when I lifted the glass. Ellie, always eager to get her hands on a shiny new toy, reached for it. I carefully shifted it away from her so it wouldn't spill, then looked in the glass.

"Oh," I said, surprised. "It actually worked." I tipped it upside down. The frozen water stayed solid at the bottom.

Sarah held her hands up. "No way. I wanted them to fail."

"How'd you do it?" I asked.

"Mom." Sarah rolled her eyes. "A magician never reveals his secrets. Everyone knows that."

"But it's not a trick," Spencer said. "It's real."

"Uh-huh." I tried to check if they had a second glass hidden under the table, but I didn't see a thing. Weird. Maybe I could get Spence to reveal their secrets once Shelley left. "Shelley, are you joining us for dinner, or do you have to get home?"

"I invited her for dinner," Spence said. "She's staying."

"Great. Then I guess you better wash up. It's almost time."

"Not quite," Kate said. "Come out to the living room first."

I followed. The living room was filled with balloons and a banner that read CONGRATUATIONS! Someone forgot the L. I pretended not to notice. "Wow, thanks, gang. It's really special."

"And the best part." Sarah led me by the hand to the table. My favorite cupcakes from the South End Bakery near Kate's old apartment were arranged in a box, each one bearing a letter that together spelled out GO, BENNIE!

"Cupcakes! Now I can retire happy."

"Retire?" Kate looked alarmed.

"Kidding. I had a really good day, actually. No retirement in my future. At least, for now. Tomorrow, I go to the actual office. We'll see what the job really entails."

"It can't be any worse than working with Josh all day, right?" Kate winked. Her interest in Josh fueled my suspicion that she really had been trying to play matchmaker, but I still wasn't sure.

"Honestly, it wasn't that bad. He behaved. For the most part. At least, once I got off screw duty."

"Screw duty?" Kate struggled to raise her eyebrow. "Sounds kinky."

"Not. I spent the morning sorting screws into piles."

"Exciting." The oven timer went off, interrupting Kate. "More after dinner. That's the corn bread. Time to eat!"

* * *

After dinner, driving Shelley home, and insisting the kids do their homework and get ready for bed, I settled on the family room couch in front of the TV next to Kate and a wide-awake Eliana.

"I tried putting her down," Kate said. "She cries every time we leave the room."

"No problem. Let her stay up and watch football with the big girls."

"We're playing the Colts and we're both undefeated. It should be a great game." Kate bounced Ellie on her lap. The camera zoomed in on Marc on the sidelines and Ellie squealed and pointed.

"That's weird. She's acting like she can tell that it's Marc on the screen."

"Maybe she does," Kate said. "She has been surprising me lately."

"Even with the helmet on? Of course, we shouldn't be surprised that she's brilliant." I tweaked her toes. "She has our genes."

"It's her father's genes that give me pause. Who knows what he passed on?" She wrinkled her brow in concern as she looked at her daughter.

"He had some good genes, too." I shrugged. I was glad Nick hadn't called. It made it easier not to have to tell Kate about the connection. "Nothing to worry about there. Except maybe Ellie will be the first brunette in the family, not counting Spence with his Miss Clairol. I can't believe she totally missed out on your blond hair."

Ellie was born with a dark coating of fuzz on her head that our mother was convinced would fall out to be replaced with golden wisps. So far, no such luck. Ellie's hair had gotten thicker and darker. More like her father's.

"Hmm." Kate stared off in the direction of the television, but she didn't seem to be focused on anything. "That was a strange trick with the ice, wasn't it?"

"Kids. You remember when you were in your magic phase? You had that ridiculous kit with the hat and all the gadgets from the toy store."

"And you would beg me to let you be my assistant."

"Yeah. I couldn't believe it when you actually let me."

"It was a big show. We raised a lot of money from the neighborhood kids for muscular dystrophy. But you were mad when I made you donate your cut of the profits, too." We both laughed.

"I remember. That was the same summer Dad left."

We both grew quiet and pretended to be engaged in the game. The quarterback threw an interception. It looked like the Colts would take an early lead. Our father had abandoned us when we were kids, but he came back into our lives last year. Kate found him, actually. I loved having him back, but sometimes I wasn't so sure Kate had fully forgiven him.

"Dad's coming for Thanksgiving next week," I said finally. "That'll be fun."

"Maybe the kids can do their magic trick." Ah, so that one was still on her mind.

"Didn't you notice that it was water when you picked up the glass, but it turned to ice after Ellie touched it?" She paused. "And not only that, but the trick never worked when Ellie was out of the room."

I looked at her, then looked at Ellie. Ellie smiled up at me. "Do you hear that, Ellie? Your wacko mom thinks you're a lucky charm."

"Or maybe she's doing the magic. I told you her father had skills."

Skills? "Well, he certainly charmed you. But I think you're worrying over nothing. Ellie's a perfectly normal baby. My kids are the tricky ones."

"I guess." Kate didn't sound convinced. The Colts scored a field goal, turning our attention back to the game in earnest. "Oh, man. I know Marc wants to be out there."

"His knee was feeling good on Sunday. You never know."

"Doubtful."

"So, how about you and Marc? You seem to be getting along pretty well these days." I baited her, hoping she would reveal something.

"He's a great guy."

"Phenomenal. For both of you." I stroked Ellie's soft baby hair.

"I kissed him," she said in a low voice, as if making an illicit confession. "I don't know what I was doing. The last thing I want to do is lead him on."

"But were you? Leading him on? You really like him. Maybe you're ready for more."

"I'm not ready for more. I just gave in to the moment. I had put Ellie down in the crib and turned around, and there he was. I bumped right into him. And I looked up, and my stomach did this flip thing. Suddenly he looked so hot. I haven't thought anyone was hot for about a year. Not even Brad Pitt."

"I haven't thought Brad was hot since he dumped Jen."

She shrugged. "It was weird. For a second there, I stopped thinking and just went for it. And it was pretty good."

"Nothing wrong with that."

"But there is. He deserves more. I can't possibly ever love him as much as he loves me. You've seen the way he looks at me, Ben. He does that all the time. He doesn't even deny it. The man is bursting with it."

"With love?"

"Yes. And when I tell him he should stop seeing so much of me and go out and meet other women, he laughs. *You're the only one for me. I've known it since the day I first met you, at your sister's party.*" She did a deep-throated impression of Marc's husky voice. "It's not fair."

"He's a big boy. He'll know when it's time to give up."

"I don't know if he will."

"Maybe he doesn't have to. You said you thought he was hot."

"For a few minutes."

"It's a start. You actually showed signs of physical attraction. Give it a chance."

"How long can he sit around waiting?"

"As long as he wants. You can't control the way he feels." Maybe that was exactly her problem. Kate liked to be in control. "And maybe there's nothing wrong with him loving you more. They say one partner always loves more."

"Is that how it was with you and Patrick?"

"I loved him with all my heart, but he loved me more. He had a bigger heart." I smiled, thinking of him. It was true.

"And are you really ready to move on?"

"To move on? No. Is there such a thing as moving on? I'll always love him. But I'm willing to see that there might be other men out there. Maybe not the great love of my life, but I want to have some fun."

"Anyone in mind?"

I hesitated. I couldn't exactly say I'd thought of Nick without her asking more questions, or encouraging her to take the chance to talk up Josh.

Ellie started fussing. We looked up in time to see some commotion on the field; then Marc emerged with the ball and started running. "What? When did they put Marc in the game?"

"I don't know. We missed it. He must be so happy."

Ellie squealed as if she knew exactly what was going on. *Interception.* The Patriots went on to lose, but that Marc had a chance to get back on the field made it feel like a win for us. I smiled at Kate's excitement. She had to end up with Marc. It was only a matter of time. I wished for her happiness with all my heart, more than I even cared to think about my own.

The next morning, I had Kate drop me off at the station so I could take the T into work. Why go through the hassle of driving into the city when we had such handy public transportation? Besides, I felt good, doing the right thing for the environment. I was eco-friendly and proud. And looking good in my tailored black department-store-label suit. It allowed me to show Kate that I was not all about designer clothes. Good thing she didn't recognize the shoes as Jimmy Choo.

I sipped at my coffee as I waited for the train, Gucci messenger bag safely tucked under my arm. I sized up the other people waiting. There was a woman in a brown pantsuit that made her look like a

Brownies troop leader and a man in a poorly cut suit pacing impatiently while typing on his Black-Berry. Oh yes. I was a professional. I fit right in. Better than fitting in. I looked like I could be the Brownies leader's boss. I definitely had better shoes. Hers were scuffed loafers.

Finally, the train arrived and we were off. My heart started pounding when we pulled into my stop. Boston. Work. Here I was. At last!

My workday had been going swimmingly. I was in my element making phone calls, soliciting dona-tions. Some said yes, some would get back to me, some were "maxed out." I knew all about maxed out and never pushed too hard. Still, it felt great to be productive. It felt even better when one of the donors called me.

"What are you wearing?" It was a good thing I rec-ognized his voice or I might have hung up on him. I probably should have hung up. I had no business getting any closer to Nick Angelos. Unfortunately, the mere idea that he was off-limits suddenly made him all the more tempting. It was only a phone call. Kate never had to know.

"Black. Low cut. Tight." I wasn't shy—or entirely truthful. My outfit was black, at least. The skirt hugged my curves, though the suit wasn't actually tight. The jacket buttoned up to a V-neck silk shell that wasn't exactly low cut.

"Tell me you're wearing heels."

"Peep-toe spectator pumps." My feet were killing me. From now on, I would follow Brownies Leader's example and wear old loafers in to work, then switch at the office.

"Mmm." He purred. "I can imagine what they do to your legs."

"Besides cause an almost unbearable searing sensation up my calves?"

"Not the kind of pain I had in mind, but it speaks volumes for your power of endurance."

My stomach flipped. I struggled to catch my breath. "Yes, well, and what can I do for you today, Mr. Angelos?"

"First, you can put me down for another donation. What do you suggest? Will a grand do?"

"Hmm. I don't know. Could you consider ten grand?"

"Done."

"No, I was teasing." I perched on the edge of my desk and twisted the ancient phone cord around my finger. "We have this spiel we do when soliciting. Usually people aren't willing to contribute, so we suggest a low number and talk them up from there."

"I see. You were trying to get me for a hundred grand. Clever girl. No problem there, but I'm going to demand that you have dinner with me. You did say you were soliciting?"

My cheeks flamed. "Donations. Soliciting donations."

"A shame. I had something else in mind."

"I didn't think I had to solicit for that." I smiled at my sharp comeback, trying to ignore the fact that I was getting a little carried away. Why encourage him? Seeing him again was a really bad idea.

"Touché, Mrs. St. James. Touché. So, we're on,

then? I'll pick you up. Let's see? The sooner, the better."

My heart raced. *The sooner, the better.* An incredible man wanted to see me again and I was going to turn him down? Maybe it wasn't so bad that he was Owen's nephew. Maybe Kate never had to know. It was only dinner. One meal. What was the harm?

"I'm done here at five." I glanced at the clock; four thirty-two.

"And it doesn't sound as if you have to go home and change. Black, tight, and low cut works for me."

Be still my heart. "Ah, but one problem. You never told me what you're wearing. Turnabout is fair play."

"You can see for yourself," he said. "I'm standing on the other side of your office door about to come in."

I nearly fell off the edge of the desk. Fortunately, I maintained my balance and managed to straighten my jacket and cross my legs at the ankles, just like they taught us in pageant school. "Well, come in, then."

He entered and took my breath away. He wore what first looked like a black suit but turned out to be a deep dark forest-green that brought out his eyes. He had a pale green shirt underneath, opened at the neck to reveal a hint of his tanned skin, enough to remind me of what he looked like without his shirt. His blond hair was slightly tousled, calling to mind a wild mane, and he moved like a lion with lean, economical steps.

He stopped at the edge of the desk, reached for the phone in my hand, and hung it up. "I can't believe they've left you here all alone. On your very first day."

"Second, technically. And you know we don't have a large budget for staff. It's mostly volunteers."

"Still, you'd think Leslie would stay and open up a bottle of champagne to welcome you."

I shook my head. "I don't think it's allowed on the job. But that's fine. I told her to go home, that I could handle it. She showed me how to lock up. There's really nothing to it."

"Then get busy. We have reservations."

"Oh? Where?" I moved around to the other side of the desk to power down my computer, and for safety's sake. I didn't trust myself not to reach out and grab him. I hated to give the wrong impression.

"The Oak Room. I hope you're a carnivore." When he said it, he bared his teeth ever so slightly.

"I love steak. But I don't know."

"About the Oak Room?"

"About you. No doubt *you're* a carnivore. Sometimes you look at me as if you might be ready to eat me alive." And there was that Glendower thing.

"Eating you is definitely on my agenda." He raised a golden brow. Tingles shot straight down my spine. "I think you're on the menu for tonight's dessert."

Check, please.

The sensible side of me reared up in protest. What exactly did he have in mind? Dinner? Or an affair? What did I have in mind, for that matter? I knew I should beg off, maybe some other time. Or just agree to a drink instead of a whole dinner. Yet, somehow, I didn't want to be sensible anymore. I wanted to have some fun. "Just let me call home. My sister's watching my kids, but I want to let them know I'll be out."

"Late."

I crinkled my nose. "The kids have school tomorrow. I can't be too late."

"Not too late, then." He nodded as if it didn't bother him at all. "I'll work around it."

Whatever that meant. I picked up the phone and dialed Kate, relieved when she didn't answer. Maybe she took them out for a quick bite before Sarah's hockey practice? If they waited for me to get home, Sarah wouldn't have a chance to eat. Besides, practice lasted over an hour. I could leave her a message for now and call her back from the restaurant. One dinner, why not? After our little talk last night, I felt confident that she would probably be happy for me. If not, she had my cell phone number and I could go straight home if she called.

"Kate, hi," I said at the beep. "I've been invited to a little celebratory dinner and I'll be home a little later than planned. Not too late. Thanks for watching the kids. See you later." *Click.*

I looked at Nick Angelos, all six-foot-something of towering body-built-for-sin. I needed this. Damned if I didn't deserve it, too, after the year I'd had. It was time I took pleasure by the horns.

Or, you know, whatever else Nick Angelos had to hold on to . . . growl.

I stood up, ignoring my wobbly knees. "I just need to lock up and we're good to go."

Chapter Eight

As I'd come around the desk to lock the doors, Nick's arm slid around my waist and he didn't let go until we got to the car. I missed the warmth of him as soon as we broke contact and climbed into the car.

"Morrison's with us again, I see?"

Nick opened the door and placed his hand on the small of my back to ease me in. "Never mind Morrison. Pretend he's not even here." He slid in beside me, his hand finding a new spot on my knee.

I met his gaze and smiled. Morrison started the car and drove away from the curb.

"It's hard to pretend he's not even here when he's up there driving the car." I caught Morrison's grin in the rearview. He didn't seem the type to enjoy being ignored.

"I think I can make you forget." He leaned in and brushed his lips to mine.

I forgot my name. I forgot everything but the warmth at my core. I opened my eyes slowly. "What?"

He chuckled from low in his throat. "That's better."

"Much better," I agreed.

"We're here," he said.

"So soon? How did we get here so fast?" I looked out. Sure enough, I looked out to see the bell entrance of the Fairmont Copley Plaza.

"I like speed. I give Morrison permission to go as fast as he pleases."

"Which is still much slower than you would like," Morrison added, only to get a sharp look from Nick in response.

"I haven't been here in years," I said.

"I thought I might arrange for us to stay the night." His gaze dipped down to my cleavage and back up again. "But I guess it's out of the question on a school night."

"It's out of the question on a first date, but nice try." I smiled. First date. There weren't supposed to be any more. But why did my stomach flutter with excitement instead of dread? I wanted more, so help me. Only dinner? Suddenly I didn't want to stop with one night. I was having too much fun. The man had a dangerous effect on me.

"Apologies are unnecessary. We have all the time in the world."

"All the time in the world," I repeated, liking the sound of it a little too much.

We lingered over dinner. The Oak Room was masculine to the extreme, as if testosterone tainted the very air and made me light-headed. Or maybe that was the wine. Nick ordered a bottle of something that sounded French and tasted expensive. Wine had been Patrick's territory at home. I didn't pay much attention beyond red, white, and sparkling.

Animal heads hung on almost every wood-paneled wall. Nick looked at home in the setting, as if he might have been the sole hunter filling all the room with his various trophies. I identified more with the stuffed creatures.

"Do the animals intimidate you?" he asked, leaning in.

"No. Well, maybe a little. No doubt the poor things barely stood a chance."

He looked around. "You're safe with me."

"I'm not so sure." I met his gaze. "Your eyes are wild. You have that golden mane. You remind me of a lion."

"A lion." He seemed amused. "I've never heard that one."

"No? It really fits. You move with a feral grace."

"Grace? How masculine." He oozed sarcasm.

"Very masculine. Everything about you says *macho*, right down to the flared nostrils."

"Now you're making fun of my nose?"

"More like enjoying the view across the table." Inside, I was giddy. It felt wonderful to be out to dinner with a man. A very handsome man. I'd seen the way our waitress looked at him, as if she would like to knock me out of my chair and take my place.

"You've barely touched your chateaubriand."

"It's delicious. Really. It's hard to focus on the food with the lion sitting right across from me."

"I won't hurt you, little lamb."

"Oh?" I arched a brow. "Not even a little?"

My heart raced with the thrill of flirting. Perhaps I was more hunter than prey after all.

"I don't think so." His gaze narrowed. "No woman wants to be hurt. Not really."

"I meant it in the naughty way. Not in the literal sense."

"I see." He finished off his wine and waved the server over. "We're ready for our check."

The waitress glared at me again, but I took it as a compliment. I had what she wanted, if only for a few hours. Nick was with me. Tonight, it was good to be Bennie St. James.

Morrison met us exactly where he'd dropped us off. It was a leisurely meal, but service was prompt thanks to the server's apparent fascination with Nick Angelos. Still, it felt late and I had no sense of how long we'd taken.

I hadn't worn my watch, and I'd left my bag in the car so I couldn't check the hour on my cell phone. Very careless of me. I should have worn a watch. I should have kept my phone close. What if Kate had been trying to call? I felt a pang of guilt at the lack of responsibility. I had kids. What was I thinking?

"You're a good mom," Nick said, as if he had read my mind. "To plan to get in early because your children have school."

"Most moms would, so I would like to think. My kids are everything to me."

"I understand."

"Do you?" I looked at him. He wouldn't know a thing about the demands of parenthood, would he?

"Bennie, I don't mind that you have children." He stroked my cheek. "I'm incredibly attracted to the woman you are now. That includes accepting everything that came before me. Husband, children. I have a past, too."

"Of course you do." I hadn't even thought about *his* past. Eventually, we would get around to revelations. For now, being with Nick kept me focused on the present, on all the new feelings he stirred in me. What would it be like to be with him? In bed. My chest tightened. The thought made me nervous and intrigued all at once. Subconsciously, I'd already accepted that I planned to see him again. How would I explain it to Kate?

Morrison held the door this time, but Nick assisted me into the car.

In the car, he slid in beside me, his arm around me, leaving no room between us. "I would like you to call me," he said. "Later. When you're all tucked into bed." His voice dropped to a low purr.

I nodded. "Another one of those *what are you wearing* calls?"

I could get into phone sex. Talking came easy and I didn't have to worry about his reaction to any visible cellulite around my upper thighs.

"Mmm. What do you wear to bed?" He nuzzled my hair and I could feel his breath heating my neck. My mouth went dry.

"Depends on the night. When it snows, I wear flannel." I looked out the window. No snow.

He noticed, too. "No sign of flurries. Good. Flannel's out."

Gulp. "I do have some really heavy cotton nighties. If there's a chill in the air, I cover up."

His hand ran along the back of my neck and paused at my nape. "It's not that cold out, for November."

"Cold enough."

"Really?" His lips brushed my ear. "I could warm you up."

"You could."

"Call me. I'll make sure you're warm enough to wear silk to bed."

"Silk?" I wasn't sure I had any silky bedtime clothes. It had been so very long for me to need anything that favored form over function.

"At least. I prefer to think of you going to bed in nothing at all. My number's programmed into your phone."

A blush heated my cheeks.

"But how did you—" I'd left my phone in the car. Morrison must have been busy. I could have been angry, but that Nick wanted me to call badly enough to have Morrison program my phone brought a smile to my lips instead.

"Your sister called," Morrison said, interrupting my conversation with Nick. "Numerous times. Not to worry, I told her you were otherwise engaged as a guest of Mr. Angelos."

"Oh." I cringed. Man, was I in trouble now! "And she said?"

"That it wasn't important and she would catch up with you later."

Kate code for it was not an emergency, but it was important to her, and I was so busted. It wouldn't be pretty. Damn.

"Thank you, Morrison." I closed my eyes and snuggled deeper into Nick's arms, against his solid chest. "I wish I could stay here all night with you."

And I would definitely be warm enough to sleep without wearing a stitch.

"If we had all night"—he paused to kiss the top of

my head—"I wouldn't stay here. I'd find us a nice comfortable bed. And the things I would do to you."

"Yes?" I turned to meet his gaze. What would he do to me? My palms began to sweat. I wanted to know.

"Let's just say that you wouldn't be worried about your sister, or getting your kids to school on time. You wouldn't be able to think. And I promise you wouldn't regret it."

"I like the sound of that." Oblivion. Sexual oblivion. Sign me up. I only wished it wouldn't have to wait for a more convenient time. Tonight, I had Kate to face and kids to tuck into bed. "I hope we can do it again sometime."

"We'll do it. Soon."

I couldn't find my voice.

A mental image of Nick's hands smoothing over my naked body somehow jumped into mind and I couldn't chase it. Then it was as if I could feel his hands doing what I'd imagined, stroking, moving down my chest, pausing to cup my breasts. My nipples tightened in response. I closed my eyes to savor the sensation.

"We're here," he said, his voice soft in my ear.

I straightened up and opened my eyes as Morrison pulled into my driveway. "So soon?"

"I'm afraid so. I may have to rethink the speeding."

It took me a minute to get my bearings enough to say good-bye. "I would love to ask you in, but I don't think it's a good idea."

"Not with the children ready for bed and your sister gunning for bear."

"Exactly. It's probably not even safe to see me to the door."

"Not to worry. You'll see me sooner than you know." He planted a chaste kiss on my forehead.

"I'm counting on it. Thank you for dinner. I had a wonderful time. Well worth the risk."

He nodded in acknowledgment and I got out of the car. I waved once before turning and heading inside to face my family. The air was cool, but tinged with the comforting aroma of burning wood. Perhaps Kate wouldn't be such a pill. She might actually understand that I'd needed some time with Nick. Of course, it had been selfish of me to just assume she would stay longer than planned and handle the kids through homework, hockey practice, and dinner. Not that I hadn't been happy to have Ellie longer than planned on myriad occasions when Kate found herself running late after an open house or a business meeting. She would understand, I decided, right before I walked in and realized that I'd read her wrong this time.

Kate, hands on hips and slippered foot tapping, waited just inside the door. Not exactly the posture of an understanding sister. "Nice of you to come home."

"I left a message. I told you I would be late." More guilty than annoyed, I breezed past her, dropped my bag on the couch, and headed to the kitchen for a glass of water, a handy substitute for a cold shower. Not that I needed either with Kate ready to put a damper on my fun.

"You left a message." She followed me, her white chenille robe trailing behind her to lend an angel-of-justice quality to her appearance. "And did you even think to leave one with Josh Brandon?"

"Josh? Why?" I sipped my drink as I headed back

out to the living room. That's when I caught sight of the embers burning in the hearth. "Oh, crap. It's Tuesday."

"Yeah."

I tried to think of a way to spin the facts to make me look less guilty of blowing off a friend. "Well, did you and Josh have a nice time?"

"Unbelievable." She ran her hand through her hair, the other hand still firmly planted on her hip.

"That sums up my evening," I said, eager to break past her anger and talk about it. When was the last time I'd had a date?

"So glad you had a good time while you were standing up Josh. He's got a thing for you. How do you think it made him feel?"

"A thing for me?" I sat down in front of the glowing remains of the fire. "Ridiculous. He's too old for me." Possibly not ridiculous. I couldn't say I hadn't had my suspicions. But I didn't want to think I'd hurt his feelings. I hoped it wasn't true.

"He's barely forty. In case you haven't checked lately, you're well into your thirties."

"A little into my thirties. And I take good care of myself." From the looks of things this morning, so did Josh. But that was beside the point.

"God, you're vain."

"I'm realistic." I downed the rest of my water.

"Vain. And selfish. Josh stuck around waiting for you all night. He fixed the fireplace, a dirty job. He ended up covered in soot. I let him use your shower. Then he gave up waiting and drove to get the wood. So it would be here, he said, for when you got back."

"And it's lovely. I'd forgotten how much I love the smell of burning wood." I tried to remain optimistic, but Kate's words hammered into me. I'd made a horrible mistake and possibly hurt a friend.

"He stayed late to tend the fire, determined to keep it burning. I invited him to join us for dinner and he finally decided that he would eat something and hit the road. He seemed heartbroken."

"Are you sure you're not reading too much into it? Maybe you're just upset because you tried to do a little matchmaking of your own and it didn't work out as you planned?" I hoped that was it, that maybe Josh wasn't counting on anything other than making the friendly gesture of restoring my fireplace to working order.

"You bitch."

"Excuse me?"

"You heard me. You're being a major bitch. After all he tried to do for you?" She gestured to the fireplace.

"I'll apologize and thank him tomorrow. What more can I do?"

"You could try being human. Showing up, or maybe calling him when you had a change of plans."

I sighed. "You're right. I wish I'd remembered."

"I think that's what hurt him most. That you couldn't even bother to remember."

I shrugged. "I forgot. People forget things. Is it a crime?" Maybe not a crime, but I didn't need Kate to tell me that it was a pretty nasty thing to do. I did feel bad. All I could do now was hope that he would forgive me.

"Well, fine. I hope Fabio was worth it."

"He does not look a thing like Fabio." As if. I cringed at the thought. "The next time I see Josh, I will apologize. Profusely. I didn't mean to hurt anyone. I had a date for the first time in forever and I got carried away with the thrill of it all. I couldn't wait to come home and tell you about it. So much for my support network."

She softened a little around the eyes, but she didn't seem entirely taken in. "You know I'm here for you. And I'm happy for you, I really am. But you can't steamroll over people who care about you just to get what you want."

"I didn't steamroll." Finally, I was getting angry. Really angry. Yes, I messed up. It was jerky and not fair to Josh. But did I deserve to get a verbal pummeling from my sister? As if she'd never messed up? "I made an innocent mistake. Maybe you can't forgive me, but I'm sure Josh will."

She clucked her tongue. "Yeah, well, consider yourself lucky. That man would forgive you anything. He's head over heels."

I still didn't believe it. Head over heels for me? He didn't exactly seem it when he was yelling at me about my nailing technique and keeping me away from the paint and power tools. Then again, that was when I first had started volunteering with Habitat for Humanity last spring. Yesterday, there'd been no yelling. And then that bit about wanting my opinion? Maybe it could be true that he had some interest. But head over heels?

"It would be nice if I could count on forgiveness from my own sister, but maybe that's too much to ask." Too easily, I fell back on my old reliable trick of turning a situation around so that Kate became the guilty party.

"You're impossible." She sighed. "I'm going up to check on Ellie."

I stood. "I'm going up to say good night to my kids. Thanks for keeping an eye on them."

"You've done the same for me when I needed you, and I'm sure you would again," she added, a tad reluctantly, on her way up the stairs.

After I checked in on Spencer and Sarah and changed into my pajamas, I returned downstairs to turn off the lights and lock the doors. It had been a long day. I was ready for bed myself.

Imagine my surprise when I turned and caught a fully dressed Kate with a bundled-up Ellie headed for the door. "Where are you going? It's late."

"It's not even eleven. I think Ellie and I need some alone time. We're going back home." It was a twenty-minute ride at best, but it wasn't like Kate to leave after Ellie was settled for the night.

"Suit yourself." I closed the distance and kissed Ellie on the forehead. "Be good for Mommy, sweet pea." Translation: keep her up all night with fussing. You can always catch a nap tomorrow. "Sleep well, Kate." Translation: don't miss me now that you're stuck with your own crying baby. Who's a bitch now?

"You, too." She opened the door and stomped out to her SUV.

Fine. She could be that way. I'm sure she did need some alone time. She always needed alone time when she got in her moods. I think she spent her entire sophomore year of high school, minus the school hours, alone in her room. As Sarah would say, whatever.

I locked the doors, turned off the lights, and prepared to head for bed, where Bert and Ernie would smother me with their own special brand of puggy affection. People could be a real disappointment. My dogs never let me down.

Chapter Nine

Before heading upstairs, I heard a noise at the front door. Ernie, at my feet, barked and crossed the room. He'd heard it, too. Bert, unconcerned with anything that kept him from bed, stayed at the foot of the stairs.

My heart pounding, I walked slowly across the room and peeked out the curtain of the window next to the door. Nick. I breathed a sigh of relief only to tense up again a second later when I remembered our conversation in the car.

Determined to act braver than I felt, I took a deep breath and opened the door.

"Flannel," I said, gesturing to my flannel pajama pants that I wore with a long-sleeved cotton tee. "Does that answer your question?"

He flashed the wolfish grin. "It's more charming than I expected. Cold front on the way?"

"I got one from my sister for coming in late, thanks. You just missed her. She went home for the night. Come in before Cujo here attacks."

Ernie sat at attention, his tail thumping the floor wildly.

Nick came in and rubbed him on the head, prompting Bert to come running for the same. Bert would never stay on the sidelines if being petted was a possibility. Not that I could blame him. Being petted by Nick looked to be a worthy reward. He'd changed to jeans that hugged his taut behind when he leaned down.

My admiration turned rapidly to fear as he straightened up and looked me over again. Why was he here?

"It's late," I said. "We were just headed up to bed."

"We?" He arched a blond brow. "You and the dogs?"

I crossed my arms over my chest, mainly to hide the reaction of my braless nipples to the chilly night air. "They do keep me warm at night."

He closed the distance. "Lucky dogs. I wouldn't mind taking over the position."

I laughed lightly. "I'll let you know when I'm hiring."

He slid his hand under my chin and tilted my face up to meet his gaze. "How about tonight?"

A tingle raced up my spine. Fear, or excitement? "Tonight?"

"Mmm. Tonight." He dipped his head to kiss me. His lips were soft but firm. He didn't do anything more than touch them to mine, but he didn't need to do more.

I reacted. *I remembered.* The rush of adrenaline. The blood pounding. The tightening between my thighs. The aching need. This was what it felt like to yearn. It had been so very long for me.

"Nick." I placed my hands flat against his chest,

holding him off but not pushing him away. "I'm not sure. I need more time."

Time. My pulse raced, panic setting in. I remembered what it was like, what to do, but was I ready? *For that?*

He kissed my forehead. "I got home and couldn't stop thinking about you. I could still smell your hair, the shampoo you use. Or maybe it's your perfume. Something, some bit of you rubbed off on me. You give off an incredible scent."

"Thanks." I blushed, my gaze averted.

"I got back here as soon as I could."

"I didn't hear your car." It just occurred to me that I should have heard him pull in.

"My Lamborghini purrs like a kitten. It's fast, but quiet. Plus, I parked down the street."

His hand, on my waist, slid to my hips.

My heart beat faster. "The kids are in bed, but they could get up. It's not a good time."

"They're prone to getting up in the middle of the night?"

"No, but it could happen." I rubbed my hands together. My palms were sweating.

"Not on my watch."

I gnawed my lip, wondering, what was the worst that could happen if I didn't chase him off? Kissing? I could handle kissing, but would I be able to go any further? What would he expect?

"You can't exactly stop kids from getting out of bed without alerting them to your presence."

"True, but they'll sleep through my being here. They won't even know." Confident, he dropped a trail of light kisses along my jawline. Despite my better instincts, I rolled my head back and savored the feel of his lips on me. Just a few more minutes and I would have to ask him to leave.

He stopped kissing and looked down at the dogs, sitting patiently at our feet.

"They're ready for bed," I said.

"So let's put them to bed. Where do they sleep if they don't sleep with you?"

"They have beds out on the porch." I gestured to the back of the living room. "It's glassed in and heated. They like it there during the day because they can look outside and they have a doggy door."

"Perfect," he said, whistling to the dogs. "Come, boys."

I laughed. "They won't follow you. They'll only go with me or one of the kids."

Unless food was somehow involved and then all bets were off. But, to my amazement, the dogs snapped to attention and trotted off after Nick.

"Incredible," I said.

"I'm good with animals. You just have to know how to command them."

"They may rebel once they realize your intentions."

"They'll be fine. Trust me." He led them to the porch. They went willingly, no whining or fuss. He came back out and shut the door behind him.

"Now then." He closed the distance.

"Now then." With Bert and Ernie out of the way, I might as well indulge in a few more kisses. I would hear the floorboards creak if the kids got out of bed. "Can I get you a drink or something?"

He reached out and stroked my cheek with the back of his hand. "Or something. I'm not thirsty."

He cupped my face, drawing me to him to indulge

in a kiss, this one slower than the first one, deepening as our mouths came into contact, his tongue begging entry between my lips. My reservations drifted off. Our bodies pressed together in a way that felt organic, so right. His erection grazed my hip. The excitement of being wanted fueled my desire.

I allowed my hands to slide around his waist, over his back. His muscles were rigid under my fingertips. I moaned from the back of my throat as his tongue slicked over mine, smooth as liquid glass.

His hand ran under my shirt, up to my breast. He grazed his thumb over my nipple, provoking an instant reaction there and lower, my body tightening like the strings of a guitar being tuned.

"Let's go upstairs. I want to look at you."

My legs wobbled, barely supporting me. Even the words nearly made me come undone. I shook my head. "Too risky."

"They won't even know I'm here."

He kissed me again and I began to believe him. He'd parked down the street. We could be quiet. As long as he was out at a reasonable hour . . .

His hands moved down to cup my buttocks and I was in his arms before I knew it, my legs wrapped around him. A second later—or so it seemed, I had no recollection of moving—we were up the stairs and in my room.

He closed the door behind us and lowered me to the bed. "How did we get up here? I barely felt us moving." His kiss was consuming, but was it that disorienting?

"I'm fast. I told you so."

His hands gripped my shirt at the sides and he

began to tug it up. I pulled it back down. "You really are fast."

"Too fast?" He propped himself on his arms, hovering over me. A golden gleam twinkled in his dark green eyes, lending him an air of mischief.

My heart raced. "Maybe."

"All right. I can go slower." He cocked a brow and leaned in for a kiss. A deep, slow kiss. So slow it made me crazy. It made me long to speed him up.

Atop me, his body moved in an equally slow rhythm, his hips shifting forward, then pulling back, his erection pressing into me, then easing away, making me eager for its return. I ground against him, finding my own, more urgent rhythm.

"You feel so good." I didn't mean to say it out loud.

"So do you." And before I knew it, he stripped my shirt off over my head. "And you look as good as you feel." His eyes widened at the sight of my naked breasts.

I tingled again, deep down, as the cold air, and his warm gaze, met my bare nipples. I brazened it out, determined to fight the instinct to cover up. Nick's smile of appreciation helped, and when he dipped his head to take a rosy tip between his teeth, nipping gently, I lost my senses.

I arched my back, relishing the feel of his mouth on me. Unable to hold on much longer, I reached for him, eager to feel him, too. My fingers worked at the button of his jeans and eased his zipper down. He groaned when I found him, my hand closing around his thick shaft and stroking down, then up, and down again.

Back up to speed, he shifted and tugged his jeans down his hips and off in seconds. I stared. Wow.

Frantic, I worked the buttons of his shirt, eager to strip him bare and see all of him, every inch of his amazing body. He pulled off his shirt and reached for me, giving one sharp tug at the fabric around my hips and pulling. I kicked my pants off the rest of the way.

He kissed me again, as if to reassure me that I was safe with him. It worked. I stretched out under him. His gaze lit with appreciation as he trailed his hands down my waist, down my legs, urging my thighs to part for him. I still wore my underwear, safety in layers.

Or maybe not. His head dipped, following the path of his hands, pausing over my cotton-covered mound. He licked the cleft through the fabric. "So wet."

I trembled at the sensation of his tongue, the sound of his voice. He twisted a finger in my waistband and slid my underwear down my hips, revealing the rest of me to him. He rose, slipping the white cotton down my legs and off, then returned to intimate proximity.

"Oh. Oh. No." I didn't think I could take much more.

He arched a brow. "Yes."

He blew on me, his breath hot and tempting. His hands smoothed up my thighs, parting them to allow access. His tongue darted between my legs, circling my delicate nub and lapping until I nearly cried out. I tangled my hands in his hair. He looked up, lips curled in the wolfish grin. "You taste as good as you smell. I don't think I could ever get enough."

My body clenched, the need spiraling out of control.

"I need you inside me," I panted, ragged. "Now."

"Now?" His voice was a velvet whisper.

"Now."

He poised over me, resting his weight on his arms, before he blazed a trail of kisses down my neck, along my collarbone. I felt his erection against me, centered against my silken folds, and then in. All the way in.

I was prepared for the shock, for the newness of the way his body fit with mine. I wasn't prepared for how warm he felt, how utterly amazing the sensation was. I didn't remember how good it could be. How it heated the blood and sent my head spinning in the very best of ways. How it made me wild with euphoria.

He stroked me with his finger as he plunged himself deeper inside me than I imagined he could go, and I lost all track of thought, all track of time, all track of everything save for the sensation of being overwhelmingly, completely fulfilled.

Lights danced, colored fragments falling like confetti behind my eyelids before everything went blindingly white. I pulsed around him, tightening, holding on to every inch of him. I didn't want to let him go. And then his liquid heat coursed into me and I knew it was over, for now. He stayed atop me, resting his weight on his arms for several minutes to steady his breathing and meet my gaze.

He rolled off to my side and stroked my face. "Incredible."

Lacking words for my cathartic journey, I said nothing but drifted to sleep with Nick still stroking my face.

* * *

Fortunately, I woke before my alarm went off, well before it was time to wake the kids. Nick, as breathtaking as a figure from a Renaissance painting, slept beside me.

True, he had captured my attention. Most definitely, he inspired my lust. But was what I felt for him love? From the first day with Nick, I'd been carried away by the idea of him as a romantic hero. What did I really know about him? And why did Josh Brandon hate him so much? Why was I even thinking of Josh while lying in bed with Nick?

In the light of morning, everything suddenly seemed so serious. I'd done what I never thought I would do—snuck a man my kids had barely met into my bedroom overnight. I cringed. How could I be so irresponsible? I hadn't even considered using protection. So careless. I'd had my tubes tied after Sarah's birth, so pregnancy wasn't an issue. But diseases? I hadn't even given it a thought.

Despite my guilt about bringing a man into the house with the kids at home, I didn't feel I'd betrayed Patrick. I'd changed my bedroom around since he died. Patrick never wanted flowers or lace, too girly. I'd gone on a shopping spree and replaced it all, new comforter in pale blue satin in gold swirls, new sheets. I painted the walls a creamy taupe and hung some framed prints of Monet's *Waterlilies*. I'd even replaced our mattress. The old one held a faint eau de Patrick and I ended up in tears every night when I crawled into bed. Patrick still lived in parts of the house, but the bedroom was all me.

And now I'd christened it with a new lover.

At last, I knew I could feel again. I remembered how much I liked making love. I'd never had sex without feeling a strong emotional commitment, and no doubt that commitment was not yet there. Maybe it could be. I loved *being* with Nick. I needed to give it a chance. Sex that mind-blowing was definitely worth devoting more time for investigation.

I wanted to slip from the bed to shower, but I wasn't sure leaving Nick alone was such a good idea. What if he woke? What if one of the kids woke and came to find me?

"Hey, sleepyhead." I shook his shoulder gently. The smell of him, a heady musk, made me feel warm down to my core. The guilt slipped away. The euphoria returned. Maybe it could be love. "Time to wake up."

He stirred and met my gaze with those amazing eyes that, this morning, seemed lightened to more peridot from their usual deep emerald. "Good morning."

"The kids will be up soon. I don't think it's a good idea that they find you here."

"I understand." He sat up and ran a hand through his tousled blond hair. His biceps bulged and his chest was still amazing, his abs still well defined. He squinted at the clock, five A.M., and grimaced. "I'll get ready to go."

"Sorry it's so early. I can put on a pot of coffee and be right back. I want to check on the dogs, anyway."

"Don't go." He reached for my hand and laced his fingers with mine. "I want to be with you. I can't stand the thought of being away from you until absolutely necessary."

My stomach flipped. Perhaps he was falling for

me more than I realized. "All right. But we can't stay in bed all day. I have the kids, the dogs, and work."

"What if I could stop time? We could stay in bed all day."

"That would be lovely." Truly. I couldn't remember the last time I'd stayed in bed all day. "But we'd have to eat."

"The minions would feed us. One snap of my fingers and they would bring us our heart's desire."

"It must be nice to live in fantasyland." I smiled.

"Oh, it is. I could make you queen. Queen of Fantasyland. What do you think?"

"We'll have to delay my coronation. I have nothing to wear."

"The minions could take care of that, too, but I wouldn't want to deprive you of the pleasure of shopping."

"You know me so well."

"I'd like to think so."

"You don't really have the power to stop time." It was a statement, but also a bit of a question. All his talk of minions and some of the little tricks he had pulled last night, along with Kate's accusations of Nick's uncle being the devil, fueled my imagination.

He clucked his tongue. "I'm afraid my powers are limited to smaller feats."

Suddenly he pouted as if it honestly made him sad. I was eager to bolster his spirits. "What you did last night was no small feat."

"I had brilliant inspiration." He lifted my hand to his lips and kissed the tops of my knuckles. "So I guess we need to get dressed, go downstairs, and say our good-byes."

I nodded. "I get the kids up in just under an hour."

"So there's time to shower."

"Definitely."

He arched a brow. "It would take less time if we showered together."

I sighed. Showering together seemed the ultimate in intimacy. But it also sounded tempting. The bonus was that if the kids happened to wake up and come looking for me, they would assume I was in the shower unaccompanied, as usual.

"Good idea. I'll go start the water." I started to get out of bed, but he pulled me back.

"No," he said, springing out of the covers. "I think I can figure it out. I'll start it. You join me when you're ready."

I watched him prowl across the room, half male model, half lion. All perfection. My gaze traced a line down his back to the dimples at the top of his backside, his tight rear, and the long muscular legs that made short work of the walk to the bathroom.

Once he was behind the bathroom door, I reached for my bathrobe and ran to the bathroom down the hall to freshen up before joining him.

A blessed mist enshrouded my bathroom by the time I entered. I'd freshened up, but nothing could enhance the appearance like shower steam, nature's airbrushing. I dropped my robe, opened the glass door, and stepped in behind Nick, who faced the nozzle.

"Hey," I said by way of greeting as I reached for the shower gel and squeezed a generous amount into my palm. I rubbed it into lather and smoothed my hands over his back, down to his perfect backside, and slipped around to his front. The soap made it easy to slide my hand up and down his shaft.

Pressed against his sudsy back, my nipples hardened. He spun around and caught my wrists.

"Naughty girl. I didn't think we'd have much time to fool around."

"We don't." Standing so close to him, I found it hard to keep my wits about me. I lost all reason. "But you're hard to resist."

"I'm hard." He gripped his erection in his palm. "Rock-solid. Thanks to you."

I let my gaze drop, following the golden trail of curls down under his navel. "I don't mind taking credit for that."

"Then you're going to have to pay the price." His lips curved into that wolfish grin.

He eased me up against the natural earth-toned tile and kissed me breathless, his leg sliding between my knees, urging my legs to open around him. "Oh no. Too conventional," he said. "This time, I don't want you to see what's coming."

My mouth went dry. Before I could protest, he spun me around, my backside pressed against his hardness.

"That's better." Slowly, he bucked against my buttocks. His hands wrapped around to cup my breasts, fingers working at my nipples, kneading, tugging lightly.

I arched into him. "Yes."

He spanked me. Once. Twice. "Yes, what?"

My stomach flipped. Kinky. I liked it. "Yes, please?"

He laughed, a husky rumbling in my ear. One hand stayed on my breast, the other traveled down between my legs to rub erotically. "You want me?"

"I want you."

"How badly?"

"So badly." His fingers dipped inside me. I bit my lip to keep from crying out. "Very badly."

He positioned my hips to rise, arching into him, granting him access. I braced myself against the slick wall as he entered me from behind. His hands continued to explore me, the delightful tingles fluttering all through my body before centering at my core. Again, the dancing colors, the blinding white, and his liquid heat filling me. He worked in my system like a drug. Instant euphoria. I didn't think I could ever get enough.

Chapter Ten

After the shower, we rushed to dress and head downstairs so that there was time to grab a quick cup of coffee together before saying good-bye.

A bedraggled Kate, holding a cooing smiley Ellie, greeted us in the kitchen. Not the first time she'd popped in unexpectedly, but I was surprised to see her so early. She looked like she hadn't slept a wink.

"Kate. Rough night with the baby?" I asked, ducking my face to hide my red cheeks.

"Rough night," she said, not elaborating. "Nick, hi."

"Nick was just leaving," I said. "Before the kids get up for the day."

"I would expect so. I've made a pot of coffee. Help yourselves." She took a seat at the table and bounced Ellie on her knee. "I don't know how she has so much energy."

I was glad for Ellie's distraction. Her new favorite trick was to be held on someone's lap and bounced.

"It's morning. Your fault. That's what you get for naming her—"

"Daughter of the sun. Of course," Nick said. "I just got that."

"Got what?" Kate asked.

"Mugs are in the left-hand cabinet." I gestured to the row of cherry cabinets above the granite countertop, interrupting for fear Nick would reveal himself as Owen's nephew. Now was not the time to drop that one on Kate. I wasn't sure there was ever a time. I would have preferred keeping my fling with Nick a secret for a little while, at least until I knew if it was just a fling or something more. "Let me get one for you."

I moved around the center island, keeping close watch on them over at the table in case I needed to interrupt again.

Nick would not be deterred. "The meaning of her name. She must be precious to you."

I breathed a sigh of relief.

"She's everything to me." Kate spun Ellie around in her arms and kissed her pink cheek. "Aren't you, pumpkin?"

"She's a beautiful child." Nick moved closer to examine her in the first rays of light just beginning to filter in through the bow window behind the table. My nerves remained on edge. "Extraordinary."

"Extraordinarily gifted at keeping her mother awake nights." Kate laughed. "We didn't sleep a wink."

"That explains the appearance." I set three mugs of coffee on the table, one for each of us. "You look awful."

"Thanks. Showering every morning is a luxury not all of us can afford. I see you two took advantage." Meow. Kate could work her way from passive-aggressive to plain old aggressive in a matter of minutes.

"You're more than welcome to use mine. I can watch Ellie for you."

"Thanks. I think I'll take you up on that." She stood and handed Ellie into my waiting arms. "Good-bye, Nick. Nice to see you again."

Once she was gone, I let out the groan I'd been holding in. "Sorry. I had no idea she would be here so early."

"She probably wants to apologize."

"Apologize?" How would he know?

"Last night? You seemed to think she wouldn't be pleased to see you come in late. I'm guessing you had words." He lifted his mug to his sensual lips and blew, then sipped. For a moment, his simple gesture commanded my complete attention.

I snapped out of it and shook my head. "Kate, apologize? No way. She probably wanted to rake me over the coals again. I apparently blew off plans with Josh Brandon to be with you last night."

"Oh." He sat a little straighter in his chair. "I'm always happy to beat Josh Brandon to the prize."

Was I a *prize*? "What do you mean?"

"We've had a little friendly competition for years now."

"Years? You've known him that long?"

"About ten years ago, Josh used to work with Glendower Enterprises. He developed some of our more complicated real estate projects, like the condos on the Charles."

"Glendower Place." I nodded. "Nice."

Pricey. Patrick had been charged with some of the resales and they went for a million and up.

"Uncle Owen couldn't break away from his more complicated ventures at the time, so he put me in charge of overseeing construction of Glendower Place. Josh and I were at odds from the start about building materials and project costs. He had no appreciation for luxury, but we were building for an upscale clientele."

"I can imagine." I'd witnessed animosity between Nick and Josh, but had no idea they had such personal history. I placed a very happy Ellie in her exersaucer to devote more attention to Nick. I took the seat recently vacated by Kate and sipped at my coffee.

"We were at odds about something else, too." He glanced up from his coffee, as if to gauge my reaction. "A woman. We both fell for the same one, a friend of his. I asked her out first, and apparently Josh didn't like the idea of my getting close to someone he'd planned to romance."

My stomach clenched, shades of déjà vu. If Josh was interested in me, as I'd begun to suspect, how would he react to the news that I was seeing Nick? Last night might have been harder on him than I suspected. In a few short hours, I would have to face Josh. I'd just begun to appreciate our newly friendly working relationship. In fact, I liked him. But now? He would probably hate me, and I couldn't blame him.

"So, how did it end?" I gnawed my lower lip. I could only predict: badly.

"It didn't last. I broke it off when my business was done at the Boston office. I thought it was for the best. But you know Mr. Brandon. He was all righteous indignation, stepping in like some kind of hero to make me see the evils of my ways."

"Evils? Did you break the poor girl's heart, then?"

I smiled. My heart had been through much worse than a minor breakup. He didn't scare me.

He shrugged. "I never made any promises. Molly knew what she was getting into, an affair, nothing more. Somehow Josh was convinced otherwise, that I'd led her on with ideas of a future together."

"Wait, Molly? His ex-wife?" I blurted without thinking as soon as I made the connection.

"Ex-wife? Aha. It figures. Josh got what he wanted after all."

"Haven't you read any fairy tales? The hero always gets the girl." I tried to keep it light even as I realized what it meant for my own situation.

Nick wasn't necessarily the bad guy, but he was no hero. What I could expect was a wild affair, some fun beneath the sheets, and nothing more. It suited me fine for now. I wasn't sure I wanted anything more with Nick. But I did know that I didn't want to hurt a friend. If Josh ever forgave me, I would have to be more careful not to flaunt my affair.

"Was it a coincidence that you came back here and ended up making such large contributions to Habitat for Humanity, or were you looking to maybe rub his face in it a little?" If the latter was the case, I wasn't sure what to think of Nick, exactly. I had to know.

"Pure coincidence. I had no idea Josh worked with the organization. I merely acted on orders from my uncle to get more involved in the community."

"All right. Fair enough." I accepted the explanation and finished my coffee.

Nick stood. "Well, I best get going. You'll have to tend the children."

"Yes. It's time." I stood to walk Nick to the door. Ellie started making babbling noises as if looking for more attention. "In a minute, little one."

I looked down. She was intrigued by a toy that lit up in a blinking motion. I'd bought her the toy, a little rattle with a moon on top and an acrylic handle filled with stars floating in a fluid that made them slowly go up and down when the rattle shook. But I didn't think the toy had blinking lights when I bought it. Odd.

"The things they can do with toys these days," Nick said.

"Um. Yes. They even put lights in kids' shoes now."

"Fascinating." He swept me into his arms. "When can I see you again? Dinner? Here?"

"Here?" I tried not to sound surprised, but I wasn't sure it was a great idea with Kate always hanging around. And with the kids. "That sounds so serious."

"Are you saying you're not ready to be more serious? After last night, I thought what we had warranted more exploration." His finger stroked the edge of my top. I felt that precious heat course through me once again.

"Mmm. But maybe we should keep it to ourselves? Just for a little while?" Until we were both sure we were headed for serious. I wanted to savor it a bit longer before risking it to exposure. What would the kids think? What about Kate? I would have to tell her about the Owen connection.

He flashed the crooked smile. "The sooner I get to know your children better, the sooner they may get used to me being here more often."

"You're ready for more often?"

He laced fingers with mine. "I'm ready to try.

Come on, Bennie. Let's take a chance, see where it leads? Consider it an adventure."

I raised my eyebrows. He was right. I could do this. It was dinner, hardly a promise of further commitment. "Far be it from me to deny an adventure. How about six? It's when we usually eat dinner."

"Six it is." His lips met mine in a slow, seductive kiss that made me hot all over. Again. "See you then."

"See you," I whispered, frozen in my tracks as he headed out the kitchen door. He seemed to move faster as he made his way down the walk. Where did he park?

"That was a big risk, don't you think?" Kate's voice came from behind me.

"Some risks are worth taking." In the second I turned to face her and turned back, Nick was gone. Poof. His car must have been closer than I realized. I guessed I just didn't see it.

"Wow." She fluffed her wet hair. I followed her back to the kitchen. She scooped Ellie out of her saucer. "You really are falling for him."

"I don't know." I met her gaze, hoping she would see beyond her anger to try to understand. "But I had a good time last night. I needed it, Kate. I needed to know I could just let go and enjoy myself again, that I could be attractive to a man and feel all those feelings again. You know?"

She sighed. "I do know. I'm sorry I was so hard on you. That's why I came over so early this morning. It wasn't Ellie keeping me up last night. I hated getting so angry with you."

"You called me a bitch." I flashed a glare in her direction.

"I'm sorry."

I softened. "I'm sorry, too. I feel so crappy about standing up Josh. I wish I'd remembered our plans. Maybe I'll buy him lunch today."

"That would be kind. Just don't play with him. If it's Nick you want, let Josh down easy."

"I wouldn't string Josh along. He's a good guy. But I hope we can be friends. It's a lot easier to handle him at work when he's not bossing me around."

"Josh will survive. The important thing is that you're happy. It's good to see you moving on. I wish I could do the same."

"Your time will come. When it's right, you'll know it."

"I hope you're right. I'm not sure I can make Marc wait it out much longer. I think he's going to come to realize that I'm a lost cause and move on any day now."

"Que sera sera. What will be, will be."

Kate laughed. "Remember how Gran would play that Doris Day record every Christmas? Over and over."

"And Elvis. 'Blue Christmas.' But that one was Mom's contribution to the holidays. I remember Pops being so pleased when they got the fancy new hi-fi that stacked the records and dropped them down one at a time."

"High-tech. No wonder they're so perplexed by the kids' iPods."

"They had enough trouble converting to CDs."

"Gran still thinks CDs are a savings program at the bank."

We laughed. It gratified me to have such a relationship with my sister that we could so easily abandon our tension and find comfort in familiar territory: family history.

Out of the corner of my eye, I caught sight of the kitchen clock. "Yipes, time flies. I better go get the kids up and check on the dogs. We can't be late."

"I have a slow morning. I can drive the kids to school. Wake them and send them down for breakfast."

"You sure you don't mind?"

"Not a problem. I can pick them up today, too."

"Thanks. By the way, Nick's joining us for dinner tonight. He wants to get to know the kids better. I'd like you to get to know him, too. Would you mind?"

"Staying for dinner? I planned on it."

"Great." I would worry about getting to the market and deciding on what to serve later. I wondered if now was the time to mention that Nick was Owen's nephew, or at least that he worked for Glendower Enterprises. But I had to get to work. And after all the drama of the past twenty-four hours, it seemed that I could wait and find a better time to explain it to Kate. "Thanks for coming over this morning, Kate. I'm glad we made up."

"I hate fighting with you."

"Life's easier when we get along. Besides, where would we get such affordable child care if we didn't have each other?" I hugged my sister, who smelled like my favorite shampoo, before hurrying upstairs to wake the kids and get ready for work.

By the time I got to the office, ten minutes late, Leslie was already at her—our—desk going over some paperwork.

"Sorry I'm late."

"Considering your performance of yesterday afternoon, you're free to come in as late as you like."

"What do you mean?" I hung my coat on the corner rack and took the seat across from Leslie. Not sure if I would be working in the office or on-site, I'd gone with a business casual combination of charcoal wool tailored slacks, a plum sweater, and black boots, heels in case Nick popped in. My Timberlands were in the car, just in case I had to head over to help out at the Mill Street house. "Did I do something wrong?"

My stomach lurched. Was I about to get fired? But I barely had a chance.

"Wrong?"

"Uh-oh." My heart fluttered at the sound of the voice behind me. Josh's voice. "Did someone let her near my power tools? Should I head back to Mill Street and check out the damage?"

"Ha." I turned in my chair, hoping to deliver a sharp comeback, but my wit stalled at sight of those gas-flame blue eyes.

His gaze held mine. The usual Josh, slightly sarcastic, a little playful. If my standing him up had hurt his feelings, he showed no signs of it. It should have been a relief, but it only increased my worry. Was he hiding it well or did he really not care?

"Wrong? Hello." She waved a check. "Six-figure donations don't come in every day, Bennie. Amazing work. I think Nick Angelos has a real soft spot for our organization. Or one of our workers." She smiled.

I blushed. "I'm sure it had nothing to do with me."

Josh whistled from between his front teeth as he stepped forward to take the check from Leslie. "A hundred grand. I guess you really showed him a good time last night."

Ouch. That answered my question. He was upset with me and, apparently, no longer hiding it. I certainly understood his anger, but it was a cheap shot.

"Look, I know I let you down yesterday, and I'm sorry I forgot about our plans, but please take a minute to rethink your words." I stood up, but in the close quarters it put us nearly face-to-face, without much space between us.

He held up his hands. "I'm sorry. You're right. I didn't mean to suggest you did anything unseemly to solicit a donation."

"I didn't. I wouldn't."

"I know. I really am sorry. I meant to make a joke, but it didn't come out right at all. I hope you can forgive me." His silver-black brows rose, lending him a look of sincerity.

Leslie looked from me to Josh and back again as if trying to make sense of the exchange.

"I went out to dinner with Nick last night." I filled her in. "I didn't see that it might have ethical implications, a conflict of interest."

"No conflict," Leslie said, no doubt all too eager to clear the air so there was no chance of giving back the check. "You're allowed to date donors. I can't imagine anything in any rule book against it."

"But maybe Josh has a point. Perhaps it doesn't look right. And I am sorry, Josh. The last thing I would do is willingly hurt a friend. It's not that I forgot our plans as much as I didn't even think about the day." When all else failed, I could claim complete ditziness. "It's no excuse, but with the excitement of the new job, I got carried away and I wasn't thinking at all. I hope you can forgive me."

"Forgiven," Josh said. "You wouldn't be the first woman to get carried away with Nick Angelos."

I smiled and reached out to pat him on the shoulder, but he moved a little and I missed and ended up stroking his collarbone. His pulse raced under my fingers. If only he knew how much I understood what he'd been through with Nick.

"As long as you don't start dating all of our donors, I think we're okay." Leslie winked, adding some levity to the situation. "If you'll excuse me, I have to go to the files and get some forms." She scooted by Josh and left the room.

Josh turned to me. "I hope you didn't lose sleep about blowing off our plans. I had a good time with the kids and with your sister."

I looked up through my lashes, more to avoid facing those incredible eyes straight-on. He didn't seem *too* upset, all things considered. I guessed it was a good sign. "Good. I'm glad. And I'm very grateful to have a working fireplace again. The house smelled fantastic when I got home. And I'd still like to buy you lunch, to thank you."

"No time for lunch. I have to start the roofing today. I just popped in to pick up some paperwork and I'm off."

"Oh. How about dinner tomorrow night?"

He smiled. "I appreciate the invitation. Really. And as much as I would love to give Sarah the pleasure of watching me wipe the floor with you at cribbage, I have to pass. Don't feel bad about last night. I had a great time. As for tomorrow, I have a date."

"A date?" My stomach did the flip thing, not in a good way. Why would it bother me if he had a date? "Oh. Of course. Maybe some other time."

"Tomorrow, the family's coming in to do some on-site work. We like to let them volunteer with the building stage. It helps give them a stronger sense of ownership. Would you like to spend the day on-site? We could use the help with the siding. It's our last big task on the exterior."

"That would be great. I would love to meet the family."

"If you play your cards right, I'll let you use the power tools." He winked on his way to the door. "See you tomorrow."

"Tomorrow," I repeated, pulse quickening. I didn't realize I was so excited about meeting the family that belonged to the house. That had to be it. It couldn't be that my heart was racing at the prospect of spending a day with Josh. Absolutely not. Ridiculous.

Chapter Eleven

After work, I rushed to the market and picked up ingredients for a simple meal of beef tenderloin roasted with an herb garlic crust, potatoes, baby spinach, and a salad. With no time to bake, I chose a selection of ice cream and sorbets for dessert. Perfect.

Before Nick was due to arrive, I'd had time to discuss his presence with Spencer and Sarah. They didn't seem at all bothered by the fact that their mother had invited a man over for dinner. Sarah's main concern seemed to be that Nick wasn't Josh. She'd been looking forward to settling the score in cribbage. Maybe they could get used to the idea of my dating. Unfortunately, I hadn't a chance to talk to Kate. She was occupied with calming a fussy baby and I had dinner to prepare. All I could do was hope that Nick didn't mention anything about work or his uncle.

Between learning how to process applications for Habitat houses and the process of securing low-rate mortgages for the house recipients, I'd barely had a chance to think of Nick all day. Now that I did, he didn't inspire the frenzied sort of excitement that I'd hoped. I felt surprisingly indifferent. Out of sight, out of mind.

Or so I'd thought. The doorbell rang and sent my pulse through the roof. Tingles ran up my spine. I couldn't wait to be alone with him again.

"Nick," I greeted him at the door. He must have caught my comfortable-casual vibe. I wore jeans and a V-neck light cotton sweater in clover green. His jeans and forest-green sweater delineated every muscle and made my mind jump straight to peeling them off him. So much for restraint. I found my voice. "Come in."

"For you." He handed me a paper-wrapped bouquet of flowers, luscious blooms of white alstroemeria laced with blue delphinium. Very striking. Heat rolled off him as he moved in close, palmed my elbow, and dropped a light kiss on my cheek. "Missed you."

He breathed the last bit just soft enough for me to hear.

"Thank you," I said, taking the flowers.

"And for the kids." He walked over to where Spencer and Sarah sat on the couch pretending to be well behaved and not one bit bored. "I wasn't sure what game system you preferred, but I have a friend who develops software for Nintendo. He's finished a new game. It's supposed to be like *Zelda* or a new version of *Zelda*, or, well, I don't know what it is exactly. It's not on the market yet, but he slipped me an early copy to review. Unfortunately, I haven't had time to try it. Perhaps you could give it a go and tell me what you think?"

"Whoa, dude," Sarah interrupted. "It's like *Zelda* but it's not even out yet?"

"That's what he tells me."

"And he wants people to test it?" Spence jumped up. "For real? Like, we can play it when it's not even out yet?"

Nick held out the disc and turned it over in his hand as if to study it for answers. "If you'd prefer not to, I understand. It's for something called a Wii?"

They both gathered around him. I wasn't sure if I should be impressed that he knew just the thing to win my kids over or be concerned that they were so easily won over.

"That's the coolest thing ever," Spencer said, taking the disc.

"If it works," Sarah, my skeptic, added. "Can we try it now, Mom?"

"For a little while. Just until dinner." I couldn't deny that he'd scored major points in his first five minutes. So why did I feel so on edge? "Be back down in a half hour."

"Maybe I can go up later and see how they're doing with it?" Nick asked.

"Sure. That's a good idea. If Spence allows you into the game room, it's a sign of approval. He won't let just anyone into his domain."

He smiled and squeezed my hand. I melted on contact. No need to worry. Everything was going just fine.

"So, Kate?" He turned to the kitchen where Kate lent me a hand with the meal. She'd just closed the oven after checking the meat, and the escaping aroma of roasting beef scented the air. "How are you?"

"Better than this morning, thanks," she answered, toweling her hands and coming out to join us. "Can I get you something? A glass of cabernet?"

"No, relax." Nick dropped my hand and headed toward the corner bar, where the wine stood unopened with glasses at the ready. "I can get it."

Kate charged ahead. "Nonsense. Wine duties are mine tonight. You two sit."

I had a feeling Kate was trying to make up for the morning.

"If you're not going to let me get the wine, then allow me to say hello to your charming daughter," Nick said, surprising me with his interest in the baby. I probably should have expected it, with his connection to her, but it brought on a new wave of uncertainty. Would he say something? Would he fall in love with her? What if Owen sent Nick to check on us because he wanted to take her away?

Fortunately, he seemed content to adore Ellie from afar, not *too* interested. He didn't make a move toward picking her up from the Exersaucer, where she sat and cooed contentedly with her soft toys. She was into animals lately, a little version of Noah's Ark with pairs of stuffed giraffes, elephants, and zebra. She had a zebra and giraffe on her Exersaucer tray and was currently at work on gumming the tail end of the zebra.

"That's a good girl," he said, as if at a loss, proving that he didn't quite have the knack of relating to little ones.

"You can bring her out to the living room, Ben," Kate offered from the bar area, where she stripped the foil from the top of a bottle. "We have a little while until the beef is done."

"Sure." I scooped Ellie up. She held fast to the zebra and tried to offer me a drool-covered giraffe. "No, thanks, kiddo. I'm saving my appetite for the roast."

Nick grabbed the Exersaucer and brought it out to the other room. I put her back down in it so we could watch her from the couch.

"That's a very handy device," Nick commented on the saucer as Kate handed him a glass. "She seems very happy in it."

"She loves her Exersaucer," Kate said, smiling in her daughter's direction. "Her new thing is to bounce. Constant bouncing. It gets tiring when you're holding her all day. In there, she can go to town."

Ellie bounced as if to demonstrate and went right back to her zebra.

Kate handed me a glass and settled in the chair next to us. I took a sip of wine, grateful for something to help me relax a little. I tried not to let my body language reflect that I was entirely too uptight inside. I caught a glance of Nick, the perfect profile, and calmed a little, remembering the perfect body to match, and what that body could do to me. We had physical chemistry, something I hadn't felt in a long time. Emotional bonds were harder to forge, but maybe if we got to know each other better and he hit it off with Kate and the kids, who knew? For some reason, I thought of Josh and how comfortable he'd been in my house from the start. I wanted Nick to fit in as easily as Josh had.

"So, Nick, what do you do?" Kate asked, and I cringed.

Nick shrugged. "What don't I do? I have the

benefit of being born into wealth and privilege, so I do what I want."

Kate and I exchanged a glance. Must be nice. Kate wasn't satisfied. "But specifically? Work? Hobbies?"

"I'm currently working for my uncle's company overseeing investments." Sigh of relief, no mention of the name. "I like to run."

A runner? It made sense. It was probably how he kept in shape. Except he didn't have the lean, economical musculature of a runner. I suspected that he also spent some time lifting weights. "Do you spend time at the gym?"

He smiled at me, as if he knew exactly what prompted my question. "I've honed my physique on more physical activities."

"Like the cattle herding?" The image of him at home on the range, wind whipping his wild blond mane, was still fresh in mind from when he'd mentioned it on his first visit.

"Cattle-herding?" Kate's eyes widened. "That's unexpected."

"A venture of one of my brothers. I've helped out from time to time."

"Somewhere in the Midwest?" she guessed.

"Farther south." He smiled. "Out of the country."

"And he's a musician," I piped in, remembering what he'd said shortly after we met. "How did that come about?"

"I don't really play much anymore. I used to enjoy putting together my own instruments and dabbling, but I'm not sure I would call myself a musician in the true sense of the word. Not now. No time. My uncle keeps me busy."

I was eager to hear more about his past, but maybe some other time. I couldn't afford to risk Kate's interest in Nick's family. "Ah well, we can all identify with family commitments, right, Kate?"

She rolled her eyes. "You should meet our mother. We're grown women and she can still guilt us into anything."

"I would like to meet your mother." Nick's hand, balanced on my knee, sent a charge of heat straight through me. Until I caught on his words. Meet Mother? I'd barely gotten used to the idea of having him over for dinner with Kate and the kids.

"Maybe someday," I said, not eager to put the rest of my crazy family on display too early.

"So, any brothers? I hope you don't mind my saying that you are one good-looking hunk of man. It would be a shame if there weren't more of you at home."

I shot Kate the glare. Had she drunk a bottle of wine before I'd even come home? Why was she asking about brothers? So dangerously close to leading Nick to talk about other relatives, namely uncles? I sipped my wine.

"There are more, actually. Loads of them. Half siblings. My father wasn't exactly big on settling down with one woman."

"Men. Pfft." Kate blew out a sigh. "Well, hey, and more power to 'em." She lifted her glass to men, and drank.

"So." I met Nick's gaze and blushed. He smiled as if amused. I grew concerned. Kate normally wasn't a *down with men* kind of woman. "Kate, is Marc coming to Thanksgiving?"

"He's got a game," she said. Her smile seemed

strained, her lips tight as if she wanted to say more but wasn't about to with Nick in the room. I'd been carried away with Nick, and worried about offending Josh, and excited about the new job. I hadn't exactly been busy keeping up with Kate's affairs. Had something happened with Marc? My throat clenched.

"I hoped he would join us." I continued on the Marc course with hope that she might be encouraged to elaborate.

"Eh. Not this year."

I could tell from her tone that the subject was closed. She got up to refill wineglasses. Maybe I could get her to talk later.

Ellie started to fuss.

Kate rose, but I beat her to it. "Sounds like someone's hungry. Before we have our dinner, why don't I give the little one hers? Kate, you sit. Entertain Nick while I go warm her bottle." A dangerous prospect perhaps, considering what Nick might say, but I sensed that Kate needed a moment to linger and maybe more light conversation to help her from sinking into a funk.

Ellie quieted as soon as I lifted her from her Exersaucer.

"Oh, those light up, too?" Nick asked, pointing to the tray. "You were right, Bennie. They do make everything with lights for the kids these days."

The zebra and giraffe glowed with surging pulses. The Noah's Ark animals were stuffed; they didn't have the power to light up in the dark. My heart hammered. I had no explanation.

"Yes, neat, isn't it? It keeps the tots busy for hours." I dismissed it casually, but Kate met my gaze. I didn't understand what was going on, how it was even possible. I looked at Ellie, but her sweet baby nose crinkled and she smiled sweetly before giving a little laugh. There had to be an explanation. I couldn't worry about it now. More to discuss with Kate later.

Nick stood at my side. "Let me take her. So you can get that bottle. I'm sure she'll go easy on me."

I felt oddly unsettled about handing Ellie over to Nick. Perhaps it was just his apparent inexperience with a baby. When he took her in his arms, she didn't protest and seemed comfortable, her usual adorable self.

Nick sat on the couch bouncing Ellie in his lap. She faced him and seemed as fascinated by his eyes as I was.

"I guess you have a way with women of all ages," I said, scooping her up.

In a matter of minutes, she had fallen asleep in my arms. Nick went up to check on the kids while I tucked her in for a nap, leaving me alone with Kate for a minute. I wanted to grill her on the Marc situation, but the kids and Nick came downstairs so soon that we never had a chance to talk while making last-minute preparations for dinner. Again, catching up with my sister would have to wait.

The rest of the evening passed uneventfully. The kids behaved. Dinner was delicious. And Nick left me with a kiss on the cheek and the promise to see me again tomorrow.

I was glad we'd made it an early night so there was

time to get back to routine with the kids. "He's an okay guy," Spencer said. "That game is super cool."

"Hmm. He was all right. I like Josh better. When's Josh coming over again?" Sarah asked.

Kate shot me a glance. I wanted to shoot her one right back, but I kept my attention on my daughter. "We'll see. Maybe soon. You know, he has a daughter about a year younger than you."

"I wonder if she likes hockey."

"Maybe." I doubted it. "Why don't you two go on upstairs and make sure your homework is done while I clean up with Aunt Kate?"

"Homework's done," Spencer said. "Can we watch TV in your room? That way we're close if Ellie wakes up." More like that way they had an excuse to get out of dish duty.

School nights were not typically TV nights, but considering they were so good at dinner, I allowed it. It gave me a chance to talk to Kate about Marc, and maybe I would get around to bringing up Nick's family. I hated keeping things from Kate.

"What happened?" I asked as she brought in the rest of the dishes from the table. "With Marc? Are you two fighting?"

"Not exactly. I decided to cut him loose."

"Cut him loose? What does that mean? He's a man, not a kite."

"I finally told him, in no uncertain terms, that there would be no romantic future for us. I said that if there was going to be a fire, it would have sparked. No spark, no flame."

"Oh, right. I forgot that starting a relationship was as easy as having the kindling handy."

"You know what I mean." She glowered.

"I know that your problem is that you've made yourself flame-retardant. This summer, when we scattered Patrick's ashes around the ball field, do you remember what you told me?"

"To make sure he didn't blow to third base? He really preferred the pitcher's mound, but once that wind picked up—whoosh."

"No." I play-punched her in the arm. "You told me I was too young to give up on life and pretend I only existed for the kids. You encouraged me to remember that I had a long life of my own ahead."

"Yeah. That."

"Kate, there's life after Owen, too."

"I know."

"Maybe Marc's not going to be the one. Maybe he is just a friend. But Owen's not coming back." *And hey, guess what, he's Nick's uncle!* It hardly seemed the time to mention the new reminder in our midst. I decided to save it for another time.

"Believe me, I know that. But I miss him. And I think of him. Still, the thing that scares me most?"

"You miss him less each day and sometimes, you barely think of him at all."

Her eyes widened. "How did you know?"

"It isn't any different for me. Our memories serve to remind us of what we had, not to hold us back from what still might be."

"For the life of me, I can't figure out how you got so smart."

"Are you kidding?" I finished loading, clicked on the dishwasher, and leaned back with a smile. "I've always been the smart one. It just took you a while to come to terms with me getting the looks and the brains in the family. Life just isn't fair."

Kate laughed. "You're lucky I stopped drinking in time or I might have believed you were serious."

The next morning, Nick called before my alarm went off. "Miss me?"

"Of course." I rolled over to check the time. Five-twenty. "You're up early."

"I never slept. I couldn't sleep. I kept thinking of you."

"Oh," I said, feeling a little guilty. I'd slept like a stone. I hadn't thought of him much at all. In fact, I began to think it was slightly odd the way I couldn't get enough of him when he was around, but forgot him just as easily when he wasn't. "Sorry."

"Don't be sorry. It's a pleasant kind of distraction. Can you get a sitter for tonight?"

"A sitter?" I sat up. "What did you have in mind?"

"Something special. You'll enjoy it."

"What should I wear?"

"Don't worry about it. I've got it covered."

"But—"

"I know you like to shop but you'll have to leave this one to me."

A thrill shot through me. I liked surprises. "Fine. I'll leave it to you. When should I be ready?"

"I'll be sending a car. I'll find you."

"I have responsibilities at work." Which I silently hoped would go away and leave me to some fantasy fun. Reality was suddenly overrated.

"Not a problem."

"Whatever you say." Sounded like a problem, but I didn't want to even think about it. "I'm sure Kate can handle the kids for an evening."

"A morning, too? You might be late."

"A morning, too. But again, there's that job thing."

And Kate was usually available at night, but by day she might have some appointments with clients. I would have to check and make sure nothing on her schedule interfered with driving the kids to school. Plus, I hadn't been as helpful with Ellie since taking a job of my own. I suspected Kate's assistant Val was taking over a lot of the client meetings with Kate bringing Ellie to work more often.

"Again, not to worry. I've got connections. I'll make sure they can spare you."

Part of me said I should protest. It was too soon for me to take advantage of special favors at work. The rest of me liked special favors and instructed me to shut up and roll with it. "Kate will take the kids in the morning, too. I may have to make a trade and take Ellie sometime, but it will work." Should work. I hoped it worked.

"Great. Then it's a date."

"It's a date." I smiled. How long had it been since I'd been able to say something like that on a regular basis?

"Before I let you go, what are you wearing?"

"Flannel. Head to toe."

"Ew. Tell me you're wearing high-heeled slippers? The little slip-on kind with the marabou feathers?"

"Ha. You wish. Fuzzy slippers. Big blue fuzzy slippers that make my legs look like Cookie Monster's."

"You're killing me. I'll have to remedy this situation tonight."

"Fine. What are *you* wearing?"

"Clever, turning the tables on me."

Erotic heat raced through me with the thought

of him in tight boxer briefs, or silk pajama bottoms. I rubbed my hand over my tank-top-covered breasts and my nipples sprang to life, rigid with need. "Seriously. What are you wearing?"

"Absolutely nothing. See you tonight." *Click.*

I shot a glance at the clock. No time. I wished I could squeeze ten more minutes into my schedule to stay in bed and think of him touching me again. Maybe he wasn't as out of sight, out of mind as I believed. He'd certainly inserted himself into my mind's eye. Absolutely naked. Erect. And waiting for me.

All in all, not a bad way to start the day. I padded downstairs to see if Kate was up with the baby so I could ask her my one small favor.

Sarah greeted me in the hall. I thanked my lucky stars she hadn't done that the night Nick slept over.

"Hey, baby." I restrained myself from rumpling her hair. Bad enough I'd called her baby.

"Mom." She wore her serious face, the one that warned me she was about to take issue with something I'd done recently.

"Sarah."

"I notice you haven't been letting Bert and Ernie sleep with you for the past few nights."

"I thought maybe I should let them get used to sleeping on the porch again, like they used to do when your dad was around."

"They don't like the porch."

"Sure they do."

"Not as much as they like sleeping with people."

"I'm not sure. I only started letting them sleep with me because I was lonely for a while there."

"You're not lonely now?"

"Not as lonely, no. I still miss your dad so much it hurts sometimes. But I'm trying to be more independent."

"And you're making new friends. Josh Brandon and that Nick guy."

"Don't you like them? You could tell me."

She mushed her mouth together, a good indication that I was off track. "No problem. Just that everyone suddenly has new friends."

Aha, and less time for Sarah. I would have to make sure I paid more attention. "You have new friends on the hockey team, right?"

She crinkled her nose. "They're teammates, not really friends. But it's okay. I just wondered if Bert and Ernie could sleep with me."

"Oh, is that all? Nothing else is bothering you? School's fine?" There was the little matter of her math grade slipping, but her teacher assured me that Sarah was making improvements when I'd called.

"School's not the best. Kasey, Jemma, and Kelly are making fun of me for liking hockey more than shopping."

"There's nothing wrong with liking hockey. Or baseball. Your dad played both and you know he would be so proud of you. I'm proud of you, too, for being who you want to be and not letting other kids stop you from doing what you love."

"It's just hard sometimes. I started sitting at the boys' table for lunch because they talk about cool stuff like hockey and the girls only want to talk about the boys."

"Do the boys mind you sitting at the boys' table?"

"No. Jay Peters asked me to sit with them. It's cool with the boys."

"Would they mind other girls sitting with them? Like Kasey or Jemma?"

She laughed and nodded. "Hoo, yeah. That's not going to happen."

"Maybe that's why Kasey, Jemma, and Kelly have a problem with it. Maybe they wish the boys would ask them to sit at their table, too. You just be you and don't worry about it. It will all work out."

"Thanks. But what about the dogs?"

That's my girl. No problem with staying focused. "If Bert and Ernie want to sleep with you and you don't mind their snoring, it's no problem for me."

"Excellent," she said, backing up to open her bedroom door. The pugs came bounding out and ran down the hall for their doggy door downstairs. "Because they slept with me last night and we all liked it fine."

Figured she was asking after the fact. "All right, then. Settled. Go wake up Spencer and I'll get us some breakfast."

"Toaster waffles?"

"You got it."

I headed downstairs with hope Kate would be as easy to please as my daughter.

Hours later, I had Kate drop me off at the Mill Street house. It was "meet the family" day and I was more excited than I thought I would be to see who would benefit from our efforts. Josh and a few of the volunteer construction crew were the only ones on-site when I arrived with coffee and donuts in tow. Kate agreed to watch the kids and it was *all systems go* for my date with Nick later. And for

now, donuts, good company, and work to be done.
Life was good.

"It was a Dunkin' kind of morning, guys," I said,
making the offering.

"I worship at the altar of donuts," one of the volunteer laborers said before reaching for the box.

"When will the family arrive?" I asked Josh.

"Eleven. We have work to do before they come.
Today's finishing up the roofing and getting started
on siding. Then we'll have nothing left but the in-
doors work, which is perfect with the snow coming
soon."

"Snow can stay away as far as I'm concerned."

"Really? I pegged you for a fan of the white stuff.
A real outdoorswoman. Skiing. Skating. Oh yeah."

"I do wield a mean snowball. You probably don't
want to come too close to me when it's snowing."

"Let me see that throwing arm."

As Josh lifted my arm and playfully squeezed my
nonexistent biceps, I went warm inside. My knees
wobbled. It was the way I'd felt when Nick touched
me, only maybe more intense, and it caught me
by complete surprise. I caught his gaze and looked
down to hide the rising blush. "Just what I thought.
Spaghetti arms. I am so not afraid of you. I make
snowmen who throw better than you."

"You're on." I caught my breath and looked up
again, recovered. "First snowfall, show up at my
house. I'll demonstrate my superior throwing skills.
That's not a spaghetti arm. It's rubber band snap
action."

He laughed, a big manly kind of laugh that came
straight from the gut. The thought of making Josh
lose himself in a good laugh made me feel happy,

too. Nick wasn't exactly a laugher. At least, I hadn't seen that side of him yet. "Rubber band snap action. Good one."

"You come around. You'll see."

"I'm going to take you up on that."

"Good," I said, a warmth spreading through my belly as I met Josh's blue gaze and held it this time, no looking away.

What was going on with me? I chalked it up to my horn-dog-inducing few minutes on the phone with Nick earlier. I had sex on the brain.

Chapter Twelve

"Are you feeling brave?" Josh stood beside me holding a ladder.

"Why, you want me to hold that for you?" It beat organizing shingles, which I assumed was my job for the day.

"I want you to come up with me, help me nail some shingles in place."

"You're entrusting me with a hammer?"

"I actually thought I'd work the hammer and you could hand me the nails."

"But you're letting me climb a ladder?"

"Stranger things have happened."

I followed him to the side of the house and watched while he set up the ladder.

"I'm going to send you up first. I'll hand you some supplies and come back up with more."

"Fine." I headed up, more careful than usual to firmly plant my Timberland-protected feet on the rungs. It wouldn't do to take a tumble and show Josh I couldn't be trusted after all. He paused behind me for a minute. I looked back. "What?"

I could have sworn he was staring at my ass. I'd worn my low-rise jeans today, trusting my oversized wool sweater to cover any gaps, but maybe I was wrong. I paused to feel if I could detect a breeze at my back. Nothing.

"Just taking a mental inventory."

"Of my ass?"

His lips curved in what seemed like a lecherous grin. "Of my tools. I want to make sure I have everything I need so we don't have to come back down."

"Oh. Right." I glanced over my shoulder. He still seemed to be looking at my ass, but then I was on a ladder above him. I could have been mistaken.

"I understand your confusion," he said a minute later, heading up the ladder to hand me some roofing goop. The shingles were already stacked on the tar-papered roof, left over from the previous day's efforts. "I'm sure you're used to men ogling your beautiful behind. Unfortunately, I'm too busy to notice."

"Ha. You noticed," I teased.

Was that a blush? Or the effort of lugging heavy tools up a ladder?

"I may have given it a glance. In case I had to push it the rest of the way up."

"Shut up." I laughed. I couldn't help it. He put me in a light frame of mind. Plus, the sun was shining bright for a mid-November afternoon. Nothing like the sun to improve my mood.

"Move over." He swung the tools up and followed.

"Okay. What now?"

He showed me how to overlap the shingles, prep them for his nails, and follow his trail by covering his nails with the roofing cement. He complained about the process being tedious, but I actually enjoyed being trusted with real honest labor. Finally, I felt appreciated.

"So, what do you think? Ready to take up roofing as a profession?"

"Not quite. But I like it. Let's face it, you're doing most of the work."

"I'd never get done on my own. You're helping the job go faster, and keeping me on task."

"The sooner you get done, the sooner you can stop listening to me talk?" I laughed.

He paused, mid–hammer swing. "I happen to like hearing you talk. You're open. Unguarded. It's a refreshing quality."

"Kate says I'm dramatic," I offered, to test his response.

"Your sister's pretty low-key. Maybe she could stand to be a little more dramatic now and then."

"What do you mean?"

"Well, you know, with Marc. If she doesn't tell him how she really feels, she may end up losing him."

"Oh, that. She has no idea how she feels. That's her problem."

"Really?" He grabbed a few nails, went down the line hammering, then paused. "She adores Marc. It looks pretty obvious to everyone around them. Haven't you seen the way she looks at him?"

I shrugged. "I don't know. He's always holding Ellie. It's hard to tell if she's looking at him that way or watching her baby."

"Oh no." He shook his head. "There's a difference in the way a woman looks at men and the way she looks at her children. Believe me, she's looking at him. She gets that heavy-lidded gaze going on, as if she's undressing him with her eyes."

"Kate does? I haven't noticed."

"Maybe you're too close to it. Marc spends a lot of time there. You may have tuned out those subtle signs. Plus, she tells you she's not interested in him that way. You just believe her without looking beneath the surface."

"Wow. You came up with all that from one dinner with us?"

He shrugged and hammered another nail down. "From two, actually. There was the one on Tuesday when you never showed up."

I blushed. "Oh yeah. But Marc wasn't there. Did she talk about him?"

"A little."

"And you're convinced she actually has a thing for Marc."

"Yes. And if you want her to get that straightened out, you're going to have to take Ellie off her hands for a few nights and send her off alone with Marc."

"Genius. Why didn't I think of that?"

"I'm older and wiser." His biceps caught my attention when he wiped his forehead with the back of his arm. He really was in fantastic shape.

"Older, anyway," I said, in case he'd caught me ogling.

He shot me a glance, his blue eyes piercing through me as if I didn't stand a chance. "And that's the problem with being open and unguarded. Sometimes you put things out there that might have been better left unsaid."

His mouth turning up just a hint at the corner was the only indication that he was playing around with me. After a few days of working with Josh, I had started to pick up on his tells. "It's simply the truth, old man. Maybe you want to switch roles, let me swing the hammer for a change. You don't want to get tired out."

"Nice try. Not a chance."

"It was a nice try, wasn't it?"

"Don't get crazy. You're not hammering."

"Come on. Just one?" I leaned in and batted my lashes.

He rolled his eyes. "One. Slide over here."

I slid.

"Closer. I need to guide your hand."

"I can lift a hammer."

"But can you hit a nail? I'm afraid you're going to miss and put a hole in the roof. If I guide your arm the first time, I can feel if you have any instincts."

"If I can do it all by myself?"

"Exactly. Move in." He gestured for me to scoot in between his knees.

I hesitated, my mind flashing briefly on the image of Josh in tight cycling shorts. I couldn't let a little thing like momentary interest in Josh's physique stop me from proving myself. I scooted.

"There." I reached out. "Hammer, please."

His turn to hesitate. Seconds passed before he put it in my hand, and held on, his finger making brief contact with my wrist to send a shock through me. "Ooh."

"Friction," he said. "From the roofing materials. Sometimes it causes a charge."

"And I thought we had a certain electricity." I tilted my chin in his direction and smiled.

"Chemistry," he corrected. "We have chemistry."

"We are combustible. *You* are. With your temper, if I missed the nail and hit the roof? I'm—" Apparently not as clever as I hoped. My brain froze. All I could think was that I could feel his body, so warm and solid, against me. "I can't think what I am. I barely passed chemistry."

"You're a catalyst," he said. I could feel his hips shift slightly away from my backside. "The agent that provokes or speeds a reaction. I passed chem with flying colors. All right. Ready?"

He leaned over. His arm pressed to mine, moving with mine, his hand over mine on the hammer. I broke out in goose bumps, the good kind. Was it Josh? Or was it the rush from swinging the hammer? I was off target but felt his hand guiding me to hit it square on the head.

"Perfect." I looked back at him. His face was closer than I imagined and I stopped barely an inch from his lips.

"Perfect," he repeated as if in a daze.

His lids drooped so that I couldn't see his too-blue penetrating eyes and yet the urge to kiss him nearly overwhelmed me. I could rule out the mesmerizing power of his gaze. But those lips. My heart raced.

"Hey, up there," Leslie called out, saving us from doing something foolish. "I've got someone for you to meet."

"Be right down." Josh regained his ability to speak first. "I guess we're done here for now."

"I guess," I said, suddenly uncertain. "Feels like we barely got started."

"The roof's nearly done. I'll get some of the guys

up here to finish. It will be more fun to start the family on siding."

"Siding."

"There'll be more hammers," he teased as he got to his feet and reached for my hand. "Don't let it get you too excited."

The family's excitement spread among the crew like wildfire. We worked with new zeal, getting the house half covered with dove-gray aluminum siding in a few hours. I worked with Marisol, the family matriarch, Ray, her husband, and Roy, one of our volunteers, on one side. Josh worked with thirteen-year-old twins Celia and Cindi on the other side, with Leslie and Fred, another volunteer and resident siding expert, acting to supervise both sides.

I learned more about the Habitat for Humanity program from talking to Marisol about her application process than I had in a few days working with Leslie. She wasn't simply being given the house, which I knew, but she would be working to pay off a low-interest mortgage. She'd lost her job for a brief period when the school system did layoffs of office staff, and she'd worried it would impair her application.

"Ability to pay off the loan is one of the chief considerations of the Habitat staff," she said, while I held the siding strip in place and she nailed. "I didn't know if we'd make it with Ray's income alone."

"But you got rehired?" I remembered her mentioning working with kids.

"Yeah, but for the cafeteria, not the office. It's okay. Work's work. As long as I get paid." She laughed and drove in some nails. "I'm actually glad I'm out of the office, though. Kids are little animals with their food, but you should hear some of their parents on the phone."

"Nasty?" I grabbed a new strip of siding from Ray. We worked from the bottom up, like Josh had said.

"Beyond nasty. Everyone's got a sense of entitlement. Get real. Your kids aren't any better than mine."

"No. Of course not." My kids wouldn't be busting their butts to side their own house.

"I mean, yours might be. You're a nice lady. But not some of those parents who call in to whine about too much homework or ancient textbooks. Don't get me started. Or fund-raisers. What's that supposed to do for the kids?"

"Teach business sense?" I shrugged.

"How's me buying two hundred dollars' worth of wrapping paper so the kids don't have to go door to door in a bad neighborhood teaching business sense? That's some whacked-out business, you ask me."

I laughed. "You should run for school committee."

"Oh no." Ray rolled his eyes. "Now you're going to give her a big head."

"My head is just right, thank you."

"Oh yeah, baby." Ray stepped around the siding mess to hug his wife. "You got a beautiful head."

"Have," she said. "I have a beautiful head."

"Yo, whatever." He kissed her. I looked away and caught Josh's gaze as he came around the corner.

"I would say get a room but the bedrooms aren't done yet," Josh said. "Good thing the children stayed over on the other side."

I winked. "I'm sure the kids have caught them kissing more than once."

"Nice work." Josh inspected our siding. "I came over to see if you're ready for scaffolding yet."

"Scaffolding?"

"To get the higher slats in. A ladder will get you up there but doesn't quite allow for the necessary movement or extra materials. Come on, I'll show you."

I followed Josh to the other side of the house. The scaffolding looked more rickety than I had imagined. "It doesn't exactly look stable enough to support much weight."

"Have I finally found the thing to frighten you?" His eyes widened with mock incredulity.

I whacked his arm lightly. "I'm not scared. I just don't put my manicure to unnecessary risks." When all else fails, fall back into princess mode.

He grabbed my hand and studied, my fingers feeling small in his large warm hands. "Looks like your manicure's shot."

I tugged my hands back. "Roofing. But it was worth it."

"You did a great job up there." He draped an arm around my shoulder as if he was about to offer a congratulatory hug, then backed away as if thinking better of it. My stomach fluttered with a strange sense of letdown.

Josh tucked his hands into his pockets. Suddenly it seemed safest for me to pocket mine, too. Being close to him made me feel warm inside. Pleasant warm, not the same hyperorgasmic heat that came over me in the presence of Nick. Somehow I'd gone from dreading Josh to enjoying my time with him. And it was dangerous, really.

I didn't need what I'd had with Patrick. Comfortable. Reliable. Easy. What I wanted for now was the instant rush that came over me when Nick drew near, the sexual thrill of being with someone so extraordinary.

"Too bad Roy's finishing the roof. I liked working on it," I said.

"There'll be other roofs. We have a stack of new applications back at the office. Besides, there are a lot of exciting jobs still left to do inside."

"Involving power tools?" I arched a brow.

Josh laughed. "Involving power tools. If you keep up the good work, I may just let you drill a few holes."

"Oh, baby!"

"I didn't know power tools got women so excited. Maybe I'll have to bring a few on my date tonight."

My chest tightened. "You have a date tonight?" Again.

"Yep." He beamed.

"That's great, Josh." I tried to muster some enthusiasm. Why did I care, anyway?

"Speaking of dates, your boyfriend's here to pick you up."

"Nick?" I turned to look toward the end of the driveway. The Town Car pulled in.

Josh nodded. "He called ahead to ask Leslie if she could spare you at three instead of the usual five o'clock quitting time."

He'd called Leslie to get me out of work? Part of me liked having it done for me. The other part warned that it was too easy to fall back into old habits. Plus, it was embarrassing. As if I couldn't handle my own affairs? How was I supposed to be taken seriously at work with Nick calling in to take me away from it?

"He's not my boyfriend. And if you need me

to stick around and help finish up, I'll tell him to wait."

"No need. It gets dark by four these days and we'll get enough done in the next hour without you. Go on ahead. Have a good time."

"Okay." I hated to just take off with everyone else still at work. "See you tomorrow."

"Hey, have a great night." Leslie popped around the corner in time to say good-bye. "You better scoot. I hear you have an amazing evening planned."

"Did he tell you what we're doing?"

Leslie smiled. "Maybe. But I'm not telling. You'll know soon enough. See ya."

She waved down the driveway at the waiting car. I took a deep breath and headed off toward Nick.

He got out as I approached. "Your chariot awaits, as they say. Foolish expression, really. Have you ever been in a chariot?"

Who had? "No, but I imagine they're really uncomfortable." Not unlike the way I felt stepping into Nick's arms with Josh watching from the house.

A mere embrace wasn't enough. He brushed his lips to mine, the slow friction sending a buzz to my core as if he'd brushed somewhere more intimate. I closed my eyes and let the feeling wash over me, sweeping the guilt away with it. I no longer cared about work, about Josh, about Kate at home with the kids. I was ready for a night of magic in the arms of Nick Angelos.

I allowed him to help me into the car. "Let's go."

"Hi, Morrison." I leaned over the seat. I knew Nick preferred to ignore him, but I shared a familiarity with him by now that made it seem rude not to say hello.

"*Bonjour,* madame," he answered in French. It made me giggle.

"Suddenly lighthearted?" Nick slid his arm around my shoulders. "You seemed so dour when I arrived."

"Work. We had a lot on our plate. But that was ages ago now." Five minutes. An age. What's the difference? I was with Nick and we had a whole evening at our disposal. "So, what's this remarkable plan of yours?"

"Not telling. You like surprises."

The tingle fluttered in my belly. "I do. I love them!"

"Good," he said. "Here's your first."

He reached inside his pocket and pulled out a long slender jewelry box. Not a ring, phew. But jewelry nonetheless.

"I'm afraid." I took the box. "Am I going to have to say it's too extravagant and give it back?"

"Only if you're a ninny. I'm astoundingly wealthy. Indulge me."

"I think I just had an orgasm," I said, only half joking. If allowing him to shower me with gifts and take me out of work early was indulging him, sign me up to spoil him rotten.

"You haven't even opened it." He nuzzled my neck. "There'll be plenty of time for those later."

Those, plural. I almost had another thinking about what was ahead for me.

Morrison pulled onto the Pike toward the city "We're going to Boston, then?"

"Never mind where we're going. Open the box."

"All right, all right." I opened. And gasped. And stared, speechless. Emeralds. Like his eyes. A bracelet of white gold and emeralds.

"Well?"

I caught my breath. "I'm sorry. For a minute there, I was speechless. It's gorgeous."

He smiled and reached out to fasten it around my wrist. "Now tell me, honestly, did it even occur to you to protest that it was too much?"

"It fits perfectly." I needed a moment to admire it before answering his question. "Thank you. And, honestly, the voice in my head that sounds a lot like my sister Kate said that I should give it back. Fortunately, the voice in my head that sounds exactly like me said to just say thank you, and I'm a lot louder than Kate." I smiled.

"Excellent." He pressed his fingertips together. "That was my Mr. Burns impression. *The Simpsons*?"

"Huh?" I looked at him, struck again by the likeness of his eyes to the emeralds. "Sorry."

"You've watched *The Simpsons*, haven't you? The animated show with Homer and Bart."

I placed my hand on his and became momentarily distracted by the sparkle of my gemstones. Mine! *Pretty.* "I enjoy *The Simpsons*. No offense, Nick, but your Mr. Burns needs work."

He arched one golden brow. "Oh?"

"Definitely."

"I've never heard that before. Everyone always loves my Burns impression."

I caught sight of Morrison's smirk in the rearview. "Everyone? Meaning your minions? You might want to take what they say with a grain of salt, considering you *employ* them."

He pursed his sexy, full lips as if considering. "I suppose."

"Don't pout." I placed a finger to his lips.

"Whatever works." His tongue darted out and he licked the tip of my finger with deliberation.

"That works."

He released my finger and his lips twisted into the wolfish grin. "I know."

I leaned over him to steal a glance out his window. "Back Bay?" I guessed. "Or are we headed somewhere on the harbor?"

"You could say that."

His response to my proximity distracted me from making any further guesses. I couldn't wait to be with him again.

"Give in to it." Nick's voice was a hoarse whisper. How did he know?

"Whatever you're thinking has lit your eyes with the most mysterious sparkle. Go for it. Do what you want to do." He reached for a button. A partition slid up between the seats, separating us from the driver.

I eyed the tinted glass. I couldn't see Morrison as more than a dark silhouette. But still. "Not now."

"Later?" His brow furrowed.

"Soon." I went so far as to lean in and trace the line of his jaw with my lips, opening my mouth as I neared the tender base of his neck. His pulse beat a wild rhythm under my tongue, as if to encourage me on. I blazed a trail to his hairline, catching his earlobe in my teeth and tugging gently.

He moaned aloud and nudged my arm to brush his trouser front. I allowed myself a brief and brazen stroke, my palm to his erection that burned for my touch right through the fine wool fabric. He lolled his head back and pulled me into his lap so I was straddling his hips. I could feel him there, between my thighs, even through the heavy denim of my jeans.

"God, yes," I whispered, pressing my body to him, my breasts flattening against his chest as I dipped my head down to claim his open and waiting mouth, his mouth that felt like molten ore under my tongue. I'd forgotten all about Morrison. I held on to Nick's sides, his shirt bunching into my fists, and bucked against him.

His hands cupped my backside, and slid up, over my back, under my shirt to smooth over my bare skin. I arched into them. He nuzzled my breasts through my top. I wished I hadn't dressed in layers. So it was cold, who cared? I flamed to life against him, hotter than any fire.

"We're there," he said, before he dropped light kisses along the edge of my collar.

"Almost." I reached for his belt.

He laughed. "No, my eager bunny, we're *there*."

I slipped off to his side. "Oh."

"Oh. You're going to love this. Wait." He got out and came around to open my door for me.

I adjusted my clothing and hair, then stepped out into the dusk. The air smelled of the salty sea. "The harbor. I was right."

At the end of the long wooden walkway, an enormous white yacht was moored.

"Is that for us?" I stood, frozen in awe, and not just from the cool November air.

"For us. All to ourselves. With the exception of a few crew members and some staff."

"Minions?"

"Some."

"Amazing." I'd never been on a yacht. Boats, yes. But not a yacht. "What is it, forty feet?"

He laughed and clasped my hand, twining his fingers with mine. "Bigger. They call it a mega yacht."

"It's definitely mega." I couldn't believe the size of it. Bigger than my house. Bigger than half my block.

"And it's all ours. We're going to cruise around all night. I have a few surprises yet on board."

"As if the bracelet was not enough."

"Come on. You'll see." A tilt of his head in my direction was all the encouragement I needed. I followed him down the dock and up the gangplank.

Chapter Thirteen

"It's spectacular," I said, after getting the grand tour. It had a formal living room, two parlors, a dining room, multiple bathrooms, bedrooms, a kitchen that I didn't even get to see. The staff was busy in there preparing our meal.

We paused our tour on the closed-in deck so we could watch the sun set as we sailed into the harbor, with champagne, cheese, chocolate, nuts, and fresh fruit laid out for us. I snacked happily; I was starving and the strawberries and chocolate went so well with the champagne.

"Beautiful," I said, as the sun, a big red orb, dipped below the Boston skyline, lending a crimson tint to the rapidly darkening sky. From behind, he draped his arms around and pulled me close. "Soon we won't see anything except the lights dotting the shore. But we won't need to see."

"And why is that?" I turned to face him, careful not to spill my champagne. I intended to finish every last drop. "Will we only have eyes for each other?"

"Eventually." His eyes glittered to match the

emeralds of my bracelet. "After we finish here, we're headed to separate rooms."

"Separate?" I missed him already.

"Mmm-hmm." He nodded, his hand finding a spot at the small of my back that made me go weak in the knees. "To get ready. We have a long night ahead. To prepare, you have a professional staff waiting."

"Fancy."

"A nice long massage should ease your workday tensions. Then we can just relax and enjoy each other."

"Who needs a massage to relieve my tension when I have you?"

His lips curved into a grin. "Nonetheless, a massage awaits. For now, let's enjoy the champagne. We have all night ahead of us."

Indeed, I had a staff. Once I got to the room, they reported in like clockwork. Three of them in total, Krissy, Dinah, and Kay, all young and pretty, even with their hair pulled back in severe buns and wearing matched pink cotton smocks. It reminded me of the scene in *The Wizard of Oz* when Dorothy and gang get spruced up to meet the wizard. I always loved that scene.

First, my bath. I was left alone to undress and get into the plush white bathrobe that was spread out on the queen-sized bed. I slipped into the robe and waited, taking in my surroundings. The room seemed bigger than my bedroom at home, more elegant perhaps but not as much to my taste. Everything was matched in warm hues of basic rosy beige, very hotel chic. My designer sister could have done wonders with the place.

I found my cell phone and gave her a quick call.

"The kids are fine. The dogs are fine. Ellie and I are doing just fine. Relax and have a good time." She opened with the obvious. I didn't even have a chance to ask.

"Kate, you should see this place. It's amazing."

"Where are you?"

"He whisked me away to his private yacht. Can you believe it? We're sailing up the coast. I'm not even sure which direction, looked like north. I've been plied with champagne and treats, so it's all a little hazy."

"Huh," she said. "You have to watch out for the ones who have the good sense to start off with the champagne and treats."

I ignored the warning tone of her voice. Most likely, she had some kind of flashback to her dates with the devil. "I know. It was the good stuff, too. Right now I'm calling from my own bedroom."

"Separate bedrooms?"

"Just for sprucing up. I'm getting a massage after my bath. I haven't even seen my dress yet but we're having a formal dinner for two in the dining room."

"And he likes to play dress-up. That's warning sign number two."

"Oh, please. You and all your warning signs. No wonder you're still not married." Oops. Sore spot. I said too much. Blame the champagne. "You should see this place. The bathroom's bigger than my whole kitchen. There's a huge soaking tub, with whirlpool jets of course, and a separate shower stall."

"Not unlike your very own bathroom at home."

"This one's bigger and I don't have to clean it."

"True, that's always a plus. Okay, I'm impressed. Where did you say he worked again?"

I bit my lip. I should have known better than to stay on the phone too long. The minute I got home, it would be time to have that talk with Kate. But now? Fortunately, Spencer interrupted Kate with a question before I could answer. "Spence wants to know if he can have Shelley over for dinner."

"It's fine. But keep an eye on her. She Goths it up when she arrives and de-Goths before leaving. I think I'm going to have to have a talk with that girl. I'm pretty certain her mother has no idea what she's up to and that leaves me vaguely uncomfortable."

"I'll keep tabs on them."

"I know you will."

"But, Bennie? Keep tabs on you, okay? Take it easy with this guy. Try to see the man beneath the glitz. If he didn't have it all, is he still someone you would be comfortable with at the end of the day?"

I bristled. It was nice for her to want to look out for me, but it was time I looked out for myself. "I've done comfortable. I'm looking for something else right now. And trust me, Kate, under the glitz, there's a set of washboard abs to die for."

"Nothing is to die for."

I rolled my eyes. I was very glad I hadn't even mentioned the bracelet. "God, Kate, chill out. Do I not deserve to let loose and have some fun for a change?"

She sighed. "You deserve it. Just don't get carried away."

"Thanks for the enthusiasm. See you tomorrow."

I hung up. Note to self: never put a call in to Glinda the Good Witch when counting on some good wicked fun with the wizard. I was only surprised she didn't throw in an extraneous "there's no place like home."

One sharp knock was followed by the direct entry of Dinah and Kay. One went to check on the bath, the other came to pin my hair up. For the moment, it was good to be Bennie.

It was even better when I stepped out of the bath, relaxed from soaking in a vanilla-scented foam, and straight into a warmed bath blanket being held for me by Kay.

Kay led me to a massage table set up in the middle of the room.

"Make yourself comfortable," she said. "Anya will be right in for your massage."

Anya? It sounded exotic. I did as instructed and was properly laid out and waiting by the time Anya entered.

I looked up. *Oh.* If Anya failed as a masseuse, she had a future as a supermodel. She was tall and rail-thin, but curved in the right places, with platinum hair pulled back off her camera-ready face. I suddenly got a little nervous realizing that her hands would be all over my cottage cheese thighs. I got a lot more nervous when I happened to wonder if her hands had just been all over Nick's taut, toned, all-around-perfect ass. And other perfectly formed parts. *Gulp.*

She smiled as if to set me at ease, but my mind only fast-forwarded through the mental images of her mouth replacing her hands on Nick's perfect parts. How could I follow that act?

"Relax. Stefan took care of Mr. Angelos today."

"How did you know what I was thinking?"

She winked with an eye almost as blue as one of

Josh Brandon's. "It's what they all think when they see me."

"They all?" So I wasn't the first to get the razzle-dazzle yacht date? And why would I be? I pushed the thought away.

She shrugged. "It's only natural. I used to model swimsuits. Women are jealous creatures by nature. But I assure you, you have nothing to worry about. You're beautiful, too. And he likes you very much."

Her hands started working before she was even done talking, kneading at the balls of my feet.

"Oh, that feels good." I instantly felt more relaxed. She did have good hands. My mind eased off suspicious mode and picked up on the last thing she said. "He likes me? How do you know?"

"Close your eyes. Try to clear your mind. It's more relaxing that way." Her hands moved up to my ankles, back down to my toes, and up again.

I closed my eyes and tried to melt into the table, but my mind kept working. "Stefan is giving him his massage?" A guy? How come I didn't get a guy?

"Stefan has stronger hands. Mr. Angelos likes a deep tissue massage and I can't quite deliver enough force to penetrate all that muscle."

"Right. But." The more she talked, the more my mind spun. "You've tried?"

"I may have been closer to him than you'd like."

My eyes remained closed but there was a smile in her tone that tempted me to open and gawk. Instead, I focused on the mental images involving a naked Nick and Anya in her pink massage coat, only shorter and more formfitting, paired with lacy thigh-highs and stilettos. Mother always said I was too imaginative for my own good. "Oh."

"I'll tell you a secret."

"Oh?"

"He has a spot. When you touch him there, he goes wild. He can hardly stand it. If you touched him there with your mouth, he would probably give you just about anything you asked."

"News flash, Anya. All guys have that spot. It's called a penis."

She giggled. "Not that spot. This one's different. It guarantees an immediate and very strong reaction. He's a very powerful man but this one turns him into jelly."

I didn't want to get sex advice from Anya the masseuse. But I wanted to drive Nick wild. "All right, Anya. Tell me where to find this spot."

"When I massage his scalp, I find him particularly sensitive around the ears. I found that if you trace a line from his earlobe to midway down his neck, he starts to lose control. I can only imagine if one were to apply a lighter pressure with a tongue, maybe add some light nips . . ."

Her voice trailed to a hush. I sighed, partly in relief at my overactive imagination, and partly because of the heavenly massage. "Thank you, Anya. That's very helpful information."

By the time Anya finished with me, I was butter, one big pot of melted sweet creamery butter. Bones were overrated. I'd never been more relaxed.

Sliding into the finishing touch, delicate pale pink satin Ungaro sandals with stiletto heels and ankle straps, I felt like Cinderella on her way to the ball. My dress a cocktail-length pale pink chiffon with slender straps drawing the eye to the gold sequin-trimmed décolletage, hugged me perfectly. The hem floated around my thighs, just long enough to hide my deepest secrets, not that I had any from Nick.

I caught sight of myself in the mirror as I stood up. My legs looked amazing. I never would have been bold enough to pick the dress out on my own, but Nick had been right in his choice. It could have been made for me.

Unfortunately, it didn't exactly go with my new emerald bracelet. What the hell? I wore it, anyway.

My hair was pinned in elegant disarray, a few well-placed stray curls dripping down to brush the nape of my neck. My makeup was pale, blush pinks and soft neutrals, low-key and just right. The minions knew their stuff. And of course, under my dress I had all the right lingerie designed to make a man go wild, lace-cupped push-up bra with a tiny thong that I planned to remove as soon as possible. Kate's comment about being Nick's dress-up doll stayed with me, but I forced it from my mind.

"One more thing." Dinah, one of my attendants, had come to escort me to the dining room. "These are for tonight."

She held up two perfect pink diamond, teardrop-cut earrings.

"Wow."

"Just be sure to remove them before midnight. If you still have them on when they turn into pumpkins, it will hurt like a son of a bitch."

I laughed and put them in. "How do they look?"

"Stunning. You're stunning. We do great work."

"You do. Thank you." No comment on what they

had to work with? I wasn't going to fish for the compliment. Wordlessly, I followed her out of the room and down the hall to meet Nick in the dining room for dinner.

"Wow." He stood at the bar in the parlor adjacent to the dining room. His back was to me as I entered, but he appraised my reflection from the mirrored panels behind the bar.

He turned and gave me a chance to return the compliment. "Wow," I breathed.

The man looked good in anything, jeans, business suits, bare. It didn't much matter what he wore, he was breathtaking. But in his tux? A classic black-on-white affair? With his thick blond hair that waved down almost to his shoulders and his chiseled good looks? I nearly felt my heart stop. My knees shook a little on sight of him and it had nothing to do with the height of my heels.

"Exquisite," he said, setting his drink on the bar and closing the distance between us. "More beautiful than I even imagined. Thank you for indulging me."

He took me in his arms and met my lips for a slow, erotic exploration. I tasted the vodka martini on his tongue. Dry, with a lemon twist.

"I'm the one who feels indulged. The massage was—I can't even describe it. My bones are still just growing back."

"If you think Anya gives a good massage, you should feel mine."

I felt the heat pool at my core, just from the thought of him touching me in ways that Anya just couldn't do for me. "We could skip dinner?" I smiled, but I wasn't entirely joking.

"You'll need the nourishment. We've a long night ahead."

Gulp. In truth, I was hungry. I couldn't wait to see what we were having.

"Drink? I'm having a vodka martini, but I think you might prefer one of my bartender's specialties."

"A velvet hammer?" The bartender appeared and made a suggestion. "Or perhaps a Russian quaalude?"

Sounded dangerous. "What's in it?"

"The quaalude? It's a special mix of Frangelico, Baileys, and vodka."

I regarded the bartender. "Morrison?"

"He wears many hats," Nick explained.

"I think I'd better stick to wine. Actually, I would enjoy more of that champagne."

"Coming up." Morrison went to open a bottle.

"I almost didn't recognize him without his hat," I said. "You know, he does look a lot like Jim Morrison."

"Who?"

"The singer. From The Doors. Maybe he's been reincarnated as your driver-slash-bartender."

"You shouldn't suggest such things aloud." His gaze narrowed, lending a sinister edge to his angelic appearance.

"I'm kidding, Nick."

"Of course." Nick shrugged.

Morrison handed me the champagne, making a face and shaking his head behind Nick. I laughed and took my glass.

"That will be all, Morrison." Nick waved him off.

"You do have a sense of humor," I said. "You showed me a glimpse of it when you did your Mr. Burns impression. I know it's in there."

"I have no ear for modern music. It all sounds like crap to me. But yes, I do have a sense of humor."

"Prove it. Tell me a joke."

"I'm not good with jokes. But I do enjoy pulling pranks now and again."

"Ooh." I sipped my champagne. The bubbles tickled the roof of my mouth. "Thanks for the warning. So, what's the best prank you ever pulled?"

"You first. I know you must have pulled a couple."

"Do I look like a prankster?" I held my arms out and gave a little twirl.

"You look like a goddess." He grabbed me playfully around the waist and swung me to him. "I can't wait to make you a naked little goddess."

"Ah, dinner first." I tapped his nose with my index finger.

"Mmm." He kissed me, a quick one. "Maybe. I'm losing resolve with the sight of your legs in those shoes."

"I'll tell you my best prank to distract you." I wanted dinner first. The champagne served to remind me how hungry I was. "In college, I had a ridiculous picture of my roommate. I made it into a Wanted poster and hung it all over our dorm."

"That's it? Disappointing."

"It was a hideous picture. I said she was dangerous. When she saw it, she went ballistic. Not really. She laughed. But she made me take them all down and then I lived in fear of retaliation for the rest of the semester."

"Harmless." He shook his head and went behind the bar to pour himself another martini. I guessed Morrison had outstayed his welcome. Poor Morrison. I didn't mean to get him in trouble.

"I stole my brother's herd of cattle."

"How do you steal a whole herd of cattle?"

"Very carefully." He smiled and took a sip of his drink.

"Your brother must have been pretty angry."

"He was at the time."

"Did you give them back?"

"The ones I didn't sacrifice or sell."

I raised a brow. "Sacrifice?"

"Mr. Angelos?" A minion appeared at the door, dressed in formal waiter attire, white tie and jacket, black pants. "We're ready for you in the dining room."

"Saved by the minion." I smiled. He took my hand and placed it in the crook of his arm to lead me to the table.

Our conversation remained light through the meal. The food was so incredible that it stole my attention from more than the occasional glance at my heart-stopping companion. We started with goat cheese ravioli, followed by a salad of walnuts and warm beets over greens, a palate cleanser of lemon sorbet, and a shrimp risotto that was so good it made me wonder if we'd sailed from Boston straight on to heaven.

As if all that wasn't enough, we split a chocolate soufflé cake topped with pistachio gelato after dinner.

Fortunately, I paced myself through the meal. I didn't want to overindulge in food or drink with the promise of hot sex in my very near future. As dishes were cleared, I glanced over at Nick, my gaze drawn to his ears. I thought of what Anya had said about his erogenous zone.

"Your chef is worth every penny," I said.

"They all are. There's a whole team working back there. Only the best for you."

"It has definitely been one of the best evenings I've had in a very long time."

"Only one of the best?"

"I've had a lot of good times. There's some competition."

He seemed surprised.

"Come on, I have kids. You don't think I'm going to rate their births above dinner with you? Even if you are the most handsome bachelor on the planet."

"Only on the planet?"

"In the galaxy. Universe? You are a bachelor, aren't you? No secret wives hidden away in the attic?"

"I don't even have an attic."

"Dodging the question?"

"No wives."

"Good." I didn't want to ask about girlfriends or mistresses. For now, it was enough to know he was free to enjoy my company without breaking any sacred vows.

"Did you enjoy your dessert?" He leaned in to stroke my wrist. The feral gleam in his emerald gaze brought to mind a predator toying with his food before devouring it.

"Very much. And you?"

He shook his head. "It didn't satisfy. I've a craving for something much sweeter." He brought my palm to his lips and dropped a slow, hot kiss in the center. "I think it's time I showed you the one room you haven't seen yet."

"The kitchen?" I joked.

"The master bedroom. Come on."

He helped me from my chair. My knees wobbled. He steadied me with an arm around my waist.

"I can't wait," he said, and pulled me closer. His mouth crushed to mine, his tongue darting between my lips. I tipped my head back to take him in deeper. He tasted like the pistachio gelato, smooth and sweet and delicious. My legs gave out from under me, but he had me in his arms, still kissing me.

He carried me all the way to the bedroom before I'd opened my eyes and he gently lowered me to the bed.

The room was much more masculine than the one I'd occupied earlier, dark wood and heavy brass accents. Candles were lit all along the bedside tables. The bed, king-sized with a fluffy navy blue down comforter, had been turned down to reveal inviting cotton sheets. The lights lowered somehow as if by magic until only the glow of candles remained. Seductive music played in the background, the occasional trill of a flute making itself heard over the sweeping strains of violins.

"Very nice," I said quietly, finding my voice.

He knelt at the edge of the bed, lifted one of my legs, and started to undo the strap of my sandal, then stopped as if thinking better of it. "I think I've done better than nice."

I began to understand that Nick Angelos thrived on praise and expected his companion to deliver. Not a problem. He'd earned it. "Extraordinary," I corrected. "The evening has been nothing short of extraordinary, like the man himself."

His white teeth gleamed in the candlelight. "Better."

Leaving the shoe on, he ran his hands up my ankle and over my calf. "Speaking of extraordinary."

His tongue replaced his hand. I shuddered with pleasure at the feel of him. I shifted forward to tangle my hands in his glorious mane, but he nudged me away. "I don't want you to move a muscle without my permission. Understand?"

His voice was hard with sheer authority. Normally, it might have made me cautious, but I gave in to the automatic physical response of quivering with need for him to touch me in other places. "I understand, but I'm not sure I can comply."

He flashed the wolfish grin. "Very well."

Both hands slid up my legs, calves to thighs, and urged me open to him. Before I realized his intentions, he bowed his head between my legs and licked my cleft through the lace that covered me. I moaned and leaned back.

"Sit up straight," he ordered. "I want to see your reaction when I make you come the first time."

The first time. My eyes widened. That pretty much did it. Who knew that the oral stimulation I needed to put me over the edge would come in the form of words alone? Warm heat rushed through my veins.

He dipped his head again, dropping a trail of light nips along the edge of my thong. I bucked against his mouth. Remaining upright took all my effort and I was powerless to stop any other physical response.

"That's it," he encouraged. "Lie back. Give in to me now."

My control spent, I fell to the bed. He pulled my

panties off in one fell swoop. I think he ripped them off. I barely felt anything but the river of white-hot pleasure rippling through me as his tongue met the bare bead of flesh at my core. When he swirled around the delicate nub and tugged it gently between his teeth, something primal roared within me. I eased into him, pressing his mouth to me, unconcerned with anything but releasing the feral rush of sensation.

His hands opened me wider as he suckled my nectar, making wild noises as he licked against me hungrily, as if he couldn't get enough of me. Undone, I found the strength to raise my head to plead with him. "Take me. Now. I need you inside me."

His lips curved in a lazy smile. "In due time, sweetness. Let me have my fun."

I had nothing against his fun, but I didn't want to die of chronic orgasm. On the other hand, was there a better way to go?

Chapter Fourteen

A long night of making love should have taken a toll on my body, but I felt energized at six o'clock in the morning. Nick slept soundly under the sheets at my side. I stole out of bed, picked the comforter up off the floor, and wrapped it around my nakedness so I could slip out onto the balcony and watch the sunrise.

I had no idea where we'd ended up. The coast of Maine, I guessed, looking out onto a tree-dotted rocky expanse of shoreline. It was beautiful outside, cold enough to see my breath in the air. I watched the water lap onto rocks in the distance through the occasional opening in the misty morning fog.

"Maine," he affirmed, coming up behind me to curl his arm around my shoulders.

I kissed the expanse of bronze forearm lightly dotted with sandy blond hairs. "I didn't mean to wake you."

"Come back to bed. I've got something for you." He pressed his erection suggestively into my backside.

I could feel it even through the thick down of the comforter.

"Again? I'm surprised you can function after last night."

"I can function." His voice was a sultry baritone.

A dark figure darted from the rocks into the water, stealing my attention and making me jump. Only then did I make out more dark figures bobbing along on the rocks. "Seals. Harbor seals. It *must* be Maine."

I recalled watching the seals with my sister on one of our many family summer vacations to Maine's coast.

"I said it was." He dropped light kisses along my neck, reminding me of what Anya had said about his spot. He'd commandeered my actions last night. I hadn't had a chance to try it yet. "Do you doubt me?"

"I never doubt you." I turned to him, opening the comforter to feel the heat of his silken skin against me. "I'm ready to come back to bed."

He raised a brow. "Are you sure you wouldn't rather watch the seals?"

"I'm sure." I kissed his luscious mouth, tugging his lip between my teeth before letting go. "Very sure."

From the corner of my eye, a black cloud expanded with lightning speed across the sky. I looked up. "What the—"

Birds. A flock of large black birds, flying in formation at an unbelievable speed. "Look!"

Nick looked up as a brace of feathers hailed down on us like tiny arrows. I got a quick look at the sharp quills that pierced the deck all around us before Nick, using his body to shield mine, rushed us to the open door.

"Damn!" he said.

I straightened up from where I'd landed in a heap on the floor and appraised the hundreds of tiny black sharp objects sticking out of the wood from where we'd just been standing.

"Feathers," Nick said. "Just feathers. Nothing more."

I drew in closer. "They look like arrows."

"Stymphalian birds," Nick affirmed. "They have sharp, pointed feathers. No danger when there's only one or two on their own, but when they flock . . ." His voice trailed off.

"Stymphalian? I've never heard of them. Where do they come from?"

"Not for you to worry about." He moved me away from the window and closed the curtains. "You should go back to bed. I've got to make a call."

"Now?" I glanced at the clock. "It's barely six."

"Now. Stay in bed. Don't go back outside. Don't even leave the room. I'll be back in a very short while."

His voice took on a new gravity. I didn't dare defy him. After what I'd just seen, I didn't want to go out of the room. Stymphalian birds? What were they? I'd never seen anything so frightening in all my life.

As soon as he left the bedroom, I picked up my cell and called Kate. Earlier, while we were at dinner, the minions had moved my things to Nick's room. It wasn't too soon for a call home since I knew Kate would be getting the kids ready for school.

"Hey, Kate," I said, perching on the edge of the bed.

"Bennie? A little early to call. Is anything wrong?"

"No. I just wanted to make sure everyone was up and on schedule."

"Don't worry. I've got it covered."

"We're in Maine," I said. "Off the coast, anyway. I saw seals."

"Wow. I remember when we watched the seals when we were kids. You were afraid to go in the water after that, remember? I had to show you that I could go in and get back out without seals taking me away." She laughed.

"We also saw some weird birds. Stymphalian birds. Have you heard of them?"

"Stymph—what?"

"Stymphalian. They're big and black and travel in flocks. They shed sharp feathers like arrows. Weird, huh?"

"What do you mean, shed?"

"Their feathers are big sharp quills that fall like daggers. The flock flew over us while we were on the balcony this morning. I thought we were going to be killed. But I'm sure it's my sense of drama acting up again. Never mind."

"No. It sounds scary. Hold on, I'm Googling." She paused for a long time and I thought I heard her gasp.

"Kate?"

"Yeah." She sounded fine when she came back on the phone. "Stymphalian birds? Big black birds with sharp feathers. Wikipedia says they're mythological, pets of Ares, the god of war." She exhaled sharply. Maybe it was a laugh? Hard to tell. "Well, you know Wikipedia, right? Anyone can post misleading info. You're safe now. Not to worry. I've got the kids and dogs under control. You just have a good time and I'll see you later, okay?"

"Okay." I hung up, feeling slightly reassured.

By the time Nick returned, I'd managed to drift off, though I don't know how after the fright of nearly being run through by birds with deadly sharp feathers. The next thing I knew, he was kissing me awake and I was glad to have him back under the covers with me. "How did your call go?"

"As expected. I'm sorry for the interruption."

"Not a problem." I reached out to stroke his stubble-dotted cheek with the back of my hand. "I stayed in bed."

"Where I like you best." He nudged the sheet down to reveal my rose-tipped breast. His lip curled as he watched my nipple harden in response to the cool air. "Very nice."

"I think I've done better than nice." I mocked his comments from earlier.

"Touché, my wanton little minx," he said before taking my breast in his mouth. I leaned in to explore his neck, finding his pulse with my lips and tracing it to the spot just under his ear.

His response was swifter than I imagined. He immediately reared back with a moan. His hands on my waist, he spun me atop him. I spread my legs, straddling him. His erection, thick and solid, begged immediate entrance. I obliged, shifting my hips until he filled me. I rocked with him, in rhythm. His hands glided over my skin, down my back, and up again to my breasts. The rough pads of his thumbs grazed my nipples, urging me to arch into him. I moved with him, riding him faster, until I could feel him find his release.

Dazed and spent, I rolled off him to curl at his side.

He stroked my hair from my face. "Incredible. You're the most extraordinary woman I've ever met."

His voice reflected some degree of awe, as if even he was surprised by the admission. I didn't know what to say. *You're not so bad yourself* sounded trite. True, he was physically extraordinary. And when he was near me, slaking my lust became my primary focus. But love? I didn't know if it would come, and that made me a little sad as I drifted back to sleep in his arms.

Hours later, we shared a late breakfast of croissants with jam, scrambled eggs, fruit, and champagne on the closed deck as we sailed back into Boston Harbor. The sky looked overcast yet clear in the way that indicated oncoming snowstorms.

"Do you ski?" he asked.

I tried not to shudder. "I lodge."

"Come again?"

"I stay in the lodge and drink cocoa while everyone else skis. I've never been that steady on my feet."

He laughed. "I was going to suggest maybe Thursday we could go, if it snows later today."

I thought back to yesterday's conversation with Josh. Funny how Josh seemed to instinctively understand that winter sports and I just didn't mix, though he'd made a joke of it all. Even the memory of laughing with Josh filled me with a tingly warmth. Not quite the frantic heat I had with Nick, but there was something reassuring in thinking of someone

who had me all figured out. Nick had no idea
what it would take to get me on a slope.

I shook my head. "Thursday's Thanksgiving. I
have an army to feed."

"An entire army?"

"My family. Kate, the kids, parents and grandparents. We make a day of it."

"Oh."

"What's Thanksgiving usually like for your family?"
I toyed with his hand next to mine on the table, tracing his knuckles with my finger.

"We don't usually celebrate."

"No turkey?" It made sense. I'd always got a foreign
vibe from Nick, as well as from Owen.

"If you don't count my brothers." He smiled.

"You have a lot of brothers?" I seemed to recall
he'd said that he did. "Back home. Where you're
from?" I hoped he would fill in some detail.

"Countless. And a few sisters." He remained
detached.

I pulled my hand away, feeling a little shut out.

"I hadn't imagined you came from such a large
family." I spooned jam on to a croissant.

He emptied his champagne glass and poured
some more. "We're all fairly self-absorbed. Most of
us avoid interacting at all costs."

"Harsh." But probably true. I'd begun to see that
Nick had a bit of an ego. Not that it bothered me.
Much.

"Practical." He shrugged. "We're prone to violence.
Murder is not out of the question."

A chill traveled the length of my spine. He didn't
seem to be joking. But of course, he had to be.

"Is that why you'd gone to live with your uncle?

To avoid murder charges?" I laughed, keeping it light. Nick was showing me a side I wasn't sure I liked entirely. I figured the murder and mystery talk might be designed to keep me from getting too close, and it was working. I enjoyed the getaway, but I was ready to go.

"I think it was more to save me from becoming a murder victim."

"Aha, the pranks." I recalled our conversation from earlier.

"Exactly." His eyes glittered with mischief. "My father loved me too well to watch me die at the hands of my brothers. He needn't have worried, though. I have as much a knack for bargaining my way out of tough spots as for getting into them in the first place."

He twined his fingers with mine.

"That skill must serve you well in business." And in love, perhaps. I'd thought about what he'd said regarding Josh and his mutual friend. Fortunately, I felt myself in no danger of falling too hard, too fast.

"It does." He kissed my knuckles. "Most definitely."

"Ugh, business." I wished I hadn't thought of it. I had a sudden wave of guilt for not going in to work today, especially with the sky looking so ominous, though Nick had covered my absence with Leslie before sweeping me away. "I wonder if they finished the roof."

"They could always hire some extra hands." Typical rich boy answer. Trouble? Spend more.

"The idea is to keep costs down. The family has to be able to afford the house they'll eventually move into and make their own."

"That's where creative accounting comes in."

"I can see why you and Josh got along so well in a work environment."

"Ah yes. Everything's by the book with Mr. Brandon. Poor man, trapped in such a boring existence as to be ruled by his conscience."

"I don't know. I think it's very noble of him to stick to his morals." Honorable. It appealed to me more than I'd realized.

"The noble Josh Brandon." He lifted my hand to kiss the inside of my palm. "Don't tell me you're falling for him?"

Suddenly I wasn't so sure. But I smiled and dodged the question. "Now, why would I say anything of the sort when I'm sitting here having a lovely time with you?"

"Why, indeed?" As he moved from kissing my palm to my neck, the frantic heat returned and I realized I wasn't so ready to rush off for home yet after all.

Shortly after noon, Nick dropped me off at the house. I was glad to have some time on my own to come back down to earth before it was time to pick up the kids.

Kate waited in the living room, where she had paced a path right into my carpet. She was all energy when I walked in. By contrast, Ellie had fallen asleep in her Exersaucer.

"Look at the sweet pea," I said. "She must have bounced her way right into dreamland."

"About ten minutes ago," Kate confirmed. "But she's out pretty soundly. The pugs were barking on their way out to play in the yard and she never even flinched. A good thing, because it leaves us a chance to talk."

My stomach flipped. I sensed that Kate wanted to talk about something serious. "Sure."

"Coffee?" She headed for the kitchen and took mugs from the cabinet. "I just made a pot."

Further proof that it was not going to be an easy talk. "Coffee would be good. I'm still really tired."

"Didn't get much sleep, huh?"

"Not exactly."

"Me, either." She poured.

I got the cream out of the fridge. She drank hers black but I needed mine light and sweet. "Why? What's wrong?"

"Marc's seeing someone. He called last night to let me know." Her eyes welled up as she said it.

"Hon, I'm sorry." I put down the cream and gave her a hug.

"I didn't think it would happen so fast. I thought he'd need time."

"Who is she?"

"Jill Richards, from ESPN."

"Ew. That trampy little reporter who does the post-game interviews? The one with the turned-up nose?"

Kate nodded. "That one."

"I can't picture it. She's not his type."

"Apparently, she is. He said they really hit it off. They've been out a few times now." Her tears started falling faster. "He thanked me for giving him a chance to get out and explore."

The whole thing smelled of middle school high jinks to me. He was using Jill to make Kate jealous so that she might realize her true feelings. Juvenile, perhaps, but in this case it was proving effective.

"I don't know," I said. "It doesn't seem like Marc."

"I shouldn't even be crying." Kate wiped at her eyes. "So silly. If he really found someone, I should be happy for him. It's what I've wanted for him all along."

"Come on, now. Is it really? I think your reaction shows more than you care to admit."

"I have a lot to think about," she admitted as she dried her eyes. "But that's not what I wanted to talk to you about."

"It's not?" The feeling of dread intensified.

"No. Let's go out to the other room so I can keep an eye on Ellie. And I think you need to sit down."

"That bad?"

"Maybe."

I stirred sugar into my coffee and followed her in to take a seat on the love seat opposite Kate in my wingback chair. "Why didn't you tell me Nick worked for Glendower Enterprises?" she said, getting straight to the point.

I exhaled. "I'm sorry. I should have mentioned it. I meant to talk about it. I just hated to bring his name up again when you seemed to be finally forgetting him. And then I worried that every time you looked at Nick, you'd think of Owen. It made me feel guilty for even seeing him when I thought about putting you in that spot."

"Now I know. I'm in that spot. But the fact is I'm not bothered by it."

"You're not?"

"I see Owen every time I look at my daughter, Bennie. It's not as if he'll ever really go away."

"True." I sipped my coffee. The warmth, and Kate's lack of anger, made me feel more relaxed. "I see Patrick in the kids all the time. I understand."

"How exactly did you meet him, again?" Kate narrowed her eyes.

"I went to see Leslie for some job advice, stumbled at the construction site, and Nick happened to be there. You know all that."

"Odd that he just happened to be there at the right place, at the right time. No?"

I thought back over the events. "Yes, but it's not as if he targeted me and made me fall into his arms all so I could lead him back here where—" I stopped myself. She knew he worked for Glendower Enterprises, but I still hadn't explained the family situation. What if Kate had a point? It was odd that Nick ended up being connected to Ellie through Owen. "Coincidence. It had to be."

She shook her head. "There are no such things as coincidences. I think Owen sent him."

"Sure. The devil." I widened my eyes and used my best spooky voice so she would know what I thought of her theory. She was way off.

"Hades," she corrected. "He more properly thinks of himself in the Greek tradition."

"Hades." My sister had gone over the edge. Poor thing. It was probably the thought of losing Marc adding extra stress. But then I remembered Nick's admission that they all chose their own names, his being Greek for "messenger." Coincidence, again?

"I know you don't think I'm serious when I tell you that Owen is Hades, but please believe me now. I think you might be in some kind of danger, Ben."

"Me? In danger?" The birds had been scary, but actual danger?

"What do you really know about Nick?" She crossed her arms.

I blushed. "He's pretty incredible in bed."

"Bordering on supernatural?"

"I wouldn't go that far."

"No? You sure?"

"Yeah." I nodded. "He's really good. We have fantastic sex. But that's just it, Kate. Shouldn't I be falling for him?"

She raised her eyebrows. "You're not?"

"Physically. When I'm with him, it feels pretty intense. It could be headed somewhere. I'm not sure yet." Shouldn't I be sure yet? But somehow I kept thinking of Josh. I couldn't be falling for both of them at the same time. Could I?

"That's a relief. I think you need to stop seeing him."

"The danger thing." I bit my lip.

"He might be a god." She got up and paced.

"Slow down. When did you start thinking he might be a god?"

"Just last night, after we talked. Before that, he seemed perfectly normal, if a little too good to be true. Of course, so had Owen. But he raised my suspicions with sweeping you away to his yacht. I knew he had money, but it all seemed over the top. I looked him up once we got off the phone. As soon as I found out he worked for Glendower Enterprises, I knew. I remembered the talk at dinner the other night, his evasive answers about his past occupations and his family, his numerous half

siblings. It all clicked with what I know of Owen.
If not a god, Nick might be a minion."

"Minion?" My heart raced. "He calls his staff minions. His driver, Morrison."

"As in Jim?"

"Dead ringer."

"Hades had Byron."

I laughed. "The poet? Kate, get a grip."

"I'm serious."

"You think Morrison's the real Jim?"

"Could be." She shrugged. "At first, I thought Nick
was a minion, but then I wondered if Hades would
trust looking after Ellie and me to just any minion.
It seemed a bigger job. And if he was going to send
a minion, why not Byron?"

"The poet?"

"Byron's still with Glendower Enterprises. He
sends occasional correspondence."

"Child support." I nodded. Of course.

"But he didn't send Byron. He sent someone who
could get in and observe."

"So Nick's using me to get to you?" I struggled to
keep the anger out of my voice.

"To watch out for me and Ellie somehow. Yeah.
Maybe there's some kind of danger coming, or
maybe he just wants to know firsthand how we're
doing. I haven't quite worked it out."

"Maybe Nick couldn't resist my charms and it has
nothing to do with you."

She shook her head as if distracted. No, that
couldn't be it. Unreal. "There's something to it.
Maybe Hades is worried about Ellie's powers."

I rolled my eyes. "Here we go again."

"You saw her with the water-to-ice trick? And all that stuff with the lights?"

"I'm sure Spencer has some kind of explanation for the water trick." But the lights. Her toys were lighting up and there was no explanation for it. No natural explanation. I couldn't deny what I'd seen for myself.

Kate's nervous energy was making it hard for me to sit still. I got up and stretched my legs.

"Kate, you're jumping to conclusions. Kind of crazy ones at that. Even if you think Owen was a god, it's kind of a jump to assume that there's a supernatural plot at work, and that Nick is in on it. Maybe you need a vacation?"

"What about the Stymphalian birds?"

My skin prickled with the memory of those freaky birds and their daggerlike feathers. "What about them?"

"Look." She picked her laptop up off a side table, clicked a few buttons, and turned the screen to face me.

It was a good thing I'd put down my coffee. The screen was on a Web site for mythological studies that featured Stymphalian birds, black birds with iron knife-sharp feathers that heralded the arrival of Ares, god of war. "That's exactly what they were."

"Convinced?"

I took a deep breath. Was crazy contagious? "No way he's a god of war. He prefers lovemaking. Eros?" I could buy that he was god of love.

"Hermes," Kate said, clicking a few more buttons. "Messenger to Hades. Angelos is Greek for messenger. Which also makes him—"

"Hades's nephew," I said. I didn't need to read

the screen she'd called up next on Hermes to know. Nick had been perfectly honest from the start, at least as far as his relationship to Eliana was concerned. "Cousin of our little sweet pea. I knew he was Owen's nephew, Kate. I did. But how could I have suspected the whole god thing? So he did have the ability to know to be in the right place at the right time. He was using me all along."

"Not entirely. I think he really likes you. He hasn't exactly spent a lot of time here."

"True, but—"

"But he came here for a reason."

"And that reason wasn't me." It felt disappointing, sure, but I wasn't exactly devastated. In a way, I was relieved. I knew I wasn't falling in love with Nick. But I also understood more why my sister had had so much trouble letting go of Owen. "So you knew all along that Owen was Hades?"

"He told me after I'd started to fall for him. It almost changed my mind about him, but I couldn't help what I felt. I love him for all that he is. I always will."

"And that's what is keeping you from Marc, isn't it? You think he'll come back?"

She shook her head. A single tear glided down her cheek. "He can't come back. I know that. He made a deal with Zeus that keeps him for eternity in hell, but enabled him to give me Ellie."

"Our little sweet pea." I looked over at my delicate baby niece, her little rosebud mouth puffed out as she slept slumped over in her Exersaucer seat. "What would we do without her?"

"I'm sure we'll never have to find out. Her father's looking out for her. It explains why Nick's here.

Hades wouldn't have wanted to interrupt my life with an obvious intrusion, but he probably wants a firsthand report on how Ellie's growing."

"And on you. If he misses you as much as you miss him, it's painful for you both. He must want to know how you're faring." I thought of Patrick and how I missed him. But Patrick was human and there was more finality to how he'd gone from me. Maybe it was easier that way. I didn't want to ask if Kate knew from Hades what happened after death. It wouldn't change the fact that my husband was gone. But what about Kate? Did she have a chance? "You'll never see him again?"

"We know we won't be together again for a long time. He told me to live my life. To love again."

"So you're free to be with Marc."

"If that's what I really want, yes." She nodded, but she seemed somehow uncertain. "I'm not sure I'm ready to let go. Maybe he's not, either. Maybe that explains Nick. For Nick, dating you is the perfect way to keep tabs on Ellie and me and allow him to have a little fun in the process."

"So I'm an added bonus? The icing on the cake?"

"The icing is the best part, isn't it?" Kate waggled her brows.

I didn't mind so much when she put it that way. "True enough."

"I just don't want you to get hurt, and not just from a broken heart. What about the Stymphalian birds?"

I stifled a shiver at mention of the birds. "I'm not in danger of breaking my heart, don't worry. But I agree about the birds. Pets of Ares? Yet another god?"

"Maybe it's nothing to do with us." Kate shrugged.

"Maybe we're wrong about Nick. Maybe he's just an ordinary guy who happens to work for Glendower Enterprises."

"Maybe. The birds really startled me. I guess it's possible they were just passing through the area. But as much as I had a good time with Nick, I have to admit something felt off to me somehow. It was seriously weird the way he talked about his family. There wasn't a lot of love and admiration to go around." More like mentions of murder and mayhem, but I didn't want to scare Kate more. Ellie belonged with us, but she was part of Nick's family, too. What could it mean for Kate and Ellie? "You really think Ellie has powers?"

I approached and stroked her soft brown curls, carefully so as not to wake her. "She's half god."

"Wow." I shook my head.

"Wow," Kate agreed.

"So the mystery remains. Why is Nick Angelos here, and what do the Stymphalian birds have to do with him?"

"It's a good question. I think we should be on our guard."

"Nick wouldn't put Ellie in danger," I said. "He's loyal to his uncle, as far as I can tell. He must be here on some official purpose. I'll find out."

"Not now," Kate said, gesturing to the clock. "It's late. You're going to have to go pick up the kids."

Chapter Fifteen

"My brother." Hermes allowed himself to fall out of character as the mortal Nick to welcome Ares into his office at Glendower Enterprises. Not the ideal place to meet, but it was the most protected from exposing their powers to mortals. Who knew what rules Ares would choose to break or follow in this realm, considering he'd felt free enough to let his vile birds loose in near daylight? "What brings you to visit?"

Hermes remained seated behind the desk, a position he felt gave him the upper hand. Ares was the physically superior of the two of them. No need to remind him of it.

Ares sank into the chair opposite him and let out a sigh that sounded more like a fierce beast's growl. "Our father, of course. He has been watching you, Hermes."

"Me?" For all Hermes knew, Ares worked in Zeus's interests even now. He had to be careful not to reveal more than he intended his father to know. He valued his freedom too highly to let any of Hades's treasured secrets be revealed. "What would he care what I'm up to, considering it's all boring business of our uncle's? Hades likes to *keep his finances secure, no doubt in case Zeus ever relents and lets him come back here."*

"Zeus never relents." Ares looked damned uncomfortable in the scrawny little desk chair meant for human builds. Hermes enjoyed watching him squirm. He'd always found it much easier to adapt to the earthly customs than his hot-tempered half brother. "Hades must know better than to expect it."

"Of course." Hermes shrugged. "Hades is no fool."

"Fool enough to bargain with Zeus." Ares tried to arch a brow, but the scar that ran the length of the left side of his face prevented it from budging much beyond a fraction. Neither could he open his eye wide on that side of his face, the heavy-lidded gaze lending the god of war a more sinister air than any of the other gods of Hermes's acquaintance.

Aside from the scar, the two looked remarkably alike despite having different mothers. They took after their father, Hermes supposed.

"Fool enough indeed," Hermes agreed with a laugh that sounded as cruel-intentioned as his brother looked. In truth, he bore no ill will to his father or his uncle.

His interest lay mainly in looking out for himself. He would end up on whichever side was more advantageous to him in the end. In most cases, Hermes had learned from experience, his best chance was to play each side against the other and stay in the good graces of all parties involved.

Hermes sat forward in his chair. "Let's cut to the chase, shall we? We both know you didn't come for a social visit. You don't like me all that much."

"I like you better than most."

"You don't like anyone."

"Aphrodite's all right, when she's horny." Ares laughed,

a great big bellowing sound that would have had his uncle's minions come running had the office not been properly soundproofed.

"Yes, well, you've both caused your share of grief for the sake of getting together."

"Suffered from it, too." He rubbed his face as if trying to rub out the memory of being trapped naked with Aphrodite for all of Mount Olympus to ridicule. "I'm here because I owe you, brother. You saved me from the giant's jar when everyone else would have left me there to rot."

Hermes nodded. "True."

In fact, when the two giants, Otus and Ephialtes, had trapped Ares in an urn, all the other gods and goddesses intended to let him remain there. Even Ares's favored Aphrodite. But when the giants' stepmother, the beautiful Eriboea, had come to Hermes for help, he couldn't resist her charms. He'd saved Ares's pitiful life. Besides, he figured Ares would owe him for the favor and that one day might benefit him. As it happened, the day had possibly come.

"Zeus has been mistrustful of Hades's intentions for creating life."

"For love of a mortal woman? Not reason enough for dear old Dad?" In truth, Hermes had questioned his uncle's logic as well, until recently. He'd begun to come around to Hades's way of thinking. Bennie breathed a refreshing burst of cheer into his stay. He found he could hardly stop thinking of her, even when she wasn't with him.

"Zeus suspects a plot. He has planted spies among Hades's staff."

"Spies?" Hermes stood at attention.

Surely he would have known, would have suspected, if someone wasn't who they claimed to be? Perhaps not. So many minions, both here and in Hades's own realm. Any one of them could be secretly in his father's employ.

"Spies," Ares repeated, his lips curving into a grin. "Zeus thinks Hades may have gifted his child with godlike powers as part of a plot to take over Mount Olympus."

Hermes laughed and settled back in his chair. "Preposterous. If the child has powers, it would be a mere fluke, probably an oversight of Zeus himself when he granted Hades the privilege to reproduce."

Ares shrugged. "There's no telling Zeus it's anything but a plot. If the child has powers, I've been instructed to deliver her to Mount Olympus."

"But—that would be a deliberate affront to Hades. It would mean war."

"I know." Ares smiled.

War meant loss and destruction. Loss of things Hermes held dear, potentially his freedom, and destruction of things he liked best, like his uncle's most excellent wines. Not to mention what might happen if a war of the gods carried over into the human realm. No. War had to be prevented, at all costs.

On the other hand, if Hades could be overthrown, Hermes might persuade his father to give him his uncle's entire kingdom. "So, why are you telling me this, again?"

"I owe you, as I said." Ares narrowed the unscarred eye. "I'm repaying my debt by giving you fair warning of Zeus's intentions. Anything you report to Hades will be known not long after by Zeus."

"So if I discover the child possesses unique abilities?"

"As soon as it is confirmed, I take her."

"And if she's under my protection?"

"You'll side against Father?"

"Perhaps," Hermes bluffed.

"You're willing to stand up against me?" Ares stood. This time, he managed to arch the brow, scar be damned.

Hermes shrugged. "Whatever it takes. But I'm sure it won't come to blows. I've seen nothing to indicate the babe is anything but disgustingly mortal."

"Good." Ares brushed his hands. "I would hate to do battle with you after you were kind enough to free me."

"One more thing and I'll consider your debt to be paid in full."

"One more thing?" Ares cursed under his breath. "You've always been piss-full of nerve, Hermes."

"And you've always been crude." Hermes smiled. "But yes, one more thing. Send me a sign in advance if things go badly and Zeus intends to send you for the child. I would like to allow the mother a chance to say good-bye. It would curry more favor with Hades until I choose a side. But don't send the Stymphalian birds. Keep them home at Thrace. Too suspicious. Send the vulture and I'll know what it means."

"None of it will be necessary depending on what you report to Hades." Ares paused on his way toward the door.

"I know. But I have to decide what suits me best before I make the report."

The brothers exchanged a glance, each one knowing the other's mind too well to mistake that Hermes would report what he wanted depending on his intentions, to prevent a war or to make one.

Chapter Sixteen

All weekend, I'd been trying to contact Nick Angelos to no avail. Kate got in touch with Byron at Glendower Enterprises, who confirmed that Nick was spending some time "in corporate conference" with Owen Glendower, aka Hades. Byron also confirmed that while Nick had a visit from his brother, the brother had returned to his home. It helped to know a few good minions, I guessed. Kate and I felt reassured that all was well, for now. I would learn more when Nick returned and started calling me back.

Feeling guilty for having missed a day of work, I threw myself into the job on Monday morning. I'd secured a sizable donation from Nick Angelos, true enough, but I wanted to prove I could do better at raising funds on my own.

"Leslie," I said, only after I had the planning well under way. I'd had the weekend to mull over some ideas. "How about a football toss?"

"A football toss?"

"As a fund-raiser. We could set up a raffle for a

chance to throw a ball through a modified goalpost. We could sell raffle tickets, giving us cash donations, and we could give tickets away based on hours volunteered to help build houses. It boosts our donation income as well as our volunteer force. The winner would get a chance at fifty thousand dollars, half of the donation from Glendower Enterprises. We need to spend money to make money, right?"

Leslie shrugged. "Maybe."

"I think I could get some of the Patriots to show up. It would help us complete another house for a new family by Christmas."

"Another house? In a matter of weeks? Are you insane?"

"Not if we buy a foreclosure. I still get e-mail notices for real estate listings at one of Patrick's old addresses. One came up yesterday that looked promising. I could have Josh check it out to see if it can be restored with little effort, and not too much money."

"It's a thought. The Mill Street house is almost finished. If we get the manpower in the form of volunteers, it could be a good opportunity."

"A great opportunity. With some football stars there, I could get good press coverage. Besides, I contacted the mayor about donating the Christmas tree on Boston Common. If the mayor shows up, we'll get even more coverage."

"Donating the tree?"

"For lumber. I saw Al Roker on *The Today Show* say they were donating the Rockefeller Center tree to Habitat for Humanity in New York. Why not here? It's not as if they'll do anything special with it once Christmas is over."

"That's a great idea. I wish I'd thought of it."

"Me, too. But no harm in taking a good idea and making it work for us."

"No harm indeed." Leslie nodded. "You really think we could get people to volunteer a whole day of hard work just for a chance to throw a football for money?"

"If they're getting coached by a star quarterback to do it. Not to mention they can rub elbows with some Patriots players during the day. I'm pretty sure I can get some to show up. I have a contact on the team. They have a bye week coming up."

"Marc Ramirez. He is so delicious. If your sister wasn't with him, I would beg for the chance to lick him all over."

I wasn't about to touch that one. Besides, if I could get Marc and Kate together in the same place, it would be a start.

"It will be fun," I said. "And we could raise money. If corporations or even small businesses think there will be a press presence, they'll be feeling charitable. We'll raise more than the fifty thousand we give away."

"More?" She was catching on.

"More. Think of all the houses we could build, all the families we could help."

No mention of raising salaries, the hazards of working for a nonprofit. Leslie and I split a salary. Josh hired out for independent contracting jobs, probably to make up for what Habitat couldn't afford to pay him. He stayed because he believed in the work and I respected him for it.

I couldn't imagine Nick generously giving his time without the assurance there was something in it for him. And even though I had memories of

Nick Angelos's naked perfection to spare, I couldn't stop thinking about the curve of Josh's butt in his bike shorts. Or the spark that had flown between us when he handed me the hammer. Or the way he made me feel when he'd trusted me to do some of the roofing work, or asked my opinion on the setup inside the house.

Nick really appreciated how I looked in the dress he'd picked out for me, but he'd never even asked if I liked it. Josh would have asked. Josh would have come shopping with me instead of choosing a dress himself and laying it out on the bed for me to put on and model for him.

"I think it's a great idea."

A thrill shot down my spine when I heard his voice directly behind me, as if I had conjured him with my thoughts.

"Josh." I turned to face him. "I had no idea you were coming into the office today."

His aquamarine eyes brightened in intensity as he met my gaze and smiled. "We're even. I had no idea you'd decided to come back to us."

"Of course I came back. I work here. Duh."

"Duh?" His smile widened. "It's not duh. It's d'oh. Don't you watch *The Simpsons*?"

"In fact, I do," I said. Enough to recognize that he did a perfect Homer. I wondered about his Mr. Burns. "They're no Flintstones, but they'll do."

"I loved *The Flintstones*," he said. "I haven't seen them in years. My favorite was the episode with Ann Margrock. Did you see the one with Ann Margrock?"

"I did. She had a way with Pebbles."

Josh nodded. "But she was no Wilma. Give me

Wilma Flintstone any day. They don't make 'em like that anymore."

Be still my heart. "No, they don't."

Leslie looked from me to Josh and back again. "*The Flintstones?*"

"Perhaps they were a little before your time, Leslie," I said.

"No, I know *The Flintstones*. They're just not that funny."

Josh shook his head. "Then you really don't know *The Flintstones*."

"Whatever." Leslie rolled her eyes. "So, you like the football toss idea?"

"With the Patriots? Are you kidding? We'll attract all kinds of people to that event. It's a great idea."

I scooted behind Leslie and angled the monitor so she and Josh could see what I'd been working on. "I've designed invitations to send potentially interested VIPs. And print ads to attract people. And here's the house. What do you think? Can we pull it off?"

"As long as we can get the house. Do you think we can get it? On short notice?" Leslie's excitement seemed to be growing now that she'd wrapped her mind around my idea.

"I have my contacts. I think I can work it out," I said, confidence growing along with Josh's and Leslie's faith in me.

"Nick Angelos." Josh said the name with as much distaste as if he'd been eating octopus brains. Not that I'd ever had octopus brains, but they sounded pretty disgusting.

"No. Actually, the daughter of one of Patrick's old friends is the Realtor. Patrick got her into her first house. I think she'll feel tender toward the cause and help us out. It's worth a shot, anyway. I've put in a call to arrange a showing. With the way the market is headed, and at this time of year, I think they'll be willing to unload it."

"Impressive." Josh nodded, then he reached out and patted my back, making me tingle. "Nice work, St. James."

"Thanks, Brandon."

"So we're going to do it?" Leslie asked. "We're going to have a football toss?"

"I don't see why not. I've got the address list ready to go. I can have the invitations printed and ready to mail by the day after Thanksgiving. We'll try and schedule it for the week before Christmas, when people will be most in the mood for giving. We can call it something catchy, like The Great Snowball Toss."

"I like that, as long as people don't think they're throwing snowballs," Josh said, as he helped himself to a cup of coffee. "Excellent idea. Let me know when I can look over the property to make sure it's a sound investment, and what else I can do to help."

"If you're free to check the house this afternoon, I'll try to get the Realtor to let you look around."

"Great," Josh said. "Timing will be tight with Thanksgiving at the end of the week."

"*This* week?" Leslie nearly jumped in her seat. "Already? I'm going to have to get to the market and prepare to start my baking."

"Or, forget baking," I said, riding the waves of creativity. "How about Thanksgiving dinner at my house? We can take some time between dinner and dessert to address the invitations." I got a little carried away with enthusiasm, but why not? "Josh, you come, too."

"I've got Thanksgiving with my mom, sorry." Leslie made her apologies. "I'm bringing the pies."

"Josh?"

"I would love to come, but I've got Kyrie. Her mom's going out of town."

"You can both come. She'll get to hang out with the kids."

"And your dogs. She loves dogs. She wants a pug. She'll be thrilled to meet Bert and Ernie."

"She wants a pug? She has great taste in dogs. I think I'm going to love your daughter, Josh."

"And yours likes hockey. Maybe we should trade." He laughed. "It sounds like a fun day. We'll be there."

"Fantastic." I felt a warm wave course through me from top to toe.

"Great, well, see you then. I've got to finish up some jobs. Call my cell if you can get me in to look at the house."

"Are you working at the Mill Street house today?"

He shook his head. "No volunteers with Thanksgiving coming up. Besides, we're pretty well set for now. The wiring's done. We're ahead of schedule. I have some independent jobs I contracted out on that I want to finish before the holiday. A little trickier now that we have some snow on the ground, but not bad. It's melting fast."

"Of course. It's almost fifty degrees outside." Weird for late November, but not unheard of.

"I just came in to drop off the Mill Street keys." His biceps flexed as he dropped the keys on Leslie's desk. At least, I imagined it flexing under his heavy jacket. I clung to the visual image of him swinging the hammer on the Mill Street rooftop, coupled with the tactile memory of the way I felt, so small and protected, in his arms.

Then there was his scent. I stepped an inch closer and inhaled, eager to get another whiff of the piney, spicy, musky odor that was eau de Josh.

"Bless you," he said.

"What?" I opened my eyes, stared straight into his crystalline baby blues, and realized I'd stepped a few inches closer than intended. Almost close enough to kiss him. Oops.

"You looked like you were about to sneeze."

"Oh." I massaged the bridge of my nose. "Oh. Right. I was, but it didn't come out. Don't you hate when that happens?"

Josh smiled. "Have a great Thanksgiving, Leslie. Bennie, see you Thursday." He winked as he made for the door. I nearly melted on the spot.

"Thursday," I repeated, staring after him as he left.

Thanksgiving morning dawned clear and unseasonably warm. Kate and I got up early for preparations and made great time in the kitchen. I'd given up trying to get in touch with Nick. He hadn't returned my calls. If he'd given up on me, and on whatever drew him to me, it was just as well. I didn't need to risk getting more interested in him if he didn't plan to stick around.

"Do you remember last Thanksgiving?" I asked Kate, as I moved the knife through carrots and celery for the corn bread stuffing. It was nice to have Kate's help on such a labor-intensive holiday. For so many years, I'd handled the cooking on my own while Patrick managed the kids and straightening up the house. "Patrick made a toast to friends and family, and he winked at you. He knew about Owen, didn't he? More than I'd caught on at the time, obviously."

Kate, a dreamy sparkle in her eyes, looked up from peeling potatoes. "I think he knew, yes. Maybe even more than I did. I had no idea where I was headed with Owen and I'd agonized over it all day. It was the day I decided to have a baby, no matter what Owen wanted or if he ended up in my life or not."

"Wait, what?" I put the knife down. "I thought Ellie just happened? You planned her?"

"No. I had no idea that Owen would be the one to make my dream come true. I went for an artificial insemination with donor sperm right after Thanksgiving, but it didn't work."

"God, Kate." I stepped around the butcher block to give her a hug. "All on your own? Why didn't you tell me?"

"I felt awkward about it. You had Patrick and the kids. You were just back from your Disney trip and you seemed so darn happy. I wanted that, too. I wanted a family like yours."

"Odd how that turned out, for both of us. One year later and we're both single moms." I brushed back a tear. I didn't want to cry. I missed Patrick, and the holidays were proving to be especially tough, but I was done with misery and self-pity.

"I should have come to you. I know you would have been supportive. But I didn't want to bother you with the details, and I feared failure. What if I'd found out I couldn't have kids? I can't imagine life without Ellie now that I have her."

"She's quite the bundle of joy." I stole a glance at her hunched over in her Exersaucer, sleeping with a trickle of drool running down her chin.

"Yeah." Kate laughed. "My graceful baby girl. I'm just lucky that she's a part of what Owen and I shared together. It's like I'll always have a part of him with me now."

"You really think she's like him? I mean, with special powers?"

"It's possible." Kate shrugged and went back to peeling. "More likely than not from what I've seen, but I don't think it's anything that will get out of control."

"It could make for some interesting situations, though. I can't help thinking of Tabitha from *Bewitched*." I wiggled my nose à la Samantha Stevens.

"I don't think she can do that kind of magic. But who knows? Her father had the mind reading down, plus some funky control over dark and light and hot and cold." She paused, as though remembering something private between her and her Hades. "And a whole bunch of other stuff I don't even want to think about for her now."

I'd always suspected Ellie could read my mind. Maybe there was something to it. "Special powers could come in handy for making dinner happen on time. We still have to get dressed."

"Plenty of time," Kate assured me as she clicked on the oven light to check the turkey. "Everything's on track. I think I'll go change Princess Blubber before she gets a rash from the drool."

"You do that." I smiled as I watched Kate carefully scooping a very sleepy Ellie into her arms. She stayed asleep. Amazing. Kate was getting better at this mom stuff.

As they left the kitchen, the lights went out after them as if set to automatically extinguish with Ellie's departure. Light and dark. Spooky. Good thing she hadn't started to play around with the thermostat. Then again, maybe my niece could eventually save me a bundle on heating bills. The possibilities were endless.

Everything in the kitchen was under control, so I headed upstairs to take a shower.

What to wear? What to wear? Josh seemed to appreciate me dressed down as much as he liked me dressed up, if not more. I had no idea if he liked me any way at all, really, but there was wishful thinking at work.

It still amazed me to be filled with tingly warmth when I thought of Josh Brandon. Josh Brandon! The man who, up until very recently, had made my blood boil with annoyance rather than attraction. Or maybe it had been attraction all along and I'd just refused to see it for what it was.

Right in time for the first doorbell ring, I'd made it down the stairs in my favorite jeans dressed up with a wine velvet blouse and paired with matching pointy-toed flats, so last year but who cared? It was a good hair day.

"Hi, Mother, Hal." I tried to hide my disappointment that they weren't Josh arriving early.

"Your grandparents are right behind us." Mother shoved a warm casserole dish into my hands. "I'll go help Gran get the pies."

As much as I argued that they didn't have to do anything but show up, Mother and Gran always brought corn pudding and pumpkin pies. I learned to stop making my own pumpkin pie years ago to leave the honor for Gran. I had a pecan pie backup for Pops, who preferred almost anything to pumpkin.

I carried the casserole dish inside and set it on the counter until it was time to reheat it in the oven, currently occupied by a turkey so ginormous it left little room for much else. Mother and Gran found their way to the kitchen.

"Now, where's my great-grandbaby?" Gran barely said hello anymore before setting off in search of Ellie, and it was fine by me. The less she picked on my weight, always too skinny for Gran's liking, and the way I'd done my hair, never pulled back enough to show off my pretty face, the better.

"Ellie's upstairs getting pretty for you, Gran. She'll be down in a minute."

She wandered off in search, taking my mother with her. I laughed to myself. It used to be I could never get them out of my kitchen. Thank you, Kate.

"I hope she put her in a dress this time." I could hear Gran muttering all the way out to the living room. "Last time she had her in little dungarees as if she were a boy. She's going to turn her into a tomboy like—oh, hello, Sarah. You look—your hair looks nice today."

Sarah had insisted on her favorite Patriots jersey over khaki pants. I was lucky to get her out of sweatpants these days. How many kids had real authentic signed Pats merchandise, anyway? I just hoped Gran didn't have a heart attack when she finally caught sight of Spencer. His jet-black spikes hadn't faded much, but he was sporting some nice blond roots at least. With any luck, he'd agreed to my earlier suggestion to go makeup free in honor of the holiday.

I poured myself a little wine from the leftover bottle of chardonnay in the fridge, just in case, and went over my mental checklist for dinner. The whole house smelled of roasting turkey.

"Got any more of that wine?" I turned to greet my dad, decked out in a Hawaiian shirt decorated with hula girls and dress pants with no socks and loafers. Typical dad since he returned from Vegas as a big winner from the slot machines to lead a life of retired leisure. "I'm going to need it if I have to spend all day with your gran casting the evil eye my way. Better yet, got anything stronger?"

"You're the first to ask, so I'm designating you today's official bartender. You know where the bar is. Get to work." I gestured to the other room. "But bring this out with you, please." I handed him a basket of crackers.

My gran had never liked Dad, going back to when he had met and started dating my mother, but her loathing increased with his abandoning us years ago and remaining absent in our lives until recently. Thank goodness Mother had eventually found Hal, her knight in shining tool belt. Mother didn't like to be alone.

Dad, on the other hand, thrived on independence, though occasionally I caught him staring at my mother with a mixture of longing and remorse. Good. Just because I'd forgiven him for leaving us didn't mean I didn't want him to suffer just a little, on occasion, to make up for what he'd put us through in growing up without him.

I poured the cocktail sauce and arranged the shrimp over a bed of ice on a decorative platter.

"Your gran's hogging the baby again," Mother said, coming back into the kitchen. "I barely got to hold her for one minute before Gran grabbed her and ran off to the porch."

"I can bring the dogs in from the backyard. She won't stay on the porch once Bert and Ernie reclaim their domain."

"That's all right." Mother sighed. "I'll help you in the kitchen. Eliana will wear the old lady out before too long and I'll get my chance, unless your father beats me to her. Have you seen her? Kate put her in an adorable little velvet dress. She matches you, actually."

I smiled. I knew something had been telling me to wear the wine velvet this morning. "Perfect."

"So, can I do something?"

"The cheese trays are ready to go. You can bring them out. The turkey has another hour of roasting, so there's time before the rest needs to be done."

"I'm on it." Mother was halfway out of the kitchen with the trays when the doorbell rang.

My heart raced. *Josh.* "I'll get it."

"You're on shrimp duty. Let the kids get it."

Apparently, Spencer got it because I heard the sound of Josh's voice a second later. The mere timbre of his low voice sent a wave of heat right through me.

I tossed the rest of the shrimp on the ring of ice around the cocktail sauce, washed my hands fast, and carried the tray into the living room.

"Josh." A rising blush stung my cheeks. "So nice to see you."

"And this is my daughter," he said, with a tone of pride. And no wonder. She was lovely, about Spence's height with long white-blond hair and glowing green eyes. Even though she wore jeans and an emerald sweater that matched her eyes, she had the air of a fairy princess. "Kyrie, this is Mrs. St. James."

"Wonderful to meet you. Make yourselves at home." A second late, I realized I was standing there holding a platter of shrimp. I offered it up. "Shrimp?"

"Don't mind if I do." Josh grabbed one. I watched as he ate it, taking it between his lush lips, and wished I was the shrimp. My attraction to him had smacked me in the gut like a sucker punch.

Kate made the rest of the introductions while I put the shrimp down in an effort to hide my burning cheeks. Josh greeted my mother and accepted a drink from my dad, probably an Irish whiskey. He looked amazing in a simple Irish knit sweater paired with a perfectly fitted pair of khakis. *Josh.*

"You might get a little warm in that sweater," I said. "I seem to be having a heat wave. I mean, we— we seem to be having a heat wave. It's hot outside. For Thanksgiving."

"Yes." Josh flashed a smile, all perfect white teeth. "I can take it off if I get too hot. I have a lighter shirt on underneath."

My mind snapped to an image of him peeling the sweater off his rugged workman's frame, minus the lighter shirt. I felt the blood rush to my nipples. "I better get back to the kitchen."

I turned and ran before my state of arousal became obvious to all present. In the kitchen, I stuck my head in the freezer, an attempt to restore my senses. I had dinner to make, people to entertain. I couldn't afford to get all light-headed and goofy around a man.

"Can I help with anything?" Josh's voice came from directly behind me.

I straightened up. "Um. No. I think I have it all under control." Except for my raging hormones.

"The kids took Kyrie upstairs to play. They really hit it off, I think."

"Good." I smiled. "That's really good. She's sweet, Josh. I'm glad you could bring her."

"Me, too. She could use a few more friends in my neighborhood. It makes it easier to keep her entertained."

"You two are always welcome to drop by when she's in the neighborhood. And, I mean, when she's not. You're welcome on your own, too."

"Thanks." He stepped closer. I looked into his gaze and instantly became dazzled by the blue. "Good to know."

"Good," I repeated, still dazed.

He stepped closer still. "We should probably go back out, don't you think? Your family might start to worry what we're up to in here."

"Yeah." I laughed lightly, nervous laughter. "My grandmother's got a great imagination. She could come up with all kinds of kinky scenarios."

"Oh." He was almost pressed up against me, my back to the fridge. His lips curved into a grin.

"Maybe I like your grandmother more than I thought."

The heat went straight to my cheeks and, truth be told, to other more delicate parts. Did he want to get kinky *with me*? *Kiss me kiss me kiss me,* I willed silently. Instead, he reached for my hand and laced fingers with mine. "Come on. Let's go join the clan."

Chapter Seventeen

Thanksgiving dinner was one of my favorite meals of the year, but I could hardly eat. I sat at the table and watched Josh eat. I admired his easygoing manners, the way he made conversation with my family. He seemed to know exactly the right things to say to everyone. Kyrie displayed her father's wit and charm and got along with my two as if she belonged with us. Both of them fit right in.

I tried to imagine Nick at the table. He would probably brag about his golf scores instead of asking my grandfather's opinion on putters, as Josh had. Would Nick know that the fastest way to impress my mother was to compliment her on looking too young to have grown daughters, as Josh had pulled off without seeming disingenuous? Gran would find fault with anyone given enough time. And Dad? Nick would probably try to dominate the conversation, while Josh recognized that my father liked to be the loudest voice at the table. Josh worked with guys like my dad, the kind of guys who did what they had to do to make a living, but kept looking for the fastest route to easy street.

"Mom, you should see what Kyrie can do," Spence said between bites of his favorite mashed potatoes. His spoon, Tiffany silver in the pattern I'd picked out for my wedding, clinked against the classic white Lenox plate. "It's amazing."

"What is it you can do, Kyrie?"

"She likes magic tricks," Josh interrupted. "What were you showing the kids, peanut?"

Kyrie blushed. "Nothing much, Dad."

Sarah was apparently too excited to be politely silenced. "She made fire shoot out of her fingertips. It was super cool."

"Fire?" Kate met my gaze over the tea lights, interspersed with silk versions of autumn leaves, that spread across the table between casserole dishes. I knew she wasn't worried about Ellie getting hurt as much as Ellie being the instigator. "You weren't watching Ellie at the time, I hope."

"Don't worry. Ellie was down here with Gran. I can't wait until Shelley comes over again," Spence said. "Kyrie, you have to come back and show my friend Shelley."

"Shelley thinks she's a witch. Ha." Sarah wasn't all that impressed with Shelley. Kyrie, on the other hand, seemed to have won Sarah over.

"No more magic talk," Josh said in an authoritative tone. "Let's just enjoy the meal. Bennie, everything's incredible."

"Especially the corn," Kyrie said. "I love the corn."

Mother beamed proudly. Corn pudding was her special trick, one I could never quite master. "Thank you. I made that, my secret recipe."

"I've got dish duty," Kate called, as if we were still kids fighting over not having to do them. "You can dry and put away."

"Fine," I agreed. "But, Josh, my sister and I can handle it. You sit, watch football with the guys."

"I would rather stick close to you. Besides, I love cleaning up."

"I knew he was a keeper," Gran said.

"Come on, then." Kate grabbed him before I could. "You'll be safe from Gran in there, at least."

I thought about ways I could get rid of my sister. "Kate, how about you watching football? Isn't Marc playing today?"

She turned and glowered at me. "He's out of state."

"Out of state where?"

"Don't they play the Dolphins this week?" Josh asked, bringing an armload of dishes to the sink.

"Yes. And Jill Richards just happened to grow up in South Beach. Her parents still live there." She sank her hands into the running water.

"How do you know this little tidbit?" Josh asked.

"Google," I answered for her. "She did a little Internet investigation of Jill Richards. Kate Googles everyone, and everything."

"Marc hasn't told you he wants to be with her, then? Because as far as I could see, that man only had eyes for you. And little Ellie, of course." Josh assisted as I scraped the leftovers into containers.

"You think?" Kate whipped around so fast that she sent soap bubbles flying into the air.

"I know. He's not interested in Jill Richards."

"Then why is he in Miami now? They don't play until Sunday night."

"It's warm." Josh shrugged. "Maybe he needs some space to figure things out, or the extra time on the field. Who knows?"

"He's playing you," I said, taking half the plates out of Kate's range and placing them in the dishwasher. We would be here all night if she thought she was going to do everything by hand. "He wants you to be jealous so that you catch on to what you're missing. Duh."

"How many times must I tell you?" Josh said. "It's d'oh. Not duh. D'oh."

"But that's so eighth grade." Kate paused as if to consider.

"Josh can't help it. He's into *The Simpsons*," I defended.

"No, I meant the making-me-jealous tactic, so eighth grade."

"Doesn't love turn us all into middle schoolers?" Josh winked at me when he said it. Just as I began to wish more ardently that I could get rid of Kate and have Josh all to myself, the sound of baby cries rent the air.

A second later, my mother ducked in. "Ellie needs a mommy break. There's nothing the rest of us can do to keep her quiet."

Kate dried her hands. "We're almost done, anyway. I'll be right there."

"Go ahead." *Please go.* "We've got it under control."

"We'll need our pie to go," Mother said before ducking out again. "Gran's got a tummyache. She wants to get home."

"All right. Let me get that together for you." I put aside dish drying to disseminate servings of pie and whipped cream in plastic containers.

"You have a nice family," Josh said, placing one last plate in the dishwasher before coming over to help me dole out pie. "Thanks for letting us be a part of your day."

"Some days I'm on the fence but I guess I'll keep them. What's yours like?"

"My family? Passed away."

"What, all of them?"

"My parents had me when they were older. Only child. Mom died of breast cancer and Dad followed not long afterward. I always thought he couldn't take the idea of going on without her."

"It could be true. I can't imagine my grandparents surviving without each other long. But that's so sad. How old were you?"

"Nineteen when Mom passed, twenty for Dad. It was rough."

"You've been on your own a long time."

He shrugged. "I've got friends."

"Yeah, but it's not the same."

His hand met mine as we both reached for the knife to slice the pie. "Sometimes it is. Some friends feel like family."

His eyes smoldered with white-hot intensity. I felt the heat right down into my gut. "Like brothers and sisters?"

My teeth clenched.

"Kate feels like a sister. With you, there's something else."

"Cousin?" I hoped not.

He laughed. "Nothing too closely related, but something close all the same."

"Something close. Like . . ." *Lovers.* The word

formed on my tongue but I couldn't say it out loud. I didn't dare.

The doorbell rang, interrupting our conversation. "Sounds like you have more company," Josh said.

"I'm not expecting anyone."

"No?"

"No." But even as I said it, I knew who was at the door.

Seconds later, Nick's voice rang out as he introduced himself around the room.

I expected Josh to be unhappy with the new arrival, but I wasn't prepared to see a look of hurt on his face, as if he'd been betrayed. "Josh, I didn't invite him. I haven't heard from him in days."

"That's fine. I knew you two were seeing each other, so it shouldn't exactly take me by surprise. We should be going, anyway. I'm not sure if Kyrie has homework."

"She has all weekend. Why don't you stay a bit longer?" Josh's reaction affected me more than I suspected it would. In that moment, I knew I didn't feel for Nick what I'd been beginning to feel for Josh. Not even close. "Please stay. I don't want you to leave."

"We'll stay for pie. Kyrie's having a good time upstairs and I don't want to tear her away just yet."

"Thank you." I reached out and squeezed his hand. Bold, perhaps, but I wanted him to know how truly welcome he was in my home, even with Nick Angelos around.

"You should go say hi," Josh said.

"Let him make his own way. He can be very charming. I'm sure Gran will love him."

"Maybe he'll cure her indigestion. Considering

his magic healing touch and all." Josh made no
effort to hide the contempt in his voice.

"Funny. Would you like to wear this whipped
cream?" I shook the can as if it were a weapon.

"I dare you."

"You're bluffing."

His eyes sparked like glass in the sun. "I double
dare you."

That did it. I reached out and sprayed. All over
his cheek. I couldn't get close enough to do his
nose.

"Now you've done it." He chased me around the
butcher block, caught me, and disarmed me. He
held me up against the counter, the spray poised
and ready to deliver a whipped cream mustache.

"No, please." I laughed so hard I nearly ached.
And then I felt him, hard against my hip, and I
ached in another way entirely. We stayed together,
both of us breathing in synch, careful and slow.
"Please."

He leaned in with a wicked smile and I shut my
eyes and closed the distance.

"I thought you might come out to greet me. I
wondered what was keeping you," Nick interrupted.

Josh exhaled loudly and stepped away from me.
"Good evening, Nick."

"Hi," I said meekly.

"I'm sorry I didn't return your phone calls." He
approached and the weird tingly feeling came over
me. Suddenly I was more uncertain than ever about
my feelings for him. What, exactly, did I want with
Nick? A chance to at least find out where we could
be headed, just more mind-erasing sex, or a clean
break? "I've been out of town on business."

From the corner of my eye, I could see Josh stroking the back of his neck. I recognized that gesture in Josh. It was the same gesture he made when I'd pounded nails in crooked when I first volunteered at Habitat for Humanity, shortly after Patrick had died. I hadn't seen that gesture in a while.

As if aware of Josh's annoyance, feeding off it, Nick leaned in and kissed me, a quick brush of the lips. Desire flooded my bloodstream, as effective as a shot in the arm. Nick worked like a drug on my system. He did it on purpose, I guessed. He needed to get close to me to have an excuse to stay close to Kate and Ellie. The theory began to make sense. *I was being used.* At least now I knew it, but in a way, I'd been using him, too.

I took a step away from him. Wanting him was the last thing I needed, next to giving in. "I have to get pie boxed up for my grandparents, Mother, and Hal. They're getting ready to go. Why don't you go out to the living room and I'll join you shortly?"

The eyebrow arched. I'd surprised him. Clearly, he wasn't used to the idea of my taking control.

"Very well." He turned, walked by Josh, and headed to the other room.

"We'll always have pie," Josh cracked, once Nick was gone.

I burst into laughter. Again, I felt a rush of emotion for him—no chemical tricks or druglike jolts to my system. I really liked being with Josh. We finished dishing out the pie in companionable silence, and then he helped me carry the containers in a bag out to my family.

"Here you go," I said, handing the bag to Mother. The kids came down to say the obligatory good-byes and headed straight back up to the game room. My dad decided to cut out early with the rest of the gang. After they'd all gone, it was just Josh and Nick with the kids, Kate, and me. We settled down in the living room.

"It's cold in here now." I hugged my arms. "All of a sudden."

"The temperature dropped outside," Nick said. I caught Kate's gaze over his shoulder where she sat cradling a now sleeping Ellie.

"Let's light a fire," Josh suggested. "I'll go get some kindling."

"Great idea." The wood was stacked and waiting as Josh had arranged on his last visit.

As soon as he stepped out on to the porch, Nick stepped up to the hearth. A second later, a fire blazed.

"How did you do that so fast?" I asked, amazed.

"I have my ways." He smiled, and began to unbutton and roll up his cuffs as if getting comfortable. He planned to stay awhile.

Kate met my gaze. Perhaps it was good that Nick showed up after all. If he stayed late enough, we would be able to clear the air once Josh and Kyrie went home for the night and the kids went to bed. But I was in no hurry for Josh to leave.

"Oh." Josh returned with an armload of small sticks and papers. "The fire's lit. How'd you do that?"

"I have a way with fire." Nick's lips curled into a grin. "Sorry to put you out."

"I'm not put out." Josh smiled as if accepting a challenge. "Your flame will die down eventually and I'll be here to stoke it to a roaring inferno."

Standing between both men, I turned to meet

Josh's gaze, but the fire gave off a sudden flare, causing everyone except Nick to jump.

It died down as the kids bounded downstairs seconds later.

"Dad, can we have some pie?" Kyrie asked, as if she'd been designated official spokesman for the group. It was then that I noticed. I looked from Kyrie to Nick and back again, and everything clicked into place. Nick had said that he had an affair with Josh's friend Molly—Kyrie's mother. At last I knew why Josh hated Nick so much beyond the fact that they'd dated the same woman. Kyrie didn't look one bit like Josh, but Kyrie was the spitting image of Nick.

Oh my God. Nick was Kyrie's father. And Josh knew. Suddenly I realized that Kyrie's magic trick earlier was much more than magic. Did Josh know about her special abilities? If he did, then he must have known about Nick. Why hadn't he done more to warn me?

Of course, it hadn't been his place to warn me. Josh knew me better than I even imagined, well enough to know how I would resent unsolicited advice and that I needed space to make my own mistakes. Nick was more the type to steamroll along, believing he knew best about everything. Much like everyone in my life had ever done, if truth be told. Kate, Patrick, they were always looking out for me, trying to protect me. But Josh had figured me out without my having to say a word. *He knew me.* And the realization stole my breath clean away.

Was Nick even aware of his connection to Kyrie? Standing right in front of her, would he not figure it out? Or was he truly that caught up in himself that he failed to see the obvious, the girl who looked just like him, standing right before his eyes. Then again, maybe it wasn't as apparent as I feared. Kate, unaware that Josh and Nick had both been with Kyrie's mother, didn't seem to notice the resemblance.

Josh narrowed his gaze and looked from Nick to Kyrie and back again. It was clear he wanted to get Kyrie out of the room before anyone was any the wiser.

"Maybe we should take that pie to go, Kyrie," Josh said. "We have plans for the morning, remember?"

"Can't we stay longer? I'm having fun with Spence and Sarah."

As much as I wanted Josh to stay, I knew the best thing to do was get him out of the house. Fast. I stepped in to help. "Kyrie, maybe you can come back some other time. Soon. We have to make it soon."

"Definitely soon." Josh looked at me curiously, as if trying to guess what I knew.

"Call me later," I said to Josh, loud enough for Nick to hear. "I would really like to continue our conversation from the kitchen."

"All right," Josh agreed, then made his good-byes. My heart surged as I watched him leave. I felt connected with him in a way that I never had before, in a way that I could never imagine connecting with Nick. I couldn't wait to see him again.

"Alone at last," Nick said, stretching his arm over my shoulder as we sat together on the living room couch. The kids were settled in their rooms. Kate had gone up to change the baby.

"Alone for a minute. Kate's probably coming right back down." I felt torn between wanting her to come back and wishing she would stay away. I liked the warmth of his body next to mine, the heat beginning to build inside me. But I had to stay focused on getting some answers.

"Your sister wouldn't begrudge us a little happiness. She knows what it's like to be in love."

"That's just it." I turned, shrugging his arm away. "Are we in love, Nick? Are we falling in love? Do we even really know each other?"

He took a deep breath, met my gaze, and took my hand. "I don't know what it is, Bennie. I've never felt this way before. I've never really felt, honestly. It's all so new to me. You have no idea what you do to me. I think of you all the time."

His eyes glittered, deep green and filled with an unmistakable tenderness. I had no idea that I'd had such an impact on him. "I'm surprised. I really don't know what to say."

"You don't have to say anything. Just know that I'm not simply enjoying our physical relationship. I like you."

"What do you like?"

"I haven't really thought about it, honestly." He shook his head, perhaps a little taken aback by the question. "I like hearing you laugh. It's so strange for me to hear laughter, and not just superficial noises, but a genuine lightness of being. I feel like laughing more when I'm with you. You're helping me learn what it is to be happy."

Wow. I didn't know he had it in him. Against my better judgment, I believed him.

"That's one of the sweetest things anyone has ever said to me, Nick." I pressed his palm between my hands, relishing his proximity. "Thank you. I

wish I could say that I shared your feelings. It's
not that I don't, entirely. It's that I feel I hardly know
you. As if there is something you're keeping from
me. There is. Isn't there?"

His eyes widened a little. "I can't deny it."

"There's really no way to say this but to just come
out with it. Forgive me if it sounds a little crazy.
Are you . . ." I hesitated. It sounded *a lot* crazy. "Are
you a god?"

His emerald eyes gleamed with apparent pleasure. "I knew you would figure me out eventually."

"Hermes?"

He pulled me into his arms and kissed the base
of my throat, right where my pulse went wild. I
could feel his desire for me. Despite my best effort
to avoid wanting him, I burned in places I didn't
want to burn. I allowed my head to roll back and
gave in to the exquisite sensation of his mouth on
my skin.

"That's it. It's hard to resist the power of a god in
your bed, isn't it? It was only a matter of time before
you guessed the truth."

A god. I'd discussed it with Kate, but a chill went
right through me at the reality of being touched by
a myth. A god? Could it really be?

His lips met mine. His hand pressed at the small of
my back, melding me to him as his tongue coursed
over mine, delving deep, making me hunger for
more, for all of him.

"No mere mortal could do the things I do to you."

An image of Josh popped into my head, and I
pushed Nick away. "You don't think so? You may
think too highly of yourself."

He grinned crookedly. "I don't think so. Give me

the chance to prove it. I guarantee you'll never forget it."

I smiled. God or man, he'd probably already proven all he needed to prove in the bedroom. But no need to feed his ego. "Nick, er, Hermes, no. Not now. We need to talk. I need to know why you've come. Is it Ellie? On that first day, did you just happen to show up at the right place, right time, or were you looking for me on purpose? To get closer to Kate and Ellie?"

I hated even saying it out loud. But I had to know the truth.

"I knew." He pulled his hand back, ran it through his hair, and then faced me again, those emerald eyes smoldering. "I'm sorry. I never intended to hurt you. It seemed that getting to know you was the easiest way to get to Kate and the baby without detection. And the fact that I was wildly attracted to you merely sweetened the task."

I nodded, avoiding eye contact. I wasn't sure I could look at him and not melt on the spot, to heck with my resolve. "I see. And my sister and the baby? Why do you need to be close to them?"

"Yes, why? Why are you here? Who sent you? And why did Ares send his birds?" Kate's voice came from behind me. I spun to face her, then turned back to Hermes, eager for his answer. No sign of Ellie. I assumed she fell asleep upstairs and Kate put her down for the night, safely tucked away so that she could join the conversation.

"Just a friendly hello between brothers." Nick shrugged as if the birds really weren't a big deal. Perhaps to him they weren't. "He never intended to hurt anyone. Bennie, you were never in any real danger. You know that, don't you?"

I shrugged. Not really.

"And what about Hades? Why did he send you?" Kate asked.

"Is it a crime for him to check up on you? He loves you, Kate. He keeps watch."

She kept a poker face, but I knew how she must be feeling. What if Patrick could keep in touch with me from the grave? What wouldn't I give to know he could still be with me, in any way, even if I couldn't be with him?

And yet I could hardly deny that I'd enjoyed my time with Nick, and that I was looking forward to a chance to get to know other men. *I'd moved on.* The reality felt suddenly stark and painful. But then, not so bad after all. I'd moved on, but I would always love Patrick, too. Loving someone new didn't mean losing all I'd had. How could I make Kate understand it?

As if Nick read my mind—and now that I knew who he was, I couldn't deny that he probably did—he addressed the issue with Kate. "He let you go to have a full life, Kate. Not so that you could keep clinging to the idea that you will be with him again."

She revealed her emotion in the form of a single tear running down her cheek. I wanted to hug her so badly, to tell her it was okay to cry, but that seemed to show vulnerability somehow. Kate wasn't one to lose it in front of anyone but her very closest confidants. My eyes welled up for her as I thought about what it must mean for her to know that Hades was looking out for her.

"And what about him? Is he supposed to just

watch over us from afar? Know that I'm happy without him? How could I do that to him?" Kate bit her lip.

Nick stood, closed the distance, and took her hands in his. "Your happiness is a balm to him, Kate. Watching Ellie, the life you created together, is his greatest joy. You should see him when she smiles."

"Really?" Kate's eyes shone with the tears she wouldn't let fall. "He watches her?"

"To a nauseating extent."

I couldn't see Nick's eyes with his back to me as he faced Kate, but I was pretty sure he rolled them.

"And he knows that Marc is good for you both. He's no fool, my uncle."

Kate shook her head. "I pity the sap who calls him one."

I shuddered. I think I'd called him worse when I believed he'd abandoned my pregnant sister.

"He did send me to look after you," Nick confessed, turning to face me. "But who could tell that along the way I would end up smitten with your sister? I'm not sure what it means, but I would like to explore these feelings more, Bennie. If you'll give me a chance."

When he put it like that, it was hard to say no. Still, I had more questions. "But what about Ellie? If Hades can watch out for Kate and Ellie from afar, why did he need to send you?"

"For more firsthand information. A closer look." Nick had answers at the ready, but he seemed credible. "He wants to know how she's growing, what she's like to be around. I can tell him once I learn more. I'd like more time with you all."

His eyes held a look of sincerity. I wished I knew more about the Greek gods. I only knew what I'd learned as an English major. All accounts of the so-called mythical gods were contradictory as far as their trustworthiness went.

"It's all right with me. Kate?" I looked at my sister. She still seemed so unhappy. No doubt from all the talk about Hades.

"Yes, fine." She waved the question off. "I'm sorry. I can't stop thinking about Marc and Jill Richards. I need to call him. He needs to know how I feel."

"Let me make a suggestion," Nick said. "Do it in person. Let me make a call and I can have a jet waiting. Your sister's here to watch the baby. Go meet your Marc in Miami. It's what Hades would want for you."

"You really think so?" Kate's nose crinkled in disbelief, but she looked so much happier, as if an invisible weight had lifted.

"I know so. Go. Lead the life you're meant to live."

Nick had given Kate such a gift, more than he could ever know. I appreciated him for it. But did my feelings run any deeper than that? I thought of Josh, who had been the first to suggest I let Kate and Marc have some time away alone. Josh had the good intentions, but Nick had the power to help make it happen. Both men impressed me with their thoughtfulness toward my sister. But I couldn't have both men. Which one did I really want?

Chapter Eighteen

The next morning, I'd just finished cleaning up after breakfast when the phone rang. The kids were upstairs keeping Ellie busy. I answered the phone, and my heart beat a tattoo at the sound of the voice on the other end. *Josh.*

"I'm sorry. I realize I bailed last night before we got any work done on those invitations. How about I take you to breakfast and then we can get to work?"

"Ooh, I would love to go but bad timing." Damn. I *would* love to go. "Early risers here. We've all had our breakfast. Besides, I finished the invitations last night. Ellie kept me company."

"You did them all on your own? Now I feel like a colossal jerk."

"No, don't. I'll let you lick the stamps."

"I hate to break it to you, but they have those sticky stamps now. You don't have to lick them."

"I know, but I wanted to make you feel extra useful. Besides, the kids wouldn't mind seeing Kyrie again." And I wouldn't mind seeing Josh. "How about you two come over for lunch? We could use some help in getting rid of the leftovers."

"Lunch sounds good."

"A man's got to eat."

"I would rather take you out, though. I want to make up for the way I left you last night. I didn't mean to run out so fast."

"Take me out another time. I'm watching Ellie for a few days, anyway, so getting out might have to wait. I won't let you off so easy, don't worry."

He laughed.

"Besides"—my voice lowered with new seriousness—"after last night, I think we have a lot to talk about, Josh."

I heard him sigh. "You think you have it all figured out."

"I think I know more than you realize. And there are a few things you should know, too. For Kyrie's sake."

"I may know more than *you* realize. It would probably help to compare notes, but we'll have to be careful. I don't want to risk little ears overhearing things that may be too big for them to comprehend at this time."

"I understand. How does noon work for you?"

"Works. I'll see you then."

A shock of excitement raced along my spine, fanning out into my central nervous system. It was the kind of charge I'd felt for Nick from the start, only there was something more to it, a certain sweetness spreading with it. I'd thought all I wanted with men for now was a good time, some great sex. But maybe I really wanted more. Maybe I needed more. Being with someone who knew me and

loved me for all that I am held tremendous appeal.
I never imagined I would get a second chance to
have all that again after Patrick, but I could see
myself sharing a future with Josh. More than seeing
it, I felt myself *wanting* it. Wanting him.

But what did Josh want? I had the impression
that he was attracted to me, too, but beyond that, I
had no idea. At last, I felt ready to find out.

As the hall clock with Westminster chimes, a wedding present from Kate, struck noon, Josh's truck
pulled into the driveway. Punctual. I hoped it
meant he was as eager to see me as I was to see him.

I'd just put a sleeping Ellie down in the Portacrib.
Bert and Ernie followed me to the door.

"Look, Dad, it's Bert and Ernie!" I smiled at Kyrie's
enthusiastic greeting for my dogs, rocked once again
by her resemblance to Nick. She dropped down on
her knees and petted their wriggling bodies. "How
can you tell the difference?"

"It's easy once you get to know them," I said.
"Ernie has more black on his face and tail. Bert's
tail is only black at the very tip."

"Oh yeah."

"Hi, Josh. Come on in."

"Hey." He moved inside and handed me a bag. "I
brought some bread to go with the turkey for sand-
wiches. Fresh baked."

I looked him over. He wore his usual work boots
and faded jeans with a long-sleeved cotton shirt,
but somehow his rugged regular guy style seemed
so appealing.

"Incredible. Thanks so much." I peeked in. It

smelled heavenly. "Kyrie, you can go on up and play with the kids if you want. They're in the game room."

"Can the dogs come, too?"

"If you can convince them to follow you." They didn't usually venture upstairs if I was downstairs, but they dutifully followed where Kyrie led as if entranced. It reminded me of Nick's easy command of them when he'd stayed the night.

"So much for loyalty." I turned to Josh. "How about a beer? Or is it too early to start drinking?"

"It's five o'clock somewhere. But I've got a bottle of Beaujolais in the car. It will go better with the leftovers."

"Do you always come equipped with the appropriate wine?"

He blushed. "It's a new hobby. I took a wine-tasting course last year and really got into it."

"Patrick would have liked you," I blurted out before I could stop myself. Mentioning the deceased husband probably wasn't the way to a new man's heart. Still, it made me feel warmer to know that Patrick would have approved. Like Josh, I didn't think Patrick would be all that impressed with Nick Angelos.

"I wish I'd met him," Josh said, smoothing over my flub with his easy charm. "We probably would have had a lot in common."

"Probably."

"You're not really going to make me lick stamps, are you?"

I laughed. "No. I have the sticky stamps."

The invitations were addressed and stacked on

the kitchen table. "I can't believe you did all those last night."

"I had a lot on my mind. Plus, as I said, Ellie was wide awake." I opened the fridge and took out two beers. "Save the wine for lunch. We'll eat in a little while. Let the kids have some fun first."

"Where's your sister?"

"Miami." I put the bottles on the counter, popped them open, poured them into glasses, and handed one to Josh. "Nick convinced her to go meet up with Marc. He even offered the Glendower Enterprises jet. How about that?"

Josh reached up to knead the back of his neck. Not a good sign. "Are you sure it's not a setup? Like she's going to get to Miami and find Marc getting cozy at the hotel with Jill?"

"I don't think so." Now I started to worry. What if it was? "Nick seemed very encouraging."

"Of course. He probably told her it was exactly what his uncle wanted."

"You don't think it is? You don't think Owen would want her to be happy?"

He put down his beer, took my hands in his, and led me to the kitchen table. "Ben, I know about Owen. *All* about him. He's a good guy, despite popular belief. I'm sure he really does want your sister to be happy. And if he sent Nick, he must trust him. But that doesn't mean I do. I've been through too much with the man, er, whatever he is."

I felt my eyes widen. "So you really do know? About Hades?"

"Everything. I'd like to tell you how, but now is not the time. Suffice it to say, I worked for him long enough to learn things I would rather not know.

But I'm glad I do know, because it helped explain a few things once Kyrie was born."

"I'm sure it did. I'm worried about Ellie, Josh. She's showing some unique abilities, shall we say?"

"Try not to worry. Kyrie has always been able to control hers, and she's a sweet kid. We've gotten this far without anyone noticing anything odd."

"That's encouraging." His hands were still on mine. I didn't want to move and risk losing contact.

"I don't know what possessed her to go showing off the other day in front of your two. That's just not like her. She knows how important it is to stay under the radar."

"Maybe she has a little thing for Spencer? I saw the way she looked at him the other night at the dinner table. They're growing up, Josh. All he talks about is Shelley Miles. Girls are capable of anything when they want to get a guy's attention."

"You're probably right. She's been talking about coming back here ever since we left."

"Good. I'm sure they're having fun up there. No loud banging."

"Nothing burning down." Josh agreed.

"Come on. Let's take the drinks to the other room so I can be close if Ellie wakes."

We walked out and looked her over in the crib. Sound asleep, no blinking toys, no sign of the supernatural.

"How did it start for Kyrie? When did you notice?"

"She was just a baby. She started making things light up in her crib. Things that weren't supposed to light up, like stuffed bears and books, that sort of thing."

My mouth went dry. "I've seen Ellie do that with her Noah's Ark toys."

He put his arm around my waist, his palm resting at the small of my back. It felt right. "She'll do just fine with it. Don't worry."

"I can't help it. There's so much to worry about when they're small as it is."

"True. But your family seems to turn out strong women."

I laughed. "Except for me, yeah."

"What do you mean, except for you? You roof houses, install siding, and single-handedly organized the social event of the season."

"That remains to be seen." I shoved my hands in my jeans pockets, more to resist touching him than out of modesty. I caught myself remembering those biking pants. Grabbing his ass would probably reveal more than I was ready to let on.

"You're a single mother. A working mother. I can't forget the way you went to town on that roof last week."

"I do have a way with a hammer." I smiled at him and got caught, again, in the pull of the too-blue gaze. I never wanted to look away. I liked the way he saw me with those eyes. "Could you do me a favor?"

"Sure."

"Take me shopping. One day when we don't have the kids around." I needed to take back a few things so that I had more money to spend on the kids. I still loved the red Dolce & Gabbana boots, but somehow they just weren't me anymore.

"Sounds like fun. I could still use your advice on what to buy for Kyrie, anyway."

"It takes a brave man to venture into the mall after Black Friday."

"I'm up for the challenge. I told you I love to shop."

"I know. It seems too good to be true."

"There's no such thing as too good to be true. That's just an excuse for refusing to believe that we deserve the best out of life."

"Wow, Josh, that's pretty deep. How'd you get to be such a philosopher?"

"It came with the premature gray." He ran his hands through his hair. I wanted to follow suit, but didn't have the nerve. "Plus, after years of believing that I wasn't good enough for the life I wanted to lead, I'm beginning to realize that I do deserve the best."

"You're a good man. I'm sure you're right."

"And I'm willing to face any challenge to make it happen." He squared his sturdy jaw.

"So what's standing in your way?" I shifted a little closer to him.

"The usual. Pride." His smile went straight to his eyes, making them sparkle like light off broken glass.

"Pride?" I had to laugh. Josh was all about pride— pride in his work, in how he lived—but it hardly seemed an impediment. More like a driving force. "How is pride in your way?"

"Because if I take a chance and things don't go my way, it could be really damaging."

"Pfft. Is that all?" I smiled at him. "Take a chance. You're not getting any younger, you know."

He put his hand over his heart and recoiled. "Ach, woman. How you wound me."

"What? Me? If I knew it was that easy, I might have tried it a long time ago when you wouldn't let me get my hands on your power tools. But I would regret it now, of course."

"Getting your hands on my tools?" He arched a brow.

"No, wounding you. I've come to appreciate you." At last, I risked reaching out and ruffling that thick thatch of hair.

"So I'm an acquired taste?"

"Something like that." All at once, I realized that his hand was still at the small of my back and we were standing closer than ever. I had a feeling I was about to acquire a taste firsthand. My pulse went wild.

His lids lowered over his amazing eyes. His face came closer, closer still. And then his lips were on mine, his hand splayed on my back urging me closer, demanding a response. I tilted my head back and opened my mouth to him. His tongue, molten ore, slicked between my lips. I drew him in.

My emotions, a river rushing, flowed with the kiss. My body pressed to his, my feet followed as he led us back across the room toward the chair, my delicate wingback. Even as we collapsed into it, his knees buckling, me landing astride him, barely enough space for us both, the kiss continued building until the river crashed through the dam.

Gasping for air, I pulled away first. I didn't want to stop to breathe, but nature forced me. "Wow."

"Wow," he repeated.

I stroked his face, slightly rough with new stubble, my gaze trained on his. His eyes, crystalline pools, refreshed me. It was different than the way I'd felt with Nick, godly tingle aside. Kissing Josh filled me with new awe in a way that took me by surprise and very nearly overwhelmed me. Looking into his eyes, I felt a deeper connection beyond mere physical attraction. My heart constricted in a way that nearly made me ache.

His hand remained at the small of my back. I shifted my hips slightly, inadvertently grinding into him in a way that made us both more aware of our desires.

"We can't do this now," he said in a hoarse whisper. "Not here."

"Not with the children upstairs and the baby asleep in the room." I backed up off him. How could we have gone so far with the kids in the house? "Have we lost our minds?"

He laughed. "What a way to go."

I cleared my throat. "Yeah. I think I need some water. It's probably too early for alcohol after all."

"Good thinking."

"Let's make lunch. Then we can call the kids down." Safety in numbers. There was too big a risk of getting carried away now that the floodgates were opened.

"Great thinking." Josh beat me to the kitchen by a few strides.

"I'll get the turkey. You slice the bread." I handed him a serrated knife and pointed him toward the butcher block.

"By the way, you were right." He turned to me as I headed toward the fridge. "I'm glad I took a chance."

Heat rushed to my cheeks. "I'm glad, too. I hope you take more of them in the future."

"I plan to," he said in a deep-throated husk that made my toes curl. "Maybe some other time, without so many others in the mix. We need to go out.

Not as parents or coworkers, but as consenting adults. Bennie, I want to be alone with you."

I watched his mouth form the words and felt the sweet tightness take hold inside of me. I wanted so badly to kiss him on that lush, perfect mouth. But I heard footsteps pounding downstairs and toward the kitchen, so instead I only answered with a quiet "I would like that. Very much."

Our eyes met for a lingering second before the door burst open and kids rushed in.

"We're hungry," Spencer said. "Can we help make lunch?"

"I think we have it under control," Josh answered, faster to recover his senses than I was.

"You can set the table," I said, as if surfacing from a daze. "In the living room. Use the good china."

"The good stuff?" Sarah crinkled her nose. "But we just put it away after Thanksgiving."

"The good stuff," I affirmed authoritatively. "It's not much trouble to get it out again. This is a celebration."

"What are we celebrating?" Spencer and Sarah looked at each other, as if perplexed.

"New friends. We have Josh and Kyrie here for the afternoon. I think it calls for a celebration."

"Okay." Sarah shrugged. "Kind of a strange reason to celebrate. We've known Josh for a little while now."

"Hey, I'm new here. I'm worth celebrating." Kyrie tossed her head regally, a princess with an imaginary crown. Josh laughed at his daughter's antics. I tried not to think about how much the gesture reminded me of Nick.

"Absolutely," I agreed, grabbing my water bottle

and raising it. "To Josh and Kyrie, our wonderful new friends."

"To us." Josh clinked his bottle with mine and met my gaze. I hoped the children didn't notice the blush that spread across my cheeks.

We celebrated all afternoon well into the evening, when Josh and Kyrie finally had to go home.

"I'll call you about that shopping trip," Josh reminded me on his way out. I'd almost forgotten I'd asked him to take me. "And then maybe we can plan an evening, just the two of us."

"Just the two of us," I agreed, hoping it would happen sooner rather than later.

Once I was settled on the couch bouncing a freshly clean Ellie on my lap, the doorbell rang. Instinct, and that pesky tingle, told me it was Nick.

Ellie gave a loud giggle as I bobbled her over in my arms to answer. Her laughter made me smile even as I answered the door to the number-one obstacle between me getting cozy with Josh Brandon.

"Nick. Hi."

"If it isn't the little darling." He smiled at Ellie, but there was something of a sneer in his tone. She clung to me under Nick's scrutiny, as if she, too, sensed something amiss. "How is she coping in her mother's absence?"

"We get along just fine, don't we?" I held her close and tried to stay a comforting force against the new distraction. "Kate called from her hotel. The flight was just fine. She sends her thanks, again. Marc was on his way to pick her up. Fingers crossed it all goes as well."

Ellie put her hands to my lips and babbled something that seemed downright engaging, if only I understood baby babble.

"Fingers crossed." Nick made the gesture in agreement. "Can I hold her?"

"Um." I looked at her as if she could respond. To my surprise, she smiled and reached out to Nick. "Sure. Maybe she likes you."

"I have that effect on women." He said it with a wink, but he reached for Ellie as if he were reaching for a bag of something vile and slimy.

She knew it, too, because she settled in his arms, flashed him her sweetest baby smile, and proceeded to spit up all over his no-doubt expensive silk tie.

"Buggers." He shifted and cradled her forward so that the *rest* of her drool hit the floor instead of him.

"Buggers? Is that what passes as a curse at Mount Olympus these days?"

"Hardly. What passes as a curse wouldn't suit human ears. I had to tone it down a bit to fit in."

"Right." I looked at Ellie. I could have sworn she winked at me.

"You could do something," he said, still fighting to hold Ellie and avoid spreading the mess.

"Who am I to interrupt a family reunion?" He glared. I smiled. "Fine, come to the kitchen. We'll get you cleaned up."

In the kitchen, I lifted Ellie from his arms, wiped her face, and settled her in her Exersaucer.

He ripped his tie off, tossed it in the trash, and started to undo his shirt collar.

"A dry cleaner could probably get that stain out."

"And go through all the bother? No, thank you."

"You have minions."

"I also have money to burn. I hated that tie, anyway. It was a gift from one of the Glendower Enterprises sales team."

"Minions give gifts?"

"They're not all minions." He stripped his shirt off to reveal his glorious, bronzed chest.

My mouth went dry. I tried not to gape, but it was hard to hide my awe at his physical perfection. His lips curled up in the wolfish grin as he prowled closer to me, prepared to take advantage of my momentary lapse of judgment.

"No, Hermes." I pushed him away with one hand, then struggled to fight the urge to keep my hand, and the rest of me, pressed against him. Whether it was a chemical or natural aphrodisiac he exuded, it offered a potent temptation. On contact, the blood rushed to my core. "Why are you here?"

"Is it a crime to want to be close to you? I told you I wanted a chance to prove myself. You said you would give me a chance."

"True."

"I know you have the baby and Kate's not here to sit. I thought it was a good chance to combine business with pleasure."

"Business?"

"Of getting to know Eliana so I can report on her welfare to my uncle. The pleasure is in spending more time with you."

"You make it sound as if he's gearing up for a custody battle. Oh." My stomach lurched. "No. He couldn't. He wouldn't, would he?"

"Relax, love." He pressed my hands warmly between his. "Hades gave Kate the gift of life so that she would always hold part of him near. Why would he have any desire to take Eliana back?"

"Why would he? You tell me."

He let go of my hands to stroke my hair, at my temples. "So suspicious, Bennie. When did you become such a cynic?"

"I'm not." I pulled back. "I guess I'm just getting used to all this god-on-earth stuff. And those Stymphalian birds? The stuff of nightmares."

"Let me sleep here at your side. I'll protect you."

"You said they weren't coming back."

"You can't blame a god for trying." The wolfish grin made its second appearance of the day.

"As much as you think about sex, you might as well be mortal."

"You've read the myths. Not far from the truth in most cases, I'm afraid."

"I did read them. You *did* rustle cattle, you naughty god."

"Apollo's. He deserved it. I probably shouldn't have killed so many of them, though. I was a reckless youth."

"And you first created fire? Impressive."

"And music. Humanity owes me some heavy debts."

"I hope you're not holding your breath." I rolled my eyes and tried not to laugh. He liked my laughter. I didn't want to encourage him.

"I may be satisfied to earn some gratitude from one human in particular." He raised a brow and took me in his arms. Not expecting his move, I let out a startled sigh. He answered by finding just the right spot on my neck with his mouth.

Instead of melting on the spot, as usual, I stiffened.

"You're falling for that Brandon fellow, aren't you?"

"Maybe I am." I couldn't deny it.

He shrugged. "I can handle a little competition."

"It may be too late."

"Then I have my work cut out for me. I'm thinking dinner. Chinese takeway? Then family time."

"Family time?"

"Whatever it is you do to spend time with the children. I want to be a part of it. I've never really spent time with my family. Zeus isn't the most doting of fathers."

"I can imagine. I guess." It seemed weird to even consider it. I still had an image of Laurence Olivier in the role of Zeus from *War of the Titans*, the cheesy eighties film that starred Harry Hamlin. It made me think of a younger Laurence Olivier in *Wuthering Heights*. *Hot*. Still, not quite as hot as a shirtless Nick Angelos in my kitchen. "After dinner, we're gathering in front of the television to watch Christmas specials."

He winced. "Delightful."

"You're not into it. I can tell." I wanted to give him the chance to get closer to Ellie, and I was grateful for what he'd done for Kate, but I wasn't sure about spending a domestic kind of evening with Nick Angelos. Not now that I had growing feelings for Josh. If a little Christmas cheer in the form of musical cartoons chased him away, so much the better.

"I'm willing to try," he said, rallying to the challenge.

"That's the spirit."

"As long as it's not that Grinch one. Those Whos down in Whoville get on my last nerve."

It figured. "Not the Grinch one. *The Year Without*

a Santa Claus, I believe followed by *Santa Claus Is Coming to Town*."

"I'm not familiar."

"You will be," I promised. *Threatened?* "You're in for a treat."

Chapter Nineteen

Late Sunday, I picked Kate up at the airport and drove her and Ellie home. Kate was glowing from the romantic weekend with Marc.

It was official now. They were a couple. I couldn't be happier for her. And yet I was slightly sad to think of losing her near constant company. Marc, when he wasn't out of town preparing for a game, was a capable and attentive coparent, rendering my services less necessary in busy Kate's life. But as long as we were in the thick of football season, I would still have her to myself now and again.

"Isn't Marc still in Miami?" I asked.

"The game was just about to start when I left. I have to meet new clients tomorrow. Besides, I ached being away from Ellie. It's amazing that a tiny little being can come into your life and affect you so much. I've never loved like this before. I mean, Ellie. But Marc, too." She reclined on her wraparound sofa with Ellie on her lap.

"I understand. No one loves quite like a mother loves her child."

I sat in the overstuffed chair in front of her gas fireplace and thought about Josh, how he would scoff that gas isn't the same as wood. I smiled.

"Marc's pretty close. He misses her so much."

"He loves you both."

"When I told him how I felt, he cried."

"And Jill Richards?"

She clucked her tongue against the roof of her mouth. "Total nonissue. Marc was trying to get me jealous, but apparently she had designs on him and started some rumors in the press to fuel the fire. The second I met her up close and personal, I knew there was no way Marc would go for her. Too yappy. Like a human Yorkshire terrier."

We laughed. "Marc hates small dogs. He barely tolerates Bert and Ernie."

"He loves your pugs," Kate defended. "He says they're big dogs in small bodies. But he wants us to get a black Lab or a golden retriever."

"Figures."

"Not right away. Maybe when Ellie's a little older and football's behind him."

"Does he ever talk about retiring? With his knee trouble?"

"I think he has a few good years left for the NFL. As long as the Patriots will have him. I can't imagine him changing teams when he's so happy here in Boston."

"Glad to hear it." Selfish, perhaps, but I didn't want to think about Kate and Ellie moving away any time soon.

"How are things for you with Josh and Nick? You seemed to be torn between two lovers on Thanksgiving Day."

I sighed. "Josh isn't my lover." Yet. "But I wouldn't mind heading that way. I think about him all the time lately. Except when I'm with Nick, though sometimes even then."

"And Nick? Where do you stand? You can't forget what he is, Ben."

"I haven't forgotten. I just don't know what it means, entirely. He makes me feel good when I'm with him."

"And when you're not?"

"I can forget him. That's what tells me it isn't anything lasting between us. We have sizzling romantic chemistry, but that's about it."

"Can't downplay the importance of sizzling romantic chemistry."

"But with Josh, I think I could have both. He kissed me yesterday and my heart skipped some beats. Nick Angelos may have some godlike skills to his advantage, but Josh may not need any advantages. No one has made me feel quite like Josh did with only one kiss."

"Potent." Kate cuddled her daughter close and seemed to consider. "Keep in mind that you're free to play around a little. No one said you have to jump right into an exclusive relationship. Give yourself some time to explore."

"Right now I feel torn between naughty and nice. I want the one who can make me feel a little of both. It might be Josh. I'm just not sure Josh is the type to hang around long while I investigate my options."

"If he cares enough, he will. And if not, his loss. You married Patrick when you were both so young, Bennie. I don't think you ever dated anyone else."

"Not really. A few trips to the movies and holding hands with middle school boys doesn't really count. But I'm a forever kind of girl, Kate. I know I have some time to decide, but I don't like playing them against each other. A few weeks ago, I thought it might be fun to play the field. Now? Not so much. I'm not comfortable with casual sex. I like commitment."

"But sometimes you have to look around before you find the one you want to be with for the long haul. You got lucky with Patrick. He came along and bam, you knew that was it. I used to envy what you had."

"I know. A lot of people did. It was special. Magic."

"You deserve nothing less this time around. Magic or bust."

"Magic or bust." I smiled. "I'll figure it out soon enough."

"Just figure out which one you want to bring for Marc's game next weekend. They're playing at home and Marc scored us some great seats."

"All of us?"

"All of us. You, me, the kids, and an extra for you. Marc thought you might want to bring someone."

"What a guy. I'm so glad you finally made up your mind."

"Now it's your turn. Are you feeling naughty or nice?"

As it turned out, I felt nice.

Josh was the only option as a date to watch the Patriots. He'd been a fan since birth. Nick couldn't have cared less about the game, which might have made it a good time to test his affection but I just couldn't leave Josh behind when we had seats almost right on the sideline.

I asked him at work Monday morning and he practically hugged the life out of me in his enthusiasm.

"Hey, I've got connections. What can I say?"

"So it worked out with Marc and Kate?"

"Just as you said. All they needed was some alone time to get it together, and now they're headed toward happily ever after."

Except, I didn't know quite how that would work out once Kate did meet Hades again—in the far, far-off future, or so I hoped. I guessed she had time to figure that one out. Josh seemed to read my thoughts. He reached out and gave my hand a light squeeze.

"It will work out. These things have a way of working somehow. Leave it to fate."

"Fate." I wondered if all myths were true and there were three women spinning our lives like threads on a spinning wheel. Some things were better left unknown. "I hope fate is kind to our fund-raiser. We can use a lot of donations."

"For the chance to work with the Patriots and throw a fifty-thousand-dollar toss? I think we'll have a lot of takers. The bonus is that you found a nice foreclosure. The house has good bones. Sure, it needs some restructuring, but it's not as if I'll be framing a whole new structure in frozen ground. It's ideal."

"The ads should go out in today's local papers and be run again a day before the event. Plus, I dropped the invitations in the mail. Leslie's working on finding a family."

"To have news of getting a new home right in time for the holidays? They'll be thrilled, whoever it is."

"I hope to have the press there to witness it. We could get a nice write-up. The mayor's office confirmed that he'll be there."

"Bennie, you did an amazing job on this. I have to hand it to you. When you came in to talk to Leslie about a job, I had my concerns. But as soon as you showed up on that first day, I knew you were ready to work. I'm proud of you, kid."

It felt great to be commended on doing a good job. Of all the people I never would have expected to have faith in me, it was Josh Brandon. Now here he was, heaping on the praise. I got the warm gushy feeling inside. "Kid? I'm only eight years younger than you."

"I know." He smiled as if enjoying some personal secret.

I supposed he could be enjoying the triumph of my acknowledging that we weren't that far apart in age after all. Josh Brandon was most definitely not too old for me.

An hour before quitting time, Nick called. "You free tonight? I would really like to see you."

"What did you have in mind?" The tingle came over me. Why did my body always have to react when my mind was working so hard to steer me in a different direction?

"Shopping. Just you and me. 'Tis the season."

"I thought you weren't all that fond of Christmas."

"It's not my kind of holiday, but I have to admit that you won me over with the whole presents and cheer thing."

"Aw, your cold heart melted like the Winter Warlock's from *Santa Claus Is Coming to Town*. It's not just the presents, you know. There's a much deeper reason for the season."

"Let's not get bogged down in theology now, hmm? There's room for all beliefs. Honestly, it was the other one that did it."

"*The Year Without a Santa Claus*?"

"That's the one. I could relate to the warring brothers theme. Not to mention Mother Nature was a real hottie. I wouldn't mind setting her up with Zeus."

"You're very bad," I said. Downright naughty. Just hearing his voice made me feel naughty, even though I was trying so hard to be nice. "I'll call Kate and see what I can do. She owes me for watching Ellie all weekend, and Marc will still be recuperating from last night's game so I think we're good to go."

"I'll pick you up at five, unless you call and say there's a problem."

"See you then."

Something was wrong.

I felt it as Morrison maneuvered us through holiday traffic, avoided the jam-packed parking lot, and dropped us off at the door of the mall with promises to pick us up where we wanted when we were ready.

It was too easy. How many times, through the

years, had I yearned for a car service or cab, some way to make it through the holiday season without facing crowds or fighting for a parking spot? But now that it had been made easy, I realized that some of the fun had gone out of my evening before it even started. Pfft.

No scanning the lot for the jewel of an empty space or driving to the entrance to follow walkers to their cars in hopes of securing their spot. No conflict. No angst. No adrenaline racing. Nothing. I let Nick drape his arm over my shoulders and lead me into the mall.

"Are you sure you wouldn't have preferred to shop in the city?" he asked. "Higher-end stores? Exclusive boutiques."

"No. I prefer the mall." It was true. When I was a child and the mall had just been built, I'd thought it was the most wondrous, amazing place on the face of the earth. Stores, restaurants, a food court, all under one roof? Heaven on earth. It didn't get any better than that.

A great portion of my teen years had been spent in the mall. My first three jobs were at stores in the mall. Even after I married and had the kids—especially with kids, it was so easy to navigate with babies in strollers—I still did most of my shopping at the mall.

Every Christmas, it was the first place Patrick and I had shopped for the kids' toys. Really, for me, there was no other option. Even if some of the excitement was already lost without the Great Parking Space Search.

Once inside, Nick crinkled his nose as if he might sneeze from the unfiltered air.

"Come on." I grabbed his arm and led him along. "It's the mall. My happy place. Don't be a spoilsport."

"How can I be a spoilsport when I am here to spoil *you*?" He tucked my hand into the crook of his leather-clad arm and kept pace. He wore a camel leather jacket over a taupe shirt with khakis and boots. On anyone else, it would have been boring, but he made heads turn as we walked. "Where would you like to go first?"

"GameStop. Or any of the game stores. The kids want some more games for the Wii."

He stopped in his tracks. "This isn't about the kids. It's about you. I want to shop for you."

"Oh. It's just that Christmas is coming. I thought I would pick up a few things for the kids."

"Bennie." He slid a finger under my chin and directed my face up to meet his emerald gaze. "I know you like to spoil them, and you will. I know you will. But let me have my fun with you, hmm? For tonight. I've never Christmas-shopped before. I want to see your eyes light up. I want to know what to get *for you*."

I took a breath. "Sure."

"How about Nordstrom's? Shoes. I would love to see you try on shoes."

"Shoes," I repeated lifelessly. A few weeks ago, shoes would have thrilled me. A whole night of shopping in my honor, and off my credit card bill, would have been a dream come true. I realized, for the first time, that I wasn't that Bennie anymore. I'd changed. And I liked who I'd become.

Independent Bennie. Hardworking Bennie. Shop-for-other-people Bennie. How many days had it been since I'd put more than five minutes' thought into what I was wearing to work? My favorite shoes had become my pink Timberlands. Nick looked at me and saw the old Bennie. But Josh knew the real me.

He told me he was proud of me. Warmth started at the heart of me and radiated out from my core. *Josh.* "You want to see my eyes light up?"

"Yes." He walked along, distracted, stopping to look in a shop window. "That would look amazing on you."

He gestured to a mannequin in the Abercrombie window. Cropped top, barely-there bottom. I laughed. "Nick, I'm not a nymphette. I have curves."

"Not really." He held me at arm's length. "Some, perhaps, but you're actually small-breasted."

I clucked my tongue. "Excuse me?"

"I like them." He shrugged. "You know I'm a leg man."

"I'm not that small."

"Smaller than your sister."

"Why are you looking at my sister's breasts?"

He laced his fingers with mine and kept walking. "I wasn't, exactly, it's just that they're on the gazing ball so constantly it's hard to avoid them."

"Huh?"

"In my uncle's office. He keeps watch. How he pines for her. You should see him. One of the most powerful gods in the universe. The most, perhaps, save my father, and there he sits, a lovesick school-boy. It's really sad."

It was sad, I had to admit. "Yes, but you told her to be happy. She's with Marc now. It will be good for her, and for Ellie."

"Undoubtedly. Hades is pleased by the turn of events. He would much rather watch her be happy. And maybe he can start watching less as she begins to enjoy her life. For the longest time, he was so worried for her."

"It's nice, in a way, that he can love like that."

"It's weak, to love like that," Nick said matter-of-factly. "All that emotion. Not good for a god. Too . . . human," he said with a shudder.

It struck a nerve. "What's wrong with being a human?"

For that matter, what was wrong with being in love? It dawned on me, at last, that there could be no possible future for Nick and me. We'd had all we could have, great sex, some good times, nothing more. What he felt for me was new for him, a temporary fascination. And what I felt for him?

"Nothing. It's simply not as amazing as being a god."

"What?" I stopped and looked at him.

"Given the choice, wouldn't you prefer some divine powers at your disposal? It's very handy. I don't know how you do without them. Eliana, now, she has hope."

"Hope?" A chill ran the length of my spine.

"You know. If she has any powers, it could be good for her. Have you seen any signs?"

"Of Ellie having powers?"

"You know, little things, like turning lights on and off."

"Of course not," I scoffed. He wanted me to tell him something he didn't know, something new. I had no idea why, but I wasn't about to take the bait. It was as if I had Ellie in my head, telling me not to tell him. Ridiculous, when she couldn't even speak, but I sensed her. I wouldn't betray her. Maybe she'd somehow stopped him from reading my mind on the subject, because he seemed to be reaching for information he normally accessed without my being aware.

"Really? No sign of anything?"

"Nothing. Why? Is it common for children of gods to be gods? I would hate for her to miss out."

"Not to worry. Zeus likely intended her to be entirely human. He wouldn't have gifted her with extraordinary powers on purpose. I was just curious if, perhaps by accident, Ellie showed signs of divinity."

"Not a trace," I said, feigning disappointment. "Too bad for her, stuck as a human."

My excitement at the idea of shopping had faded. I felt tired, deflated, and I wanted to go home. I had the inescapable feeling that the entire trip had been designed for the sole purpose of tricking or, worse, bribing me into giving up information on my niece. Incredibly, I didn't even want to be near him. So, for the first time in weeks, I played the widow card. I needed to get home and away from Nick Angelos, aka Hermes.

"I don't feel well all of a sudden," I said. "I want to go home. Shopping tonight was a bad idea."

"What's wrong? I can help."

"No. It's work, and stress, and sadness, I guess. Being here, at Christmas, without Patrick, it's suddenly overwhelming. I'm not ready."

"Very well," he said. We turned and walked back toward the entrance we came in. He grabbed his cell phone and called Morrison to bring around the car.

Once inside the car, I huddled in my seat and thought of my brief history with Nick, of his lies when he met me, about not knowing where I lived. I thought of our first time together, the way he'd overwhelmed me and convinced me to let him stay the night in my bed, with the kids so close and impressionable.

These things should have been my red flags, but I didn't want to see them. I was blinded by a handsome face, a chiseled bod, and having the attention of a man.

I thought of his gift to me on our big whirlwind adventure on the yacht. Emeralds. To match his eyes. *His* eyes. What a lovely complement to himself. I finally turned to face him, my annoyance growing.

"Do you even know what color my eyes are, Nick?" I asked.

"Blue, of course." He didn't miss a beat. But he didn't say much, either. Blue, good guess. Many blondes had blue eyes. But he didn't specify, sapphire blue or cerulean, indigo or aquamarine. Blue eyes could be so different. None were quite alike. My mind went straight to Josh, Josh's eyes, so alive with emotion and so many facets of blue, all of them almost too bright to look at for longer than a minute.

"Blue," I repeated with a sigh as we pulled into my driveway. "Don't get out. Please, just stay. I need a few days on my own, Nick. Tonight was hard on me."

"From remembering your husband?" He raised a brow.

I sighed. "That's not all. It's not going to work between us, Nick. We're so different and we want different things. I've had a great time with you. Really. But I don't see us heading anywhere. I think it's best if we just say good-bye."

"Good-bye? That's it?"

"I don't know." I shrugged. I'd never really broken up with anyone before. It was probably time I learned how. "I hope we can still be friends."

Oddly enough, it wasn't as hard as I imagined. I'd already mentally moved on.

"Ah." He nodded. "But you're set on Brandon now, aren't you?"

"I'm not set on anything." True enough. I had no idea where things were headed with Josh. "My decision has nothing to do with him. We've had our shot, Nick. You're not really planning on staying around much longer, are you?"

"No," he admitted. "My business is nearly at an end. You're right."

"Then I think that's all we need to say." I leaned over and kissed him on the cheek. "Thank you, Nick. It has been a pleasure getting to know you."

"We'll meet again," he said, the wolfish grin firmly in place.

"Sure. I hope we do." I took it as his version of "I'll call you," got out of the car, waved good-bye as the car pulled away from the curb, then turned on my heel and started toward the house.

Home, at last.

For the next few days, I poured myself into planning the fund-raiser. I worked long hours. I looked up more contacts. I mailed more invitations. I looked into placing ads in smaller publications to reach a wider audience. Didn't everyone want a chance to toss a ball around with Patriots football stars? At best, we had an influx of cash and supplies to keep the organization running smoothly. At worst, we tapped into more volunteers to help get the houses ready for the holidays. According to Josh, they could always use more manpower at the building sites.

In the middle of the week, Kate and Marc brought dinner over to share with me and the kids because, according to Kate, I sounded sad on the phone.

"You haven't seemed right since you came home from the mall the other day. I've never seen you shop and come back with no packages. Especially with someone else paying the bill."

I glared at her, then smiled. She didn't mean anything by it. She already knew how he'd started asking questions about Ellie, but we'd made a decision not to speak of it when Marc was around, so as not to upset him. We decided it was nothing to worry about, that Nick would probably be gone soon.

"You know I ended it with Nick," I said. "I just felt that it had run its course. I'm just a little preoccupied with making sure my fund-raiser goes well. And if I seem blue, well, I have been thinking about Patrick."

"I know. It's Christmastime. It's bound to be hard."

"Next Tuesday marks one year exactly that he's been gone," I said. "One year. God, that was the worst day of my life."

"Mine, too." Kate hugged me.

Marc joined in the hug. He had come to the memorial service weeks after Hades had vanished from Kate's life, even though he barely knew Patrick. He had come for Kate. That same day, Kate had found out she was expecting Ellie. It turned the day around for me. At last, I'd found a reason to smile again.

We had come full circle.

"Let's try not to be morose, for the kids' sake," I said. "Sarah's having a hard time with it lately. Spencer's more stoic, but I'm sure it's getting to him, too."

"I brought *Rudolph*, the Christmas special, on DVD. We can all watch that after dinner." Clearly, the Markham sisters had turned to TV for emotional fulfillment just a tad too much in their misspent youth.

"The kids will like that," I said. "We watched *Santa Claus Is Coming to Town* and *The Year Without a Santa Claus* when Nick was here. I think Sarah was a little let down. *Rudolph* was Patrick's favorite, though, so maybe it will be good for her."

The phone rang. My heart raced. Josh?

"Hi, Ben, it's Leslie." Small letdown. "You've been working so hard at the office lately and I've been busy with my Web stuff. I feel a little guilty."

"No, don't. I love the work." I really did, and it no longer surprised me. I'd found something I was good at and enjoyed. "It doesn't even feel like work."

"I know, but I figured I would take over at the office tomorrow and give you a break. How about you take the day off?"

"A day off in the middle of the week? It feels like cheating. We just had Thanksgiving, so it's not as if I've been pouring it on nonstop."

"I know, but I need to go over some files, anyway, and it's crowded with both of us there at once."

"That it is." It was a small space. I could see her point. "Oh, I know. How about I call Josh and see if he needs me for building?" I got the weak, breathless happys just thinking of spending the day with Josh.

"I don't know. Looks like he's planning on taking the day off, too. Sorry. I think you're out of luck."

"Oh." Damn. "Okay. I guess I could take the day off."

"Great. And, Bennie?"

"Yes."

"Have a great time. Bye."

"Bye." I put the phone down. Have a great time? She said it as if I were headed for a tropical vacation or taking the day off to do something exciting rather than staying home and trying to figure out what to do with myself.

Oh no. A thought struck me. What if Nick planned on whisking me away again in an attempt to win me back? I felt sick with dread. I thought I'd made a clean break, but maybe he'd meant it when he said we'd meet again. I didn't know how much clearer I could be about being over him.

"Something wrong?" Kate asked as I'd set down the phone. "You look perturbed."

"That was Leslie. She wants me to take a day off tomorrow."

"Cool. You could go to the salon or hit the gym. You haven't had a lot of Bennie time lately."

"I guess I could." I hadn't even thought of indulging myself with manicures or even maintaining my figure at the gym, things that had been so important to me until recently. Of the two, the gym was more of a necessity if I didn't want my hard work to turn to cottage cheese. "The gym's calling."

The phone rang. I hadn't meant it literally.

"You better answer. The gym's persistent." Kate laughed and headed back to Marc and Ellie in the kitchen.

"Hello?"

"Hey. How's it going?"

Josh's voice, warm and familiar, filled me with heat! My knees wobbled. "Great. Leslie wants me to take the day off tomorrow. I'm a little bummed. I've kind of gotten used to the idea of having the nine-to-five gig on weekdays."

"Poor baby." Josh laughed, an easy throaty warble. "I have an idea."

"Oh yeah?" My hero. "What is it?"

"We could spend the day shopping together, until it's time to pick up the kids, of course. I need some help getting something for Kyrie."

"And I still need to shop for my two. Perfect. I would love to shop." That much was almost always true, recent experience aside. "Do you want to meet somewhere?"

"Why don't I pick you up? Then we only have to worry about facing the parking hassles with one car instead of two. One problem, though. Would you mind heading to the mall? You probably like the froufrou city shops, but I never find what I need. The mall is my comfort zone, as far as shopping goes."

Be still my heart. "I love the mall. No problem."

"Great. How about I swing by at nine?"

"I'll be waiting."

Chapter Twenty

"I hope you don't mind. I have a few things to return." I let Josh in and gestured to the bunch of shopping bags in the corner.

"Holy smokes," he said. "That's a few things?"

"It looks like more than it is. It's a pair of boots, a few blouses, and a skirt I've never worn. It will free up some extra cash for me to buy things for the kids."

"You have been picking up your paychecks, right? Leslie puts them in the top drawer every Friday."

"I know. It felt great to cash the first one. I've been using them to catch up with bills. I want to pay off my credit card debt and start a vacation fund."

"Vacation?"

"Kate set up all my other investments, like college funds and retirement, so after I figure out what goes where, I'll have money left over for more frivolous spending. It occurred to me yesterday that our last family vacation was Disney World with Patrick last year. Leslie reminded me that I get two weeks' vacation time. I need to start thinking about doing fun stuff with the kids. We're still a family even without Patrick."

"Nice thinking."

"I don't need to spend all my cash at the mall. A woman only needs so many outfits, you know."

"I have no idea, and I'll keep it that way."

"Right." I laughed. "I made coffee and muffins, if you want to fortify before facing the crowds."

"I can't resist homemade muffins. What kind?"

"Maine blueberry with crumb topping. I bought a bunch of blueberries at the market over the summer and froze them for baking. I love blueberries."

"Blueberries are my favorite. I make a mean blueberry pancake."

"Only one? Because I love pancakes and I can eat a whole stack."

He smiled. "You're in luck. I make big batches at a time."

"Maybe I'll get to try them eventually."

His eyes, reminding me of a cloudless midsummer sky reflecting the sun, shone brightly. "I can't wait to make you pancakes one morning."

I blushed. It was an innocent statement, but the way his voice lowered to a sultry purr when he said it seemed to imply so much more.

"Let's take our coffee and muffins to go," I suggested. "The mall's probably going to be packed."

I poured the coffee into travel mugs and put some warm muffins in a bag while Josh put my bags in the car. No need to reveal that I'd barely slept a wink and was up an hour earlier than usual to bake as a distraction from thinking about him.

In the car, I took an opportunity to grill him a little. "So, I'm surprised you're not Christmas-shopping for Kyrie with her mom. Molly, was her name? Don't you and Molly do stuff like that together?"

"We're close. We've always been good friends, and I expect we always will."

"Oh." I didn't like the tone of warmth in his voice when he mentioned Molly. Maybe I should have left well enough alone. "That's great for Kyrie, to have her parents on good terms. When did you separate?"

Josh jumped a little. "Separate? We were never quite together, as a real couple."

"But Kyrie thinks you're her dad?"

"We let her think that for a long time. It seemed easier than explaining the complicated truth, and I have been like a father to her since before she was born. I care about Molly. We grew up together. She's like a sister to me. We're best friends."

Best friends. It comforted me. Not lovers? "I don't get it."

"Molly's parents were strict, very religious. When Molly found out she was pregnant, she didn't know what to tell them."

"But she must have been in her thirties by then, if she's your age. What could they do?"

He shrugged. "Yeah, but she didn't want to lose their good opinion, even then. Nick had already gone back to who knew where. I told Molly I would be there for her, no matter what. We decided to tell her parents that our friendship had blossomed into more and things just happened. They accepted that. They've always liked me."

"Wow. That's a long way to go to help a friend."

"I was getting over a bad relationship and I had no interest in dating. I threw myself into work at the time, so it was nice to have this new little blessing on the way, something to make life feel worth living. I've adored Kyrie from the very first time I heard her heartbeat at a doctor's appointment with Molly. I couldn't understand how someone could just walk away from that."

"But Nick never knew, did he?"

"He knew." Josh grew quiet as we arrived at the mall and looked around the parking lot for a space.

"There's a space." I pointed to one close to the Neiman Marcus door. Josh headed for it, but as we got there someone else pulled in. He kept cruising.

"He knew, because I told him. I heard he was back in town to finish up on one of the projects we were building at the time. I went to the office to find him and tell him to man up. He laughed at me, declared it was impossible and that Molly was making up the pregnancy so he would marry her."

"You're kidding." I was horrified. This was the kind of man who had shared my bed?

"Not kidding. Oh, there's another one. Hold on." Josh stepped on the gas. I was glad I had my seat belt on. We pulled into the space just before another car rounded the corner to find it.

"Great work." I high-fived him, and then he turned serious again.

"So I insisted if he didn't believe me, he should come to one of Molly's doctor's appointments. He tried to have me thrown out and I got a little feisty."

"You hit him." I nodded. "Good one."

"But he was only down for a minute before he came up shooting flames from his fingers. I thought I was going to be fried until Owen showed up, poof, out of the blue. My emotions ran the gamut that day. First, so angry I couldn't see straight, then scared for my life with a flamethrowing freak seeking vengeance, then the company CEO just materializing? It was like being trapped in a nightmare."

"That got out of hand fast."

"It was like the whole office went into lockdown. I was ushered into a private room with Owen. Nick was taken by security to somewhere else. I had no idea what was going on. My head was swimming. It was then that Owen told me the truth."

"That he was actually Hades, lord of the underworld? That must have gone over well."

"At first, he tried to convince me otherwise, but I knew what I'd seen. I was a big fan of myth and legend through school."

I rolled my eyes. "Dungeons and Dragons, too?"

"Yes, how'd you guess?"

"Patrick was a fan." Along with almost every guy in his age group and slightly older, but I wasn't going to add that. "But sorry to interrupt."

"No problem. Hades must have decided I was trustworthy, because he confided the whole tale to me, of his identity and his nephew's, that Hermes had a mischievous streak but that I should try to forgive him. He also offered me a handsome compensation package and a dose of good advice."

"What was it?"

"He told me that it would be better to raise the baby as my own, to pretend that I'd made the pregnancy up to try to force Nick to stay with Molly and conceal the truth, that Molly was indeed with child. Hades wasn't sure what would happen to the baby if Hermes knew the truth. The gods don't exactly have a shining reputation when it comes to taking care of their own."

"Meaning?" A prickle of fear went through me, for Ellie's sake.

"According to Hades, Zeus wouldn't be pleased with the possibility and he didn't know to what lengths Hermes would go to keep the baby's existence from Zeus. If he knew, Zeus would have expected the baby to be taken from Molly and raised by Nick on Mount Olympus. He doesn't believe in taking risks where children of gods are concerned, and leaving Kyrie to be raised in the human realm left her open to exposing her powers, if she had any, and endangering the ability of the gods to roam among us undetected. Hades doubted Nick was ready for the responsibility of raising a child, and he took pity on Molly. How could she lose her child? No risk was worth taking. I took the compensation package and married Molly. Hades convinced Hermes that he fired me and had me thrown out because I admitted to making up the lie about the baby being his."

"And Hermes believed that?"

"If you haven't noticed yet, Hermes is selective in what he chooses to hear and to believe. He thought I was out for revenge, or blackmail, or something. Who knows?"

"Nick had been asking about Ellie, if she had any powers. At best, he just wants to report to Hades, but at worst?" My chest constricted with fear. "What if he wants to take Ellie away to Mount Olympus?"

Josh shrugged. "I guess it's possible, but I think he's working pretty squarely with Hades now. I doubt Hades would have sent him down if he didn't trust him, right?"

"Right," I agreed. "And why would he want to

trouble with taking Ellie to Mount Olympus? He doesn't exactly like babies, from what I've seen."

But the Stymphalian birds came to mind, and Ares. Had Ares been just passing through, stopping for a visit, as Nick claimed? Or was there more to it? I was probably worrying needlessly. Nick hadn't called, hadn't tried to stop by to visit. It seemed that he really was through with his business, and through with me. I tried to relax. "But, wait, you didn't actually have to marry Molly."

"We thought we could make it work. We loved each other as friends and I really wanted to be Kyrie's dad. But we were awkward together at best. The romance never developed. We agreed to stay friends and we lived together until Kyrie started school. Molly kept her job teaching and I only took construction jobs that allowed me to work when Molly wasn't."

A car idled behind us. I laced my fingers with Josh's. "This is a fascinating conversation, but we better go in."

He angled the rearview mirror. "I guess so. This sucker's waiting for our space. We should make sure he knows we're here to stay awhile."

He let go of my hand just long enough to get my packages out of the back and come around to open the door for me. We walked close, like lovers, into the mall.

"Where to first?"

"Macy's. I'll return my boots and we can poke around for clothes for Kyrie."

"Good plan."

"So, you never saw Nick, Hermes, after that until recently?"

"His uncle kept him busy in other places for a few years. From time to time, I would hear from Owen Glendower, though. He would toss some construction referrals my way and ask about Kyrie's welfare. The god of the underworld may not enjoy the best reputation among mortals, but I have to say that he has always been one of the good guys as far as I'm concerned."

"He introduced us, when you think about it. Remember last year? When you helped my sister with one of her jobs?"

"How could I forget?" He squeezed my hand. "I had no idea Hades, as Owen, was even back in town and then he came to me needing some assistance with moving furniture. I begged off, at first, but he said it would be worth my while."

"Really? Kate was pretty desperate for movers on that job. She had a house showing to stage and all her movers quit. She'd been so busy helping me hold it together after Patrick died that she could have put her business in jeopardy. My whole family pitched in, and then Owen swooped in to Kate's rescue. Kate always said he was the devil, but I had no idea. Hades, for real. It blew me away." But I was getting off track. "How was it worth your while? Did he pay you well?"

Josh stopped walking and urged us to a nearby bench out of the way of moving crowds. "It was worth my while because I met you, Bennie. You took my breath away. I was a goner at first sight."

"What? Back then?" My stomach flipped, the good way. I searched his gaze. His eyes flickered in that hot gas flame way that burned me right through and said he was deadly serious.

"Way back then. But I found out you'd just lost your husband and I knew I would have to bide my time. You weren't about to rush into a new relationship. Still, I suggested you might want to volunteer for Habitat for Humanity for something to do, remember?"

"You gave me Leslie's card. I remember. But then when I showed up at a construction site, you were brutal to me."

He winced and reached out to stroke my cheek with the back of his hand. "Not too hard on you, I hope. I saw you with the power sander. No offense, but you were a complete klutz. I was afraid you were going to cut your hand off. You looked like an accident waiting to happen."

I clucked my tongue in mock disgust, but really I was touched by his protective instincts. "You could have had some faith."

"I could have." He bowed his head, remorseful. "I planned to let you do more once I had a chance to teach you some proper techniques on my own. I wouldn't trust your instruction to anyone else. But it was a busy construction season and I never had time. Eventually, you stopped showing up."

"I'm sorry. I wasn't much of a devoted volunteer."

"Then Nick Angelos came on the scene and you had the nerve to appear taken with the guy."

"I'm not anymore, I assure you. My eyes are wide open where he's concerned. It took a little while, but now I know."

"Now you know?"

"He's not the man I thought he was, in more ways than one. I don't know what he's up to, but I don't trust him. There's no chance I'll have anything to do with him again if I can help it."

"That's good to hear. I wanted you to make the decision on your own, without anything I could say to influence you. I trusted your judgment."

That one simple statement touched me deeply, beyond anything anyone could ever have said to me. "You trusted my judgment? You could have said something or stepped in to protect me."

"Never." He shook his head. "It's not up to me to tell you how to live your life or choose your friends. I'm protective of the ones I love, yes, but that doesn't give me the right to railroad in and take over. Even if I think I know better. Which, in this case, I obviously did."

His chest inflated just a tad. I had to smile. "You did. You were right. But you had nothing to prove. You let me make my own mistake. Thank you."

"It wouldn't exactly have helped me win your heart to come on like a big jealous Neanderthal. What if you really ended up falling for Nick? What would you have thought of me to get in the way of it? Even if I wanted to risk getting fried to a crisp just to tell him to take a hike and leave you alone."

"You would have, too. I could see that there were times when you might have come close to hauling off and punching him." I started to laugh, but stopped on a gasp.

It just struck me that he said he was protective of the ones he loved. Did he mean—

"Yes, Bennie." He took my hands, laced his fingers with mine, and time seemed to stop. My heart skipped a beat, then started pounding so hard I could feel it pulse all through me. I looked up and met the stark blue truth burning in his eyes a second before he spoke it, undeniably, out loud.

"I love you. With all my heart. From the very first time I met you but more with every passing day."

"From the very first time?" I gasped, amazed. "You love me?"

I didn't know what to say. There was so much to say. I felt the floodgates about to open. And then an old man with a dish of ice cream in one hand, supporting his frail wife with the other, neared the bench. There were no other empty seats. I nudged Josh.

"Oh." He stood. I followed suit. "Please, take our bench."

"We were just leaving," I added.

The woman smiled. "Bless you, dears. Merry Christmas."

Would Josh and I have the good fortune to be together in our old age, sharing ice cream at the mall? I realized how badly I wished it could be true. *He loved me.* All things were possible. He loved me. All this time.

It made me feel like an even bigger jerk for the time I'd stood him up to go out with Nick. And he was so nice about it in the office the next day. He let me off the hook so easily.

"But a few weeks ago, you said you had a date." I just remembered how I felt when he told me in the office that day. I should have been relieved that he wasn't that interested in me, but I wasn't. I should have seen it as a sign that I was starting to feel for Josh, more than I'd cared to admit at the time, but I tuned it out. Until now. "Was it with Molly?"

"With Kyrie. I may have played it up to be something else. Molly's in love with a travel reporter.

That guy with the show on the Food Network where he travels the world and tastes weird food."

"That guy? I've seen his show."

"That guy. And Molly has been going on some trips with him, so I've been taking Kyrie more and more. They're getting married next year. I'm happy for them."

"That's great for Molly to finally find her happily ever after."

"Yeah. It is."

"I would love to meet her." I got nudged from behind. Caught up in each other, we were moving a little too slow for the Christmas shopping crowd.

"Soon." Josh smiled, as he elbowed a wider space for us in the throngs of people rushing from store to store. "So, how about it? Let's get shopping before we get mowed down."

"Shopping!" I bounded with new enthusiasm. I had so much to say to him, but fighting the masses wasn't quite the right setting for new declarations. "Shopping is my second favorite thing."

"What's the first?" he asked as we headed toward Macy's.

"If we finish up here early, I'll take you back to my house and I'll show you." I flashed a sly grin.

"Oh, man. You're on."

I'd never seen a man shop with such efficiency, speed, and enthusiasm in my entire life. We were laden with packages, all done, and headed home in under three hours.

"Are you hungry?" he asked as we drove home.

"Not for food." I winked. He began to drive a

little faster. "Careful, there, cowboy. You don't want to get pulled over."

"Would you mind if we went to my place, instead? Not that I don't love your house, but your sister seems to pop in quite a bit."

"You make a good point. Your place is fine with me." Besides, I wanted to see where he lived. I had no idea.

"How much time before the kids get out of school?"

I checked the car clock. "Two hours before I have to think about heading over to pick them up."

He screwed up his beautiful mouth as if he was doing mental equations. "Not much time, but we'll make it work."

We pulled up outside a meticulously restored Victorian. The place was huge. Nothing like the tiny bachelor pad I'd imagined for him. "This is yours?"

"All mine," he said. "Trashed when I bought it. I got it for a song. I knew I could put some work into it and gradually make it into something special. My intention was to sell it for a profit. I just haven't gotten around to it yet."

I nodded. "It's a lot of house for two people."

"Especially considering there's just one most of the time."

"Sounds lonely." I reached for his hand. I didn't like the idea of him being lonely. Not anymore.

"It is. I spend a lot of time at work, or finding new projects in the house to keep busy. I would love to show you around but it's a big place. Maybe some other time?" He raised a brow, hopeful.

"Some other time," I agreed. We walked in the front door to an old-fashioned mudroom complete with a bench for removing muddy boots and hooks along one wall for coats. "Charming."

"It's useful in winter. I don't have to drag muck across my hardwoods."

"Oh yes." I understood once I saw the gorgeous shiny floor in the great room. No furniture, but an enormous fireplace with a dark mahogany mantel in the center of the room.

"I thought you said you didn't have a fireplace."

He cringed. "Little white lie. I was hoping you wouldn't call me on it."

"I'm touched that you went so far to get closer to me. Fixing my fireplace must have been hard work. I can't believe I stood you up."

"Forgiven."

"Did you do the floors?"

He nodded. "And I replaced the mantel, the railing, a lot of the original woodwork. You should see what I did to the kitchen."

"Later," I said. "Maybe later. Right now I'm eager to see what you've done to the master bedroom."

"That room has furniture, a plus."

"A big plus if one of the pieces is a bed."

"King-sized. It's a huge room. Any other bed seemed dwarfed. Upstairs." He gestured with his head.

I couldn't wait to tangle my fingers in his lustrous silver locks. To think I had once thought him too old for me. I took his hand and let him lead me up the enormous curved staircase.

His room was to the left and down a narrow hall with the same polished wood floors and elegant crown molding at the ceiling. The walls were covered in a delicate tone-on-tone fabric. "Amazing work. Very Victorian."

"Your sister actually helped me come up with that," he said. "She has given me some advice on decorating from time to time."

"I had no idea you and she were so close."

"I needed to talk to someone about the way you made me feel."

"What?" I stopped in my tracks. "Kate knew all this time?"

"Only the past few months. Don't be mad."

"I'm not mad. Just surprised. I didn't know she could be trusted to keep a secret. At least, not from me."

"She has been a big help to me. You know when I dropped off your Lexus? I really did call her and she brought me the keys and devised the dinner plan."

I nodded. "She didn't like Nick. She decided it was time to clue you in to what was going on."

"This is it." He paused outside a large mahogany door. "Where the magic happens, as they say on MTV's *Cribs*."

I laughed. "I've had enough of magic, if you want to know the truth."

"Not my kind of magic, baby." He winked and made the two-finger pointing gesture that Spence sometimes made in imitation of a cheesy game show host. I loved that Josh had a sense of humor that would fit right in with my family. I loved *him*.

"Before we go any further," I said, stepping closer and putting my hand on his solid chest. Very solid. I was nearly distracted by the solidity. I allowed my hand a minute to smooth over it. "There's something I need you to know."

"Yes?"

"I've fallen in love with you, too. Deeply in love. It wasn't the instant kind of love at first sight. It took time to set in. It started when you held me that day you brought my Lexus, when you held me as I cried over Patrick. It became more clear to me when I felt so crappy for standing you up to go out with Nick. I'm so sorry about that."

"Again, forgiven." He smiled, curled his hand around mine, and nodded. "Go on."

"And then when we were on the roof and you put your arms around me to help me hammer. Oh God, you have no idea how it made me feel to be in your arms."

"I have some idea. I just didn't know you felt it, too."

"Thanksgiving, when I was having such a good time with you and your daughter until Nick showed up. When I looked at you, and I figured out that Nick was probably Kyrie's biological father, my heart broke a little for you then." I took his face between my hands and looked into those amazing blue eyes. "And finally, just the other day, when you said you were proud of me, it was an amazing feeling. My heart just burst wide open for you, Josh. I love you more than I ever dreamed possible, and it just grows stronger every day."

"Hush," he said, placing his finger on my lips. Tears glistened in his eyes, and I felt them pooling in mine, too.

"I love you," I repeated. I couldn't be hushed that easily.

"I love you, too." He met my lips in a gentle kiss that gradually built fiercer with urgency. "I love you." His voice was hot in the hollows of my throat.

His hands wrapped around my back, or one of them did, as the other opened his bedroom door and he backed us inside.

My hands found his hair at last. I pulled him to me, as close as he could possibly be. I'd never wanted anyone so bad or so completely. I sucked on his tongue, drew it deep, and imagined the ways I wanted to taste him. So completely.

His hands moved down my body, to cup my behind, and back up, curling around my back. I felt so small and protected in his arms. So cherished.

He broke contact just long enough to strip off his shirt, a thermal long-sleeved Henley. My mouth strayed to find the hollows of his neck, his pulse working furiously at the base of his throat. Feeling his bare skin under my palms, I had to give in to the urge to look at him.

Amazing. Construction had given him an even better body than a god could devise. His arms were built up from endless hammering, but it was nothing to the tan, well-defined expanse of skin across his chest and down, the taut eight-pack abs and tapered waist. I couldn't wait to get him out of his pants.

With one swift move, he spun me around toward the bed and nudged me, gently, to land atop his natural cotton spread. He undid his belt and tugged, dropping it to the floor, before he unbuttoned his jeans, unzipped, and let them slide down his very fine skin, whiter where the sun never had a chance to caress him as I longed to, so eager was I to get my hands on—oh my. On his exceptionally large penis that stood at attention, erect and ready for my love.

I got to my knees between his thick thighs. I couldn't wait. I stroked him and swirled a finger around his perfectly formed tip, lost in the wonder of him. I thought about taking him in my mouth, so deep, as far as he would go, but it would have to wait.

"Come on." He took my hands, smiling, but still in control, and encouraged me to get to my feet. "Your turn. Undress for me."

He sat on the bed. Such an intimate command I could hardly ignore. I crossed my arms over my body, gripped my turtleneck jersey by the hem, and paused. "Are you ready?"

"So ready." He sounded as if he could barely breathe.

Slowly, I rolled the shirt up over my head and tossed it at his feet. For a moment, I stood in my bra and let him take it all in. I'd worn my favorite black lace push-up number and I was glad. This morning, when I'd dressed, I had no inkling I'd be making love in the afternoon.

Small breasts? Perhaps, but his eyes widened at sight of the white mounds that strained against the lace. After he got a good look at the way I filled my B cups, I undid my casual wool trousers and slid them, inch by inch, down my hips to reveal the lacy boy-cut panties that matched the bra.

I gave my best stripper spin so he could fully appreciate my backside; then I leaned down to step out of my pants. I couldn't help it. I was an exhibitionist at heart and it had been a long time since I'd felt the freedom to put on a show. Being in love was a ticket to indulge. My legs parted, I slowly straightened up and cast a glance over my shoulder. Josh looked ready to die on the spot.

"Oh God, I'm a lucky man," he said. "I can't fathom how I ever got so lucky."

Enjoying the role of femme fatale, I approached and straddled myself over his lap, rubbing the lace of my panties against his enormous erection.

"How lucky do you feel?" I breathed in his ear before taking his lobe between my lips and sucking it hard into my mouth.

"Extremely." His voice broke.

His hands ran up my thighs to pause between them, thumbs poised over my mound. He looked up, wonder heating his gaze. "You are the most exquisite woman ever created."

I smiled. "It's nice to be appreciated."

He laughed. "And you know it's true." His hands smoothed up, pausing to unhook my bra with all the awe of a child opening a Christmas present, eager to see what was in the wrapping but devoted to taking his time.

The bra fell slowly into his lap, my breasts exposed to him. He blew on them, his breath hot and inspiring my nipples to respond by hardening against the sensation. He repeated the gesture with his tongue, licking one and then the other as if suckling honey-eyed ambrosia from sacred peaks. And when he took one in his mouth and drew it in, I moaned and arched against him, barely able to control myself against my growing need.

The lace of my panties was damp with the feral heat he unleashed in me and I wanted nothing more than to wiggle out of them and feel him inside me, blissfully, completely inside me. He seemed to be on the same wavelength as he twisted an index finger into the lace on one side and tugged. I raised my hips, arching into him, to allow him to strip me bare. I couldn't wait to feel him against the most intimate parts of me.

He exhaled as he revealed me, the triangle of golden hair and the delicate white skin of my thighs. He gripped my hips with a firm hold and spun me until I was under him.

"I wanted to take it slow," he said. "To savor every inch of you, but God help me, I can't control myself with you."

"I know the feeling." Knowing I was in love brought the wondrous joy of sex back to me.

"One second." He left me long enough to cross the room and get something out of a drawer, a small square packet.

"Let me have it." He pressed it into my hand. I unpackaged the condom and slid it over his erection, slowly savoring the feel of him against my palm.

He wrapped his arms around me, buried his hands in my hair, and sank into me, filling me beyond my imagination. We fit together just right. We moved together as if we'd always been of one mind, one body. At last, I tightened around him as I felt him pulsing hot inside me. His gaze held mine as we came together. The ice-blue flecks in his eyes dazzled like crystal snowflakes falling around me, and I fell with them in a dizzying, delightful dance of love.

Chapter Twenty-one

In the next two weeks, Josh and I became nearly inseparable, with the exception of nights, and the kids didn't seem to mind at all. They really liked having him around. Still, we didn't feel it was fair to spring sleepovers on them just yet. In time, we would meld into a family, or so I hoped. I liked taking it day by day, seeing what each new moment would bring.

Kate and Marc, on the other hand, had stepped it up a notch. Marc proposed during halftime at the Patriots' game, in the middle of Gillette Stadium with the cameras of ESPN picking it up as a morning news lead, reported by Jill Richards herself. He'd sprung for an enormous diamond, channel-set in a platinum band so it didn't have a chance of breaking Ellie's delicate baby skin. That's why he'd made sure we all had tickets. He wanted us all there to witness the special event. He'd even picked up an extra ticket for Josh to bring Kyrie along for the fun.

I hadn't heard from Nick since breaking it off with him in his car, and that was fine by me. I worried, from time to time, that he would come by to see Ellie. I even looked for him at the game, but no sign. Maybe he'd reported back to Hades and he was done with us. But his last words, "we'll meet again," stayed with me and I kept wondering where, or when. How? Had he meant it or was it simply something to say?

A week later, as we assembled for my big fundraiser, Marc's teammates were still talking about the surprise proposal.

"Marc, you sap. We had no idea you had it in you." The quarterback certainly didn't have it in him. He'd been going through actress and supermodel girlfriends like candy, but who could blame him? A movie star handsome guy is always in demand with the ladies.

Marc blushed at the teasing. "When you fall in love, you can't help it. You have to move when the time is right."

"When's the wedding?" one of the linebackers asked.

"Soon. As soon as possible. We're thinking of a small family affair on New Year's Eve."

Kate smiled at the sight of him with Ellie in his arms.

"Hand over the baby, big guy," she said. "You and your teammates have work to do, after you go pose for some pictures for the news crew."

Fortunately for me, I had ESPN on the scene as well as the local news crews. Marc had been a big hit at the network since the proposal, and philanthropy always made for a good story. I was touched by the generosity of the four of Marc's teammates who had been willing to give up an afternoon during a bye week just to come help out.

About a hundred people had already arrived and more were still coming. It was early. I beamed. It was a success! People were signing up for volunteer duty in droves, all for a chance to throw the winning pass. With so many hands to help out, the new house would be ready for a family within two weeks, giving us houses for two new families before the holidays, the Mill Street house and this new one.

Plus, cash donations and pledges were flowing. Our coffers were brimming over. The lieutenant governor showed up in place of the busy governor, which was fine since we hadn't expected either of them. The mayor came to make the final announcement of the donation of the Boston Common Christmas tree as lumber for the cause. With the additional news crews and national coverage on ESPN, more local business owners were showing up with offers of donations, from furniture to materials and money.

I turned from greeting some newcomers to run smack into Nick Angelos, wolfish grin firmly in place.

"Nick. Hi." I took a second to recover my bearings. "I'm glad you could come. It's a very important event for us."

"Happy to be here." He pulled me into his embrace and whispered "I've missed you" into my ear.

This time, no hot tendril of desire curled around me. No tingle. Nothing. I exhaled a sigh of relief and immediately thought of Josh. He was at the fund-raiser with Kyrie. I needed to find him before Nick did. Self-absorbed as he was, even Nick Angelos might catch on to his resemblance to Kyrie given any prolonged contact. It wasn't worth the risk.

"Have you seen Josh? He was milling around here somewhere."

"I saw your sister," he said. "Congratulations are in order. They make a lovely family."

"They do, don't they? I hope your uncle won't be too disappointed."

"Au contraire. He'll get a thrill from living vicariously. It pleases him to watch over Kate and know that she's happy."

"That's good, then." Even if it sounded a little creepy the way Nick chose to word it. "All's well that ends well. When will you be returning to Hades?"

The sooner, the better.

"Not too soon. I've not quite completed my work here."

I'd thought getting to know Ellie was his business, but maybe he had other duties. "To watch over your uncle's business interests?"

"Glendower Enterprises is in good hands. Byron will be resuming command. I'm doing a little work on the side for dear old Dad."

My mouth went dry. "I had no idea you were keeping up with Mount Olympus these days. What does that involve?"

Before he could answer, an enormous and ugly bird flew right overhead between us to land on a branch of the tree behind Nick. "Is that a vulture?"

I didn't think we had vultures in Massachusetts, besides the politically connected kind.

He turned, glanced, and turned back to me. "So it is. Lovely to see you again, Bennie. If all goes well, I hope to see you again very soon." And before I could find out what he meant by that, he was gone. I looked up. The vulture had flown off as well.

What did it mean? Why did I think they were connected? I had a growing bad feeling about it.

I looked around for Kate and couldn't find her. I spied Marc across the lawn.

"Marc." I ran over to him. "Marc, where's Kate? Have you seen her?"

"She went to the car to change Ellie. I'm sure she'll be right back."

"Okay. How about Josh? Have you seen him?"

"He took some of the volunteers into the house to get them started."

"Is Kyrie with him?"

"Yeah, as far as I know."

"Great. Thanks." My heart pounded. I knew something wasn't right. I could feel it. I was so glad Spencer and Sarah had stayed with my mom and Hal to make Sarah's hockey practice. At least, I could trust they were safe.

Leslie stopped me as I headed for the car. "Bennie! Congratulations. We've raised so much money, and interest. It's a big hit. You've done such a great job."

"Thanks, Leslie. But I couldn't have done it without you and Josh, too. Could you take over with the meet and greets for a minute or two? I have something I need to do."

"I'll be more than happy to keep things going here. Especially as long as the hunky football players are on-site."

"Thanks." Walking fast, I rounded the corner just in time to see Nick's Town Car pulling away at top speed. The door to Kate's Aviator was wide open, Ellie's dirty diaper left on the seat. I ran after the car. "No!"

He'd taken them. He'd taken them both. What did he want with my sister?

I found Josh in the house handing out jobs, Kyrie by his side with a clipboard. Thank God, they were safe.

"Josh, I need you for a sec." I tried to conceal the panic in my voice.

"Sure, what's up?" He excused himself from the group.

"Kate. And Ellie. They're missing."

"It's okay. I'm sure they're around. We'll find them."

"No, you don't understand." I tried to catch my breath. Tears burned at the back of my eyes. "Nick Angelos was here. Kate was in her Aviator changing Ellie's diaper and then I ran and Nick's car was pulling away and—"

"Come on now, slow down. What happened?"

I took a deep breath and explained, more calmly, what had transpired. Josh's brow furrowed. "Any idea where he would have taken them?"

I thought for a minute. "Yes. I have an idea."

"All right. I'll see if Leslie can keep an eye on Kyrie."

"No." Kyrie's voice came from behind us. Neither of us realized she had come up on us while we were talking. "I need to be there. I can help."

"Kyrie, don't be ridiculous, sweetheart. I want you to stay safe."

"I know what's going on, Dad. I can see into his head. Trust me."

We both stared. "What?"

"Yours, too." She crossed her arms over her chest, smug. "I can read your thoughts, too. Didn't you know? It's one of my gifts. And don't worry, Dad. He may be my father biologically, but you'll always be my one and only dad. Let's go. We need to hurry."

Questions would have to wait. We rushed after Kyrie to get to the car.

"What about Kate and Ellie?" I asked, after we were on the road headed toward the pier. "Can you read their thoughts? Are they okay?"

"I don't really have a connection to them yet." Her emerald eyes flared, so like her father's. "But they're safe for now. He doesn't plan to hurt them."

"Freaky." Josh looked up from the steering wheel to meet my gaze. "Totally freaky."

Kyrie shrugged, seemingly pleased to be able to freak her dad out. "I've been studying Greek mythology. Only for a few weeks now. I figured I should know my history."

"Does your mother know?" Josh didn't seem happy to think of worrying Molly now.

"Like I would tell Mom anything to worry her. No way."

"Good. I would rather she didn't worry. She never wanted you to know about Nick."

"You mean Hermes?"

"Whatever."

"I knew for a long time that I had a father out there somewhere. Mom worries about it all the time."

"She does?"

"Not obsessively, but it crosses her mind." Until the past hour, Kyrie had appeared to be a normal nine-year-old in every way. Now she seemed wise beyond her years, so much older. I wondered if Ellie would be that way, too.

"So, anyway, it was at Thanksgiving that I knew for sure. One look at him, I mean, who couldn't tell? Besides him, of course. Talk about clueless."

I laughed nervously. "Yeah, a little. Can you tell what he plans to do?"

"He thinks he is keeping them safe. He's not a bad guy. He really wants to help. He was supposed to report to Hades if Ellie had any powers or not."

"I *knew* he was too interested in the baby!" I cried.

"I know, right?" Kyrie rolled her eyes. "He hates babies. They gross him out."

"You're getting that from his thoughts?"

"No. From Thanksgiving. Did you see the way he tried to keep away from Ellie? When she was in the room with him, he watched her but he never wanted to get too close."

"Oh." Beyond her special skills, Kyrie was very observant.

"You studied mythology?" I asked, thinking of my last run-in with Nick. "Do you know anything about birds? What they might mean?"

"The vulture is a sign from Ares."

"Ares?" Josh asked. I wish I had filled him in on my concerns for Ellie completely, but there never seemed any reason to mention my time on the boat with Nick, a sensitive subject considering Josh's feelings for me at the time.

"Hermes's half brother," Kyrie confirmed. "Zeus has a spy near Hades to pass important information on to Mount Olympus. He hasn't trusted his brother since Hades asked to create life. Zeus is waiting to hear if Ellie has special talents. If Hermes reports that she does, Ares is ready to swoop in and take Ellie up to Mount Olympus."

"God, no." My heart ached as if squeezed in a vise.

Josh reached over and patted my leg. "We'll get there. We'll stop them."

"How are we supposed to stop gods?"

"Relax, I have a plan." Kyrie raised her eyebrows. "Hermes hasn't made any reports. He has been putting it off because he isn't sure if he wants to help Hades or help Zeus. He's trying to decide which position will grant him more power. I was worried right up until a minute ago. He just decided to go with Hades. Hades keeps a better house."

And, what she no doubt failed to add, choosing Hades kept Kyrie out of risk of her dad needing to take her away as well, if he figured out who she was.

"Figures. The man, er, god, has taste." I nodded.

"When Hermes saw the vulture, he panicked. He took it as a sign that Zeus was growing impatient and sending Ares for Ellie. He knows Ares won't go on the water. He hates boats. Something between him and Poseidon, not sure."

"You read all that in mythology books?"

"And some from Hermes's thoughts. He's really nervous now. I've never had such a clear connection to someone else's thoughts before now. I guess he really is my dad." She paused a minute, as if she wasn't quite sure how to feel about it. It was a lot for a young girl to take in. Fortunately, she seemed to be processing information faster than she really had a chance to think about it, but once she did? "Hermes took them out on the boat to buy some time. Not to worry, they haven't sailed yet. We'll make it."

"Okay, so they're going to sail around for now."

"For now. And then if Hermes gets another sign

from his brother or fears the worst, he's planning on taking Ellie and her mom straight to Hades."

"But they'll be gone. We'll never see them again." The tears broke through. My stomach turned over.

"We'll stop them. Don't worry."

"How can you be so sure?"

Kyrie shrugged. "I just am."

When we pulled up at the docks, Kyrie scooted forward to talk to Josh. "Dad, you should stay in the car. You're not going to like this."

Josh protested, understandably. "I'm not going to let the women I love storm into danger while I wait here in the car."

Kyrie sighed. "I figured as much. Here goes." She reached over the seat to hug him and Josh slumped over, out cold.

I gasped. "What did you do?"

"He's okay. Just sleeping. You probably didn't research enough to know that Hermes is also the original sandman?"

"The sandman?"

"Puts people to sleep? It's one of the skills I must have gotten from him." She winked. "I've been doing it for years to get extra time up late playing with my toys. Mom and Dad have no idea."

"You sly one."

"It's a shame, really. I probably won't be able to get away with that one so easily again. But worth it. He'd only get all hotheaded and go off on Hermes. It won't be good for us. We're all safer with him here."

I couldn't help but agree. "You're really something, kiddo."

"I like you, too. Come on."

She got out and we walked together to the boat. As we drew near, I began to panic.

"Don't worry." Kyrie took my hand. "He knows we're here. He's coming."

"How does he know?"

"He feels you out here. He might be reading your thoughts, too. Whatever you do, don't let him touch you. Kate and Ellie are already asleep to keep them from getting upset."

"Wow." This mind reading was a pretty powerful skill. I wondered what thoughts of mine he'd already picked up on. It felt violating. "If he can read my thoughts, how come he doesn't know about you yet? I've thought about you and Ellie near him."

"He has to concentrate and zone in on the right thoughts at the right time. For someone like Hermes, that might be harder. So many of his thoughts are for himself. Plus, Ellie could be helping to block your thoughts from him. If she's like me, she's able to do a lot more than you think."

I rolled my eyes. "Yes, that fits."

"Just in case, tell him you don't want him to read your thoughts, and then he can't."

"Just like that?"

"Just like that." She nodded. I wondered if I should say the same to her, then decided it was probably best if we stayed on the same wavelength for now.

"Bennie?" Hermes appeared at the side of the yacht. His tone was pleasant, but he couldn't disguise the look of surprise on his face. "I wasn't expecting you, but it's a nice surprise."

"I don't want you to read my thoughts," I said right away.

"And you can't read mine." Kyrie said it fast as if

trying to block him from figuring anything out before she was ready to tell him.

He rolled his eyes. "Very well. Hold on. Morrison will help you aboard."

He lowered the gangplank.

"I was hoping you would come." Nick tried to take my hand to help me aboard. I shrugged away. "And you brought company."

"Kyrie," I said. "You remember? You met her at Thanksgiving dinner."

"Right. Josh's daughter?" This time, he paused and looked her over more carefully as Morrison helped her aboard. Wisely, she averted her eyes. They would have been a dead giveaway.

"Yes. So, what have you done with my sister and my niece? I want them back now."

"I'm only trying to keep them safe. Come in. Have a drink. I'll fill you in on the plan." Nick led the way to the sitting room on the main deck.

"I know the plan, Hermes. And I don't like it."

"Here's the deal." Kyrie, so commanding for all of her nine years, looked at him. "Wake them up and we'll take them home while you make your report to Hades. You need to go soon. You're running out of time."

"And how do you purport to know all this, young lady?" Nick met her gaze, and his eyes widened with a look of recognition and amazement. "My daughter."

"Yeah, Dad, nice to meet you." Kyrie reached out, all business, and shook his hand. "Here's the deal."

I had to smile at her command. Very impressive. Josh should be proud. But he wasn't going to like that she'd told Hermes the truth.

"The deal?" He raised a brow.

She mirrored the gesture. "It won't be good for Zeus to know I exist, if you know what I mean. He won't be happy with you. There's no way to report in to Hades that Ellie has magic powers without him finding out about me, too."

"Why not? I can be selective in my information."

"Yes, but if Zeus has Ares take her, I'll make sure he knows about me. Which means you'll make enemies of both Hades and Zeus and that won't serve you at all."

"Very true, clever girl."

Very clever. I knew she had to be bluffing or very brave. If she made herself known to Zeus, she would be headed to Mount Olympus along with Ellie, letting go of the only life she'd ever known. *Of Josh.* My heart ached for him. I was glad he was left behind, oblivious of the risks she took. And I knew, as well as I knew what I would do to protect my own kids, that I wouldn't let anything happen to her, so help me.

"I've been reading your thoughts. I'm very skilled. I guess I get it from you." She even knew to flatter him, the little charmer.

Hermes beamed with pride. "I didn't even know you were there."

"You had no idea about my thoughts because you didn't even consider me for a second." She shook her head as if hurt. "All you have to do is rush off to report to Hades. Tell him you saw no signs that Ellie has powers and all of this will end. Zeus will be satisfied and call off Ares. We can all stay where we want to be. Please let us all be happy. You'll be in Hades's good graces, and no worse off with Zeus."

"Unless Hades figures out I'm lying to him." Hermes arched a golden brow.

"He'll thank you if he knows you did it to save Kate and his daughter. Just go. Please. Hurry. Ares will be coming soon."

"How do you know that?"

"Just a guess. You were pretty worried about it earlier."

"That's true. I was." He smiled. "You're really quite skilled."

"I know." Kyrie gave him a hard smile.

"But there's one thing you didn't consider. What if I'm willing to face Zeus's wrath as long as it means being with Bennie?"

"What? You can't mean it." I stepped in between Hermes and Kyrie, careful to stay an arm's length from Hermes. That he had strong enough feelings to even say it came as something of a shock. I'd thought he was satisfied with the way we'd left things. I'd never even suspected that he'd thought of a future between us.

"I do, Bennie. I think I've fallen in love with you. I enjoy being with you. I miss you when you're not around. I've never felt quite this way before."

I stared at him, stunned by what I was hearing. Was it a trick? Some kind of diversion? "Are you sure? Maybe it's just that it's all so new for you to feel? You will feel it again if you try. I'm sorry, Hermes. I love Josh. I want to be with him."

"I understand. Well, not really. I'm clearly the physically superior. But it's your choice. I can't force you to love me." But he seemed to be considering the very possibility even as he said it.

"That's right. You can't."

He stepped closer. I stepped back. "Don't startle, my love. I won't hurt you. Let me hold you. Once more. Let me show you what you're missing."

I shook my head. "You've shown me all you could possibly show me. I know how I feel. Josh is the one for me."

"Very well." He shrugged as if taking it in stride, then surprised me with a quick lunge forward. Before I could react, I was in his arms. "One kiss. One last kiss. If I have any reason to believe there's a chance for us, I'll risk angering Hades. I'll bring you, your sister, and the baby to Zeus."

"And your daughter?" I asked, my question stopping him from taking that one last kiss. I looked at Kyrie. She stood back as if considering what to do next. I begged her to stay still, not to try anything dangerous, and hoped she read my thoughts.

"I'll let her stay here. She's bluffing. She would never reveal herself to Zeus and leave her family, the life she loves."

"*Your* life will change," I warned. "You'll be responsible for us, for women and children, no freedom to roam at will."

"No matter, as long as I have you."

"But you won't. I'll still love Josh. I'll resent you for taking me from him and from my children. And every day, I'll remind you of it. No matter what you feel for me, you can't change that I don't feel the same. And you'll be facing Hades's wrath. There will be war. He'll never sit by if Kate and Ellie are unhappy."

Nick nodded, as if considering. A sound rent the air, the cries of birds.

"Ares," Kyrie said. "He's coming."

"Not to worry. He's too afraid to come near the water," Nick assured her, holding me tighter as if to protect me even as he said it. "Poseidon has a grudge to settle with Ares and we'd see a battle of a different kind before he'd get his hands on Ellie or any of you. He's just trying to force my hand."

"And?" I looked at him. I saw kindness, not cruelty, reflected back in those green eyes.

He let me go. "It would be really hard to explain to Zeus, anyway. He's likely to cast me out or do something really vile, like turn me into a goat. I'll go make my report to Hades that Ellie is perfectly human and powerless. It will get back to Zeus. You'll all be safe. Then I plan to stick close to Hades and ferret out the spy in his ranks. Eventually, Hades will learn the truth about Ellie. But I won't be the one to tell him. Not until I know who is passing information on to Zeus."

"That sounds reasonable. Thank you." I wanted to hug him but I was still afraid he would put me to sleep and take us all.

"You're welcome. And you, little skilled one." He turned to Kyrie. "I find I'm truly sorry that we haven't had much time together. I'll be away for a few years, but once I can work my way back, perhaps we'll get together again. I trust Josh has cared for you well?"

"Very well. *He's* my dad."

"I know where I stand." Hermes nodded.

I think we all knew the arrangement suited him. He wasn't cut out to be father to a little girl. When she was older, perhaps.

"Is there anything I can do to assist in your care? Something you would like or need?"

"Nothing. My parents take pretty good care of me."

"That's fine, then. If you do find yourself wanting, you can contact me through the people at Glendower Enterprises. The same for you, Bennie. Anything you want or need, I'm good for it."

"I know. You're actually a pretty good sort, Hermes. Nick, if you don't mind. I'm more comfortable thinking of you as Nick."

"Nick it is." He winked. "Time grows short. Let's go wake your sister and the baby."

Chapter Twenty-two

Christmas morning, only my second without Patrick, was one of the most joyous days in recent memory. Just before dawn, I woke up in Josh's arms.

"Josh." I shook him awake. "Time for you to creep across the hall to the guest room. The kids will be waking any minute to knock on the door and ask if they can go see what Santa brought."

"Five more minutes." He nestled me closer and kissed the top of my head.

I smoothed my hand over his warm, solid chest. "Get dressed, lazybones. Time to go. I'll see you again really soon."

"I know. I just hate to be a minute without you in my arms."

"Me, too." I smiled. His mouth found mine in a slow, erotic kiss. "Okay, five more minutes."

Thirty minutes later, he was dressed and ready to sneak across the hall to the guest room. As he placed his hand on the doorknob, I whispered through the dim morning light. "And, Josh?" He turned to gaze at me, his eyes warming me through to the core. "Merry Christmas."

Quietly, he closed the door behind him.

An hour later, the kids had us up to open presents. Kyrie, Molly, and Sam, Molly's fiancé, would be joining us later to head to Kate and Marc's for Christmas dinner, where we would gather with the rest of my family.

Sitting under the Christmas tree with my kids excitedly ripping into gifts, I couldn't have asked for a more perfect morning.

"I got you something," Josh said, turning to me after the kids opened their presents and had lost interest in us in favor of trying out their new toys.

"I thought we agreed no presents?"

"You got me something, didn't you?"

"I did," I confessed, and got down on my knees to dig the box out from behind the Christmas tree. "Open yours first."

He opened. It was a watch, subdued, nothing too expensive, but classic and rugged, like Josh. I'd had it engraved with the date and the words *All my love, Bennie.*

"I love it. Thanks, hon," he said, giving me such a look of love that tears sprang to my eyes.

"You're welcome." I returned to my seat in the wingback chair.

"Now mine." I clapped. "My turn."

He smiled, stood up, went to my hall closet, and pulled out a big, brightly wrapped box. "Open it," he said, placing it at my feet and then sitting on the floor in front of me, a smile teasing at the corners of his mouth.

"Okay." I picked it up, unwrapped it, and opened

the box. Inside, there was another box. A very small velvet box. "Tricky." My heart raced. Could it be?

My suspicions were confirmed before I opened the box, when he rose on one knee and took my hand in his. "Bennie, would you do me the honor of becoming my wife?"

It was then, staring into Josh's eyes that easily outshone the brilliance of the lights on the Christmas tree, that I realized the truly nicest combination of words in the English language next to "I love you."

My eyes began to mist. I tipped out of the chair, landing on my knees in front of him, not even concerned that the children might be watching. I wrapped my arms around his neck and kissed him until we were both nearly breathless.

"I will."

Epilogue

"She walks in beauty, like the night. Of cloudless climes and starry skies." Hades quoted from Byron. For once, Hermes was in no mood to mock his uncle.

"And all that's best of dark and bright meet in her aspect, and her eyes," Hades finished. "Oh how they twinkle. Do you see how fine she looks? How exquisitely content?"

They peered over the gazing ball to watch Kate, looking radiant in her wedding finery, glide down the aisle into the waiting arms of Marc, her soon-to-be husband. Hermes glanced over in time to see his uncle close his eyes as if lost in a dream. Had he not been barred from reading Hades's thoughts, Hermes was pretty sure he would see his uncle imagining himself in the place of the groom. But it was not to be. They were both resigned to watching their beloved mortal women from afar.

In unison, uncle and nephew sighed.

"Bennie, too, looks well," Hermes said. She wore a strapless gown in a midnight blue a few shades darker than her cornflower eyes. It enhanced her bosom and hugged the curves of her thin frame. Or perhaps she had grown curvier since last he saw her and it was no illusion *of the dress? He tipped his head, studying her, trying to decide.*

"They'll both lead long and happy lives. Our interference will no longer be welcome."

"I understand. But if I couldn't just steal down now and again to be sure?"

"No." Hades shook his head, his mouth drawn to a grim line. "It's safer for them to have no more to do with us. Not until their day has come to be with us here at last. Only about sixty years or so in their time."

Hermes sighed. "For you, perhaps. You'll have your eternity. I'm not cut out for long-term fidelity." Bennie had made clear she had no future with him, but Hermes saw no need to relay such specifics to his uncle.

Hades arched a brow. "I expect you'll content yourself with nymphs or goddesses from now on?"

Hermes shrugged. "Perhaps. But there isn't a goddess or nymph who can compare to the Markham sisters."

"Amen to that." Hades smiled. "Amen." He began to let the gazing ball image fade when something more caught his eye. The image brightened again. "Hermes, did you see that?"

"See what, Uncle?" Hermes pretended to be unaware, though he had indeed seen the babe, Eliana, contenting herself with a wee ball of light she'd created for herself from thin air. He spotted Kyrie, his own daughter, nearby. She tossed another ball in the baby's direction, possibly showing off, or perhaps eager to distract the child throughout the long wedding ceremony. "Oh yes. These new earth toys. What will the humans think of next?"

"Yes. Yes, of course." His uncle waved him away. "That will be all, Hermes. Leave me. I've some matters to attend to."

Hermes bowed and took his leave, but he paused at the door on the way out. He knew exactly what matters his uncle had to attend to. He planned to keep on watching Ellie to see what his daughter would do next.

"That's Daddy's girl," the mighty lord of the underworld cooed into the gazing ball. "I knew you had something of your father in you."

Daddy's girl. *By now, Hermes knew the feeling of paternal pride all too well from watching Kyrie work her many talents. She had mastered flamethrowing and even putting people to sleep against their will. Brilliant child, his daughter. A beauty, too. And he would expect no less. He would have to keep an eye on her through the years.*

The last thing Hermes overheard as he closed the door and stole off down the hall was the minister's voice from the wedding ceremony.

"I now pronounce you man and wife. Presenting Mr. and Mrs. Marc Ramirez."

Soon they would watch a ceremony for Bennie and Josh that would end in much the same way. Presenting Mr. and Mrs. Joshua Brandon. *Like her sister, but perhaps a little more so, Bennie would be an astonishingly beautiful bride.*

Some guys had all the luck.

Nail-Biting Romantic Suspense from Your Favorite Authors

Thrilling Suspense From
Wendy Corsi Staub

__All the Way Home	0-7860-1092-4	$6.99US/$8.99CAN
__The Last to Know	0-7860-1196-3	$6.99US/$8.99CAN
__Fade to Black	0-7860-1488-1	$6.99US/$9.99CAN
__In the Blink of an Eye	0-7860-1423-7	$6.99US/$9.99CAN
__She Loves Me Not	0-7860-1768-6	$4.99US/$6.99CAN
__Dearly Beloved	0-7860-1489-X	$6.99US/$9.99CAN
__Kiss Her Goodbye	0-7860-1641-8	$6.99US/$9.99CAN
__Lullaby and Goodnight	0-7860-1642-6	$6.99US/$9.99CAN
__The Final Victim	0-8217-7971-0	$6.99US/$9.99CAN

Available Wherever Books Are Sold!

Visit our website at **www.kensingtonbooks.com**

Thrilling Suspense from
Beverly Barton